Shakespeare's Pipe

Alexandra Mason

Images of William Shakespeare

1. Droueshout the Younger portrait in First Folio
2. Old player portrait
3. Stace portrait
4. Chandos portrait
5. Sully portrait
6. Pencil drawing of Picasso portrait,
    by permission of Bruce Allen
7. Dunford portrait
8. Soest portrait
9. Felton portrait
10. Cobbe portrait
11. Buttery portrait
12. Zucchero portrait

Image of Sir Walter Ralegh smoking (p. 4) by Frederick William Fairholt, 1859.

Acknowledgments

I have an old friend I met in a book I found in an attic when I was eleven. At first I thought his words hard to understand, but he engaged me with his tales of complex relationships, vexed choices, and high passions. The childhood me heard his voice and created a vision of that author.

Years later in graduate school, his profile became complicated, even murky for me. In that summer of 1977, I read one of his thirty-seven plays each morning and studied critical interpretations in the afternoon. Such diversity and range of humanity—and glimpses into the frailties of our minds and souls. As I learned how the entire world extolled him, I thought of him as a profound humanist, the quintessential sage mensch. But there was also such variation in understanding who this author was and what his plays meant. And little actual knowledge about him personally, except for a word from a friend or rival here and there, a legal document—will or deed. Then I saw his signature and he began to feel real to me.

A living man with that name, William Shakspeare, scrawled that inky line. But which of our inherited portraits fits that shaky hand? We have etchings and paintings of this person, all as ideas of how we conceive he ought to have been. We all desperately desire the truth of the matter. We want him as our friend and mentor, our resident genius.

So Kingsley Armstrong takes the opportunity into his own hands, and this little narrative is the result. My assurances to William Shakespeare's soul if my story affronts in any way, that it is entirely an act of imaginative possibility and not an attempted portrait of the true Bard. The clone Will capitalizes on the playwright as observer and manipulator of humanity, one vision among many and not necessarily my own. My tale also makes us wonder what renders a singular human being singular. What is the entirety of the forces that shape our humanity? Each of our choices and actions influences the entire world around us—a conclusion with which I know the actual man William Shakespeare would concur.

Paul A. Jorgensen and Gloria Johnson were the finest teachers of Shakespeare one could hope for. Through decades of teaching at university I learned from both students and colleagues, especially Richard M. Goldman, who always reminded me of Ophelia's line "we know what we are, but know not what we may be." The Tuesday Writers of Waldport, Oregon, journeyed along with me through the narrative week by week, responding with genuineness, candor, and critical eyes. Thanks especially to Brenda Croghan (reader extraordinaire) and Shirley Plummer for helpful critique. Responding to a manuscript can be a thankless task, but many graciously did so: Sue Parman, Marilyn Ewing, Marilyn Sandidge, Denise Jenkins, Ron Lovell, and, just prior to her death, Ellen M. Caldwell.

To all, my gratitude, and to Ellen, my dedication of "Shakespeare's Pipe" for decades of conversation about our man, Mr. Shakespeare, who lives on and walks among us in one avatar or another.

Contents

Part II: The Birth

Part III: Childhood

Part IV: The End and the Beginning

Part I: The Temptation

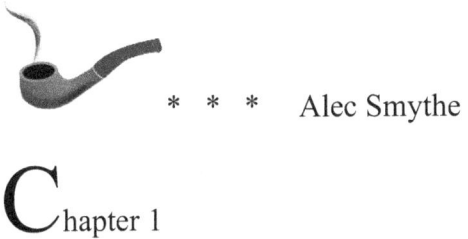 * * * Alec Smythe

C̲hapter 1

"'ere we are, then," I announced to Ewan. Our contractor's lorry eased just off the road in downtown Stratford on Henley Street. The address had led us to the Tudor house that had been the digs of old Shakespeare himself, completely recognisable to us locals and maybe lotsa arty types 'round the world. I knew it was a tourist attraction now, the whole town couldn't avoid knowing that, and my set pretty much avoided the place. Our grammar school class had visited once, and some of the facts were lodged in my brain. The original structure was almost completely gone except for a few stud walls and the hearth, having been restored from the sod up in 1857, some 225 years after the bard's death. In the meantime it had served as both an inn and the home of a butcher. The big man himself had moved up upon returning to his home town in 1613, to the house called New Place on Chapel Street.

The Shakespeare Trust had rebuilt this birthplace house in Tudor replica style and the carpenter in me could see how they saved the old hearthstone and chimney and a few of the beams. They'd made a keen run of it, timbers and lath and plaster and all, even a twee herb and flower garden in the back. Now tourist coaches rolled up from 10 'til 4 all year 'round the sign said. They'd even blocked off the original sidewalk to protect access. Seems everybody wanted a little piece of old Will.

But now the thatched roof had developed a fissure and rain had run down along the inside wall by the chimney. The work order for Ewan and myself was to remove everything to the studs and redo around the fireplace to match as well as we could. Now in early September the tourist crowds had thinned a bit, and we could set out to begin our demo before the new rains came.

"You're the lad what loves smash and crash," Ewan ribbed as we clambered out of the lorry. "Go on ahead and I'll bring in the brooms and the plaster mix."

I grabbed my toolbox and the roll of Visqueen and sauntered up to the wooden door. They'd left the key in the lock for us, and it was easy to eyeball what needed to be done right there in the hearth room.

Banging through plaster with a sledge was messy business, but I liked the brutal act of it, smashing with abandon and sheer force into the standing wall. First there was an indented crack with flaking shatters 'round the edges. I'd carefully laid the Visqueen to contain the debris best we could, and pieces of plaster were dropping like small flakes of snow. I took a step away from the wall, raised the sledge again, and put my back into it. Pow! A good-size hole was forming, and I moved my aim a smidge to the left of the growing gap.

Pow! Pow! Each stroke widened the hole brilliantly, and I began hitting lower and higher to clear the entire wall away from the joint with the mantelpiece and chimney. A tall slit about 20" wide now ran along the chimney, and I could peer directly inside. Something dark way back in there caught my eye, and I turned to my toolbox to locate my LED light.

We'd seen workers leave a careless mess inside walls before, knowing all will be hidden away from sight. We were used to finding plastic tea bottles, rags of paper or racetrack odds and betting forms, or even the remains of lunch—but this looked pretty clean. Sometimes a Jack-the-lad with a sense of humour will plant something startling or completely out of place: in the past we'd stumbled upon vampire fangs and a cap with the name of footballers, Tricky Trees from Nottingham Forest. Maybe a worker will even leave a note to the future or tuck away a slip of paper with his own name as a sign of proud craftsmanship.

With the LED torch on a strap 'round my brow, I could see what appeared to be a narrow ledge just behind the chimney but obscured from easy view by the upright support beam. The dark shadow was slight, and just above that ledge. My heart thudded, quickening. The Shakespeare vibe was strong in this room, and for a second my mind flitted to a fantasy of some scribbled parchment from 1590, some new addition to the Bard relics that would put me quids in for sure. This ledge was tricky to reach. I pushed my body into the gap and extended my arm 'til it nearly dislocated at the shoulder. With a max stretch I could get my fingers to graze the shelf, but nothing materialised. I pulled out of the wall and took a sharper angle towards the hole, twisting in and then around behind the beam. This time my fingers landed on a solid, rounded oblong object, and I grasped on with a secure grip of excitement. The object was smooth to the touch, and my mind rapidly sorted through shapes it might resemble.

"What sort-a-twist you got yourself into there, mate?" Ewan appeared in the door of the parlour with plastering supplies just as I made my catch, and my brief fantasy of securing a private treasure vanished.

"Thought I saw something wedged in back here," I muttered, my head entirely inside the wall.

"Well, pull 'er out, old sod! Prolly an empty pint-a-bitters, more's the pity."

Contorting my body to squeeze back out through the opening, and with my shoulder throbbing from the reach-beyond-its-reach, I and my hand emerged, holding . . . a pipe.

   *   *   *

Chapter 2

Not that I was a huge fan of history, but I'd seen that drawing somewhere of Walter Ralegh lounging with a pipe as long as his own body and a stem thin as a reed.

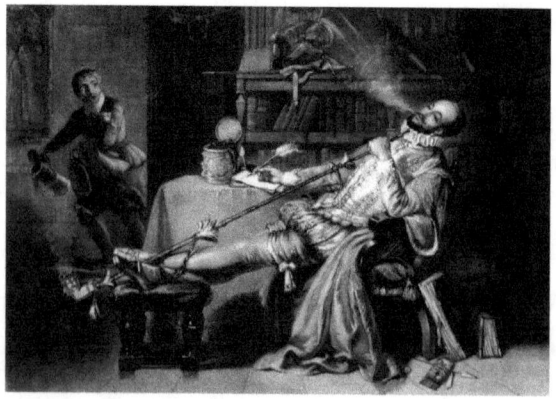

What I held in my hand was nothing like that lance, more of what they call a Bent Bulldog, about a hand-span long, made of rosewood, with a compact, thick-sided rounded bowl. I knew geezers who puffed away on them still. Ewan stood close, just across from me, both our heads bowed in a direct gaze at this find. Ewan raised my hand holding the pipe up to his nostrils and gave a sniff.

"Hmpf, thought those blokes might a' been enjoyin' some wacky backy on the job," he said.

But the aroma was identifiably of tobacco, faintly still clinging to the bowl itself, with an underscent of something else familiar. Oh, nutmeg! I recalled from history class in grammar school that the nicotine weed had made its way to England as early as 1565, on the heels of explorers returning from the New World with Indians and this strange plant enhanced with spices that was supposed to protect you from diseases and stave off hunger pangs. Crowds would gather to observe smoking demonstrations in the streets, and pipes became a common and sought-after commodity. After learning about these early smokers, I'd even experimented with the leaves myself.

Not long ago an excavation near New Place had unearthed fragments of clay pipes, complete with traces of hemp, along with tobacco and other herbs. It came to me that I'd heard about this on the news—quite a stir that our Bard might have been getting high in his time. This theory popped up to belittle those true geniuses that appear in our midst on occasion—that they were only creative when they "enhanced" their consciousness artificially. In Shakespeare's case, this was right in line with what I'd heard on radio from would-be bardologists that continually proposed someone else as the author of the poems and plays because after all, a grammar school boy wasn't noble and proper enough to have done something brilliant.

In a quick, impulsive move, Ewan pulled the pipe from my hand and put it up towards his lips. He was about to mug—a construction worker taking a toke or maybe a poet seeking his muse. I wasn't sure which, but I hastily interceded.

"Wait! You don't know where that's been!"

I wasn't a molly, and it was a silly thing to say, as we knew precisely where it had been—in the wall behind the hearth for at least 150 years, if not 420. But the origin of the pipe was a mystery, and we could not know whose lips had last put their imprint on its stem. Soon enough, we might know the answer. If it had belonged to the Bard, Ewan and I would become England's most famous factotums.

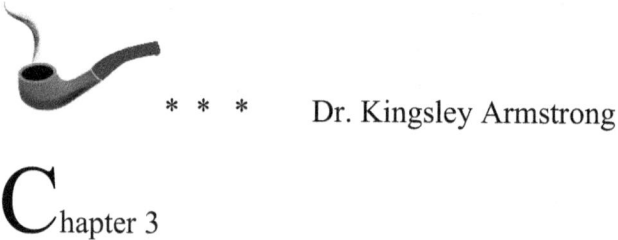

* * *   Dr. Kingsley Armstrong

C hapter 3

Mostly these days Traces, our lab, was given over to forensics-related work. The staff and I sorted through what looked like rubbish, carefully presented to us in little polythene bags, placing the bits and pieces under viewing scopes or dissecting off samples for molecular scanning and analysis. More often than not we were given body scrapings—skin cells or dried fluids or fingernail bits left on victims or scattered here and there at crime scenes. While the results could sometimes be earth-shaking or at least mystery-solving, the daily drudge was tedious and unglamourous.

Morale was always an issue in the lab. All of us were brainy and saw ourselves as scientists if not boffins. It was hard to dispel the fantasy presented to us in the cinema of vital lab discoveries, where scientists pushed the limits, performed speculative experimentation, isolated new strands, and recombined chemicals into new compounds as a daily matter of course. Instead, we sipped endless cups of tea, making sure to avoid cross-contamination as we popped open the baggies and peered through our lenses. The DNA profile programme got more and more use these days, and we took some consolation in the fact that we did help put perpetrators behind bars, locate and name fathers in paternity queries, and set folks on the sure track in seeking their ancestors.

Our most exciting job recently was this diary sitting before me supposedly written by Jack the Ripper around 1898. We remained the most trusted lab in the kingdom, so it was no surprise to receive this artifact, yet we felt solemnly important to the whole chain of history when the constable hand-delivered the sealed box. I took on the job myself, donning a complete set of protective coverings— over my head, face, body, arms, legs, and even shoes—not fearing danger for myself, but to protect the purity of the sample. It might be too much to hope for DNA of the Ripper himself on these pages, but I would see what turned up. At least we could date the artifact fairly precisely.

First I dusted the exterior and the edges of several pages for fingerprints, uncovering only some partials. Then I did a meticulous microscopic scraping, careful to bring minimal change to the sample itself, which looked, well, like it had been through a decade or even a century safe and dry in an attic, still appearing new and pristine. After I secured the scraping, I prepared the vials for separating out the two strands in the high-temp DNA melting process. Each strand then becomes a template for exponential replication. We add in nucleotides to supply the materials for new growth, and then we put the vials through temperature cycling until there's enough of the complete strands to chart and profile and enter into the data base. The machine spun its centrifugal magic, and the computer screen began to flash in nanosecond images the profiles of possible matches, scanning both the partial prints and the DNA replication.

The Royal Academy of Science had done us a great service by setting out to take cell samples from most of the nobility, as a kind of complement to Edmund Lodge's *Peerage*, so the data base was always growing. Ironic that it included primarily criminals along with swells. Some of the mitochondria were passed on most fully through the matrilinear side, so lots of links were still less than 100% sure if all we had were samples from fathers and sons. That might be key for us in the matter of principals who had no children, though we might trace the descendants of a sister. But if no female relatives survived, we could lose the chance for a confident family genetic comparison. Some scientists asserted correctly that we are "all related—it's just a matter of degree," and that was correct but not very helpful in solving mysteries.

Precise genotyping is a matter of fits and starts, as miry as the human race it tries to capture. Science was miraculous, like magic, but still it had its limits. Most of us tolerated the drudge because we were in awe of the magic. That magic made the invisible visible and the impossible possible.

The buzz of the blower interrupted my focus on the testing procedures. It was lab policy not to receive personal calls at work, but that never stopped Mum from checking on her only son. Post-graduate work at Cambridge and then my head buried in the lab had kept me from romantic entanglements, and Mum never stopped urging me to "find a sweet girl, settle down, and start a family." She was sure to harp on this again, and I didn't need the distraction. I clicked a button that would send the call to automatic reply.

The computer flashing slowed and then stilled. Two faces remained on the screen, and neither looked to be the Ripper. They were identified as Amy and Merton Barwood, not coincidentally the pair that had turned over the diary for scrutiny. No other fingerprints, and certainly no hundred-year-old DNA here. It was logical that this couple would have left their own traces on the diary in the excitement of discovery.

Now to seek the date of the paper and cardboard cover. I needed a sample of at least ten milligrams to prepare for accelerator mass spectrometry, the best method for Carbon 14 dating. We'd done this before numerous times with human remains. I shaved off a tiny bit of the edge of the diary cover from the bottom, and then I took a sliver of the paper from an outside edge towards the middle section of the pages. These needed to be put in an alkali wash to remove any contamination and then treated with graphite. I placed them into the accelerator, which would count the Carbon 14 molecules and give a ratio of them to Carbon 12 present. The longer I allowed the counting to go on, the more accurate the results would be. It would be difficult to pin down a precise date in this case, since we were only about a hundred years out from the event, not eons. The lab had been handling carbon dating for the past fifteen years or so. Agencies and private parties sent us all kinds of samples, and at £325 a test, that helped defray the considerable cost of our investment and keep us ticking along in steady business.

I was just finished preparing the sample when the blower rang again, interrupting my concentration. Once again I clicked the auto reply button as I wanted to finish the last details of this run of tests on the diary.

I set the lab back in order while the accelerator worked its magic, and then the results began to print out. Within a standard deviation of error, what I'd submitted was . . . a modern material one could pick up at any stationer's shop. I wasn't surprised, but I double-checked to make sure the results were certain. Seems our couple, whose faces still stared at me from the screen, had produced this "Ripper diary" on their own. The dating of the paper materials was certain enough; no need to examine the ink.

A clanger certainly on the Barwoods' part, but our science had saved the day on this one. History would stay buried in the past, and no Ripper profits would be garnered off this hoax. Another victory for the scientific method, yes, but I dreaded the inevitability of the results being reported to the popular press and the hullaballoo they would make, bringing the Ripper back to life on their own, so to speak.

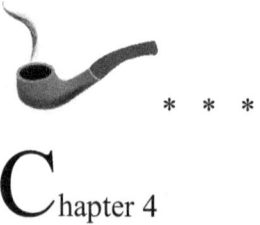 * * *

Chapter 4

With the Ripper mystery solved, I turned to the unfinished business of those calls that had been sent on to message. There was Mum's number as expected, but my eyes popped wide when I saw the caller ID from the mayor of Stratford-upon-Avon. His message was entertwined with static, but it seems a couple of the work crew repairing the Bard's

Birthplace had found an artifact in the walls. My mind raced through possibilities—a piece of pewterware or perhaps weaponry of some sort, maybe an old Douay Bible or some scribbled parchments. We could carbon-date paper, to be sure, and that would liven up the staff.

I hit the redial button with a sense of interest and excitement. The mayor was on his mobile, and our connection was fading in and out. I gleaned through his garble that a crew supervisor had insisted the find be handed over to the authorities and they'd be pleased with a little reward don't you know. Before any money, pence to pounds, exchanged hands, the county and the Trust needed to verify the provenance of the find. Something new from the Bard's days to add to the museum display would be a shot in the arm for tourism—even locals, Brits at large, would pony up the entrance fee and visit again to see a true Shakespearean item firsthand.

"We're hop--- for --- precise da--," I heard through the static. "We --- you're --- chaps who --- ---- ----." Even with the omissions I could sense the excitement in his voice. "--- send it on down --- courier posthaste."

"Right-o," I replied in a raised voice, "but what kind of testing are we in for? What sort of artifact are we talking about?"

"---- keep it mum. Don't ---- the rags to make a splash ----- threaten the safety ---- object."

"Yes, we are meticulous, confidential, and completely bonded," I assured him, "and our security is well monitored. But what's the item?"

"----- ---- they found ---- a bloody pipe!"

* * *

Chapter 5

From above, our heads must have resembled the petals of a flower opening into full bloom. The entire staff was circled around the examination table, all leaning forward to inspect the pipe I had carefully removed from the packing material.

"Wait, everyone!" I cautioned. "Put on your gloves and masks as well. We don't want any stupid contamination errors caused by enthusiastic haste." All of us were chuffed at this opportunity and its possibilities, eager to get at the examination.

They turned to fetch their safety garb, and then the flower reassembled itself, even more intent than before in scrutinising the small pipe. It was as the descriptive card stated: a "Bent Bulldog, constructed of a wooden material, 5 ¾" long, showing wear on the mouthpiece and traces of charring in and around the bowl, date of manufacture unknown, site of procurement inside wall behind hearth, Shakespeare's Birthplace, Henley Street, Stratford-upon-Avon, 10 September 2004." The police forensics collector had done her job with precision and apparent care. Lying on the pale yellow expanse of the table, the item itself seemed small, quite ordinary, and unremarkable.

"Some change from our usual dust-bin-and-rubbish remains, eh, chaps?" Their awe was palpably turning humdrum, and one by one the staff began to disperse, returning to individual stations and projects. I remained alone with the pipe and decided to just get on with it. "Probably just a worker's throwaway," I thought to myself.

I took precise measurements every which way and noted them down. Then I placed the pipe under a viewing scope and made journal entries of adhesions and markings. These mostly expanded on the original forensics description, nothing unexpected. I proceeded to scrapings of the mouthpiece and bowl areas. Certainly we would be able to identify what was being smoked, and we could date the organic compounds present in char and ash. And then if lip cells or saliva had deposited on the stem, we could tell if the smoker was a person or persons. Put the two findings together, and we might formulate a scenario—that was the really creative part of research. If there were several smokers and the substance was a drug, we could surmise a ritual of sorts. Then again, if it was tobacco and a single smoker, we surely had an ordinary pipe misplaced somehow or stashed in the hearth as a joke or perhaps in avoidance of the lashes of a shrewish wife's tongue. The carbon dating could give us a sense of the pipe's age, and, doubtful but possible, if we were extraordinarily lucky we might be able to trace the family line of any extant DNA.

The computer was making a DNA profile from the cells I was able to scrape from the stem, and I'd got the accelerator working on counting the ^{14}C from the ash and char remnants in the bowl. The rest of the staff had checked in separately throughout the week to note my progress, but I could tell their excitement had waned. I wasn't sure what the Stratford chaps were expecting. The pipe really could be from any century from 1600 on, and the odds were straight-on against it being an authentic Renaissance relic,

I'd say. I was guessing it was a workman's prank or that it had been truly misplaced—set down and forgotten in the course of building repair. I also doubted that anyone was using this mean pipe to get high, alone or in any sort of coven or satanic band. But interest in old Will was always high—same as with the Ripper—and there was enough mystery surrounding both lives that we simply wanted more, any new tidbit that would give us a better sense of the man. As Anthony Burgess, Bard biographer, had said, given the choice between discovering a new play or finding Shakespeare's laundry list, we'd "plump for the laundry list," no doubt about it.

Despite my suspicions that the pipe was simply ordinary, the possibilities had consumed my thoughts of late and I'd kept even more to myself, staying 'til dark in the lab, taking the tube home, having a drink and a wee bite, dropping off while still in my easy chair with the telly on, and stumbling to bed mid night only to rise early and begin the routine anew. This meant I had avoided, even neglected, my only steady human contact, Mum. Pater had been taken from us early on in an auto accident on the M1. I was only four at the time and hardly remembered him now. Mum had clung to me, even spoiled me—only the best of everything—and we saw ourselves as an island safe from the hostile and cruel world. It was hard on her when I left home for good, and we kept in close contact on the phone lines.

This gap while awaiting results was a good time to check up on her, and I used my mobile to by-pass the prohibition against personal calls at work.

"Kingsley! How I've missed your voice!"

"Hullo, Mum. I've missed you, too. Been awfully busy with much ado at the lab. No time to take a breath."

"I thought it was mostly the odd fingernail scraping. Has something new turned up?"

"Well, you know we've just recovered from the Ripper hoax. Just getting back to the hum-drum when we get rung up by the Shakespeare Trust fellows. A couple of workers unearthed an artifact that may be of interest, as they say. I'm running tests on it now—but hush, hush don't you know. Don't want a to-do in the *Daily Mail* filled with false sensationalist speculation."

"Oh, dear boy, what is it? A manuscript? A love letter? A pair of gloves? How exciting! Do tell Mum."

"My lips are sealed until it's all worked out. You know our rule of confidentiality."

"Oh, but now I'm absolutely dying to know. The old girls in the book circle will simply swoon when I tell them."

"That's what I fear, Mum. I've let on too much already. Let's drop it for now. . . . So, how've you been occupying yourself?"

"Well, you know my friend Gladys from Great Peter Street? Her daughter, Tessa, whom you know from school, has a friend I'd love for you to take out. She's Oxbridge all the way, Kingsley, lovely girl, works as an assistant editor at Medusa's Hair Press. Just your type, top o' the heap, brainy sort, and beautiful too, I hear."

"Oh, Mum, not again! I'm just too wrapped up in this case at the moment. Can't bear any distractions, no matter how lovely they might be."

"You're not getting any younger, dear boy, nor am I. I want to hear the patter of little feet in the parlour before I'm confined to a wheelchair."

"Mum, you exaggerate. You're a mere lass yourself. And anyway, any bird who'd get hooked up with me would have to be a pretty independent sort. You know Science will always be my first love. She'd have to put up with that mistress."

"Better than a flesh-and-blood rival, I still say, Kingsley. But do consider meeting her for a gin-and-tonic, just a sip or two. You've just been too lonely, too long."

"Mum, sure you're not speaking for yourself? How about an old geezer to liven up your evenings and the odd week end? I'll bet I can find an old scientist who'd interest you."

"Now, dear boy, you know you've always been enough for me since your father passed."

"Right-o. Well, must check on my findings here. I hear the call of the computer whirring down on its scan. Talk soon, Mum. Love you!"

The accelerator was first to spew forth a result, the range of dates emerging from a printer and simultaneously showing on a monitor. "Type of material tested, 3-[(2S)-1-methylpyrrolidin-2-yl] pyridine, commonly known as nicotine, mixed with common spices, predominantly Myristica fragrans Houtt, known as nutmeg. Burn residue. $^{14}C/^{12}C$ ratio indicates ~ 1600 CE."

By gad, we did have a Renaissance pipe on our hands!

* * *

Chapter 6

Suddenly I felt a bit more in awe of the workaday device, which had been used by somebody at Shakespeare's house during Shakespeare's own lifetime—I'd rechecked his dates, of course, and he'd been quick on this earth from 1564 to 1616. Who smoked it or why it was hidden away remained mysteries, at least for the nonce. But we did know the fellow—or lass as it might be—was puffing on tobacco and herbs, no hemp involved. Although the pipe was from our own millennium—not as ancient as bone fragments we'd tested from the Ice Age or mastodon teeth we'd dated to 9300 BCE, this result still quickened the pace of my heart and enthralled my science-loving spirit.

Somehow being next to these relics and actually interacting with their molecular composition made me part of what mattered on this globe, "this goodly frame, the earth," as Hamlet had called it. True, I was no hero called to dramatic action, but to me our planet was not a "sterile promontory," definitely not "a foul and pestilent congregation of vapours." It was vibrant and alive, the past never lost to us but still present in remnants and fragments of potential if we could find the key to reanimate its actuality.

We ourselves were walking shells containing all that had come before. Not only were we all related as *homo sapiens*, truly the same family as it were, but we rubbed space with all the molecules the internal and external matter of us had touched. We breathed our departed loved ones into our souls. Everything vibrated across spatial boundaries, merging, remixing, reacting. Matter was never lost, and I was beginning to think the same about spirit. Artifacts vibrated across temporal boundaries as well, carrying the living truth of history into our own time. Mum always said the scientist in me was really an idealist philosopher, perpetually dreaming along with the scheming. Theory *and* Practice. You couldn't have one without the other, really. That's how we could tolerate the meticulous and repetitive routine of daily lab work. It was the secret of the rotation of the galaxy that moved us along even as we did the drudge of sterilising our petri dishes.

At last the monitor showing the DNA replication had slowed to a stop, and the graphic profile of someone's life blueprint shone forth clearly. Whose, we were still to discover. I entered the profile into the data base, and the screen began to flash with possible family matches. Fairly quickly, a single face stared out at me from the screen. Oddly, in the pixilation of the image, I saw a mirror of our own solid state, more space than matter between the nucleus and rotating electrons of our atoms. We were all ghostly shadows of a sort, loosely cohered into bodies by chemical bonds.

I forced myself to focus on the face and its data. The face belonged to Audrey Thompson of Leamington Spa, recently deceased, victim of that quirky Legionnaire's disease that occasionally crops up, the virus passed from person to person easily in the confines of hotels with recirculated air flow in crowded gathering halls. How tenuous was our hold on life! I moved the cursor to find more information about Audrey's days on earth. Although of course we were all of us products of prior generations and thus prior historical eras, it felt rather immediate to know that this person's ancestor's lips had grasped the stem of that pipe that sat so innocently on my lab table and that that particular person knew or had something to do with the great William Shakespeare, the claim to fame of all England.

Audrey had been a journalist with a small newspaper in her town covering the sports beat. She evidently harboured aspirations to be a writer of screenplays and had boxes of stories half-fleshed out stacked near the desk in her flat. Broken dreams, unrealised desires . . . these always tugged at my heartstrings. No steady boyfriend, some rumours that her best girlfriend of years came "with benefits," as they say. So, no children, either.

Part of me understood this scenario intuitively, a woman with a job to keep the roof overhead who presented a conventional face to the world at large but whose secret passion drove her privately almost to the exclusion of all else. Her true self, the real record of her unique being, was in that study and lived on in the pages of her unfinished dramas, more's the pity.

I silently vowed to divorce myself from the daily tedium of the lab which so occupied my energies and come to at least a single success in my cellular research before my death. Like Audrey, even if I did not leave children for the future of our species, I wanted to leave my own trace of having lived, of having created something—from the mind, which was, after all, the miracle of mankind. Hamlet had got that right in his musings: "What a piece of work is a man! How noble in reason, how infinite in faculty! In form and moving how express and admirable! In action how like an Angel! in apprehension how like a god! The beauty of the world! The paragon of animals!"

Musings like this of my own made me realise that I probably spent too much time alone, letting my mind wander its own by-ways. I snapped myself back to the task at hand. What to do, where to go next in the matter of the pipe? Dignitaries were on pins and needles to know the truth of this discovery. History might be changed by my report. Fortunes might be created. Individuals might be catapulted into the limelight of fame—for at least fifteen minutes as that American artist Warhol had suggested.

Or was I "thinking too precisely" on the event? What did I know so far? The ^{14}C dating placed the pipe around 1600 plus or minus. So we could say it went into the wall during the Bard's lifetime. Allowing for error on both sides of that date, and knowing that Will set off for London in 1590, I conjectured that the pipe and he almost surely crossed paths. Was he its owner? Was he the smoker of tobacco laced with nutmeg? Here's where the lip cells came into play. Did Audrey, poor dear, have any link to Shakespeare or to someone he might have known? That would be my next mystery to solve.

 * * *

C hapter 7

Audrey had evidently been interested in tracing family trees, bless her, and she had posted the results of her search on one of those public genealogy web sites. I had always been drawn to the exponential expansion of relatives as soon as one began reaching back. Two parents branched into four grandparents, who branched into eight great-grandparents, who branched into sixteen great-greats and so on, not to mention the addition of aunts, uncles, cousins, and illegitimate relatives in each generation. Along with

DNA registry of the peerage and the imprisoned, the data base had grown considerably through the efforts of genealogy buffs, who individually ponied up the fee for their own profile. Though we did not have DNA samples from prior generations, when we did get a scraping and replication off an historic artifact, we could match the graphic blueprint from that sample with profiles of actual people in the data base and achieve a convincing level of certainty with a match.

Some researchers got no further than about four generations back before they lost the thread. Unless, as in noble families, clear records of lineage had been maintained, someone would have had to ferret out birth and marriage records in the legal or ecclesiastical rolls. We had witnessed this as the case with Shakespeare himself, as most of what we knew of his life, and that of his family, came from those instances of public record—buying or selling property, entering into a lawsuit, performing a rite in the church. We'd had to surmise the Bard's actual date of birth—not entered—by backtracking from the date of his baptism, which *was* entered. The problem modern researchers encountered—in contrast to the internet age's easy and quick access to almost any tidbit of information— was the fact of fires over the centuries. If a church or a county seat office burned down, there went all their records of the past and its people.

But as I paged through her results, I saw that Audrey had accomplished a heroic feat in her investigation— maybe a facet of her journalistic inquisitiveness. Following the enate, or side of her mother, I found a proliferation of common English surnames reaching back through the centuries. Evidently the families had been devout in recording each generation's tree in the family Bibles, and these had been passed from mothers to daughters. This was an English family that had stayed put, localised fairly specifically in Warwickshire, to the north and west of London, not coincidentally the location of Stratford itself. It was generally easy enough to trace a family line back to 1900, just a hundred years and three or four generations.

If the family had stayed put and kept some records, the 1800s were often accessible too, but beyond that generally records tapered out and sleuthing into traces found by other researchers was necessary. Audrey had networked well and filled in missing links, so that, as I continued to click the cursor, I saw the dates reach back and back into remote times. The 1700s were well fleshed out with daughters and their mothers, and the surnames were looking more and more like ones I'd seen in history books, with antiquated spellings. We were now into masses of relations, the exponents of ancestors forming dizzying branches on the tree.

But I kept on, mesmerised, relishing this glimpse into the family of England, noting through the names how even acquaintances I had today might be shirt-tail relatives of Audrey's extended family, Hathaways, Halls, Harts, and so forth. This process was in a sense an uncovering of Audrey's identity, similar in a way to the examination of physical forensic matter only here in its digital form. Each leaf (as it were) on this tree represented a flesh-and-blood person with habits and proclivities, trials and tribulations. I was hoping to find one of them who liked to inhale tobacco with nutmeg and who had found reason to secrete the smoking vessel in the wall at Stratford.

Something about these names on the screen was ringing a bell in my memory. I knew a little of the Shakespeare lore, of course, but did not consider myself an expert. Hall and Hart, along with Quiney, I remembered as descendants of the Bard, names of the families into which his sisters and daughters had married. Some of their children had even been named Shakespeare as a first name or William Shakespeare as first and middle names. These surnames were appearing with more frequency in Audrey's tree as we approached 1650.

I switched over to a Shakespeare genealogy web site and with some surprise found an overlapping name. John Hart, noted as a sixth-generation descendant of the Shakespeare family through Will's sister Joan, also appeared in a branch of Audrey's tree. If this was a coincidence, it was an enticing one. John Hart had died in 1800 at age forty-five, ample time for having a family. If he had left us any daughters, then perhaps Audrey really was part of the Shakespeare family, all these centuries later. My heart resumed its rapid pounding. One of John's children was William Shakespear Hart, and sure enough there was a daughter, Sarah, with seven children of her own. I was feeling much like an historical detective.

At this point, however, in a couple of generations we had lost the matrilinear branch through lack of daughters, so a match would have less statistical strength. In the absence of a continuous line of mothers' mitochondria, though, we could follow the inherited X chromosome, although it weakened the sample as male children inherited an X and Y rather than two X's like daughters. As genealogist Peter Lee commented on a web site I was reading, "Slowly but surely the pedigrees of the distant Shakespeares are converging but it is a difficult business. There are so many large voids. The evidence is very scattered." I adjusted the scan to focus only on the X chromosome of my pipe profile, and the screen began to flash faces once more.

A few minutes, and there she was again. Audrey stared out at me like an old friend sharing a secret. While statistically there was room for doubt, the coincidences overwhelmed me. In my mind it was clear: Audrey was a Shakespeare descendant, and it was our Bard whose lips had held this pipe.

*   *   *

Chapter 8

Mum had persisted in her desire for me to meet Tessa's friend Elizabeth, and I had buckled under the pressure. Looking up at the clock, I saw that I would just be able to catch the tube to Mayfair for our appointed meeting for a drink at the Dorchester bar. And oh, bother, I had told her she could recognise me by a red carnation in my coat lapel, so I'd need to make a run into the florist's shop. All around, this date seemed like very bad timing.

Right now I had an enormous decision to make, probably the most important decision of my career, even of my life. Certainly I could, and would, turn over the ^{14}C results to the Stratford authorities. The pipe dated to Shakespeare's day, that I could report with certainty. But I could not with certainty place his lips on the pipe—it may even have been his sister who had smoked it—and I did not relish sending bardologists and the popular media down the garden path. I myself did not want to be the centre of an internationally-reported hoax or scam like we'd seen in the Ripper ordeal. My personal feelings aside, I could not with any level of scientific assurance report the pipe as Shakespeare's—and, even more vital, the DNA on the pipe as that of the genius. But for now I'd have to let the matter rest in the back of my mind.

I made it on foot to the florist's but was so short on time I grabbed a black cab for the Dorchester. Poshness oozed from the decor of the bar, but I was not uncomfortable for long until an exquisite woman with light brown hair worn up in a loose bun approached me, wearing a stylish black cocktail dress.

"Kingsley, I presume."

"Elizabeth. Am I really that obvious—sore thumb, what-ho?"

"The carnation. . . ." She smiled and gestured lightly towards the crushed bloom on my lapel. Suddenly I wondered if the wind had mussed my hair unspeakably.

"Shall we find a table? May I offer you my arm, madam?" The ambience of the Dorchester seemed to demand gallantry, and Elizabeth responded like a lady. I still was mad about classic martinis, and though I drank liquor seldom these days, was looking forward to the dry, icy crispness in the inverted cone glass. This famous bar was sure to make a fabulous ritual of its preparation and presentation with its Master Morelli and his team of mixologists who specialised in "bespoke" concoctions. I wondered if I dared order my preferred three olives but held back at the last moment in a surge of decorum and restraint.

"Old Tom?" the waiter inquired.

"Oh, yes, please."

"Dry?"

"Of course."

"Up?"

"Absolutely."

"Shaken?"

"What else?"

Elizabeth, to my surprise, opted for a martini as well, but one of the modern, flavoured sort, here called the "Dorchester of London" with "Bacardi, London Dry Gin, and bespoke Forbidden Fruit Liqueur." At least we had gin in common. I took that as a good sign.

"Seems we know quite a few of the same old crowd," I ventured.

"Ah, yes, well, Tessa's quite a good friend. Has been for years."

"I wonder that our paths haven't crossed before. Of course, I've been hiding in the lab, but where have you been keeping yourself, away from the world?"

"Kingsley, you do go directly for the jugular, I see. . . . I am sort of a late bloomer, as they say."

"Allow me to compliment the blossom." (Egad, where did that come from?) Elizabeth discernibly blushed.

"I'm actually a bit of a dink. Spent my teen years with glasses and spots and my nose in books. I confess I'm an addict," she continued.

"Virginia Woolf and the Brontës, all that set?"

"*Orlando* to be sure, but more like Mary Shelley and H. P. Lovecraft to my taste. I'm less a romantic than a fantasy fan, though you wouldn't guess from my demeanour these days. It all paid off in the end, though. I adore my job."

"Cutting big author deals, late lunches with writers, fancy-dress book release parties . . . ?"

"More like page after page of potential manuscripts, I'm afraid. I'm the point of contact for agents with the next sensation. But how about you? Is there a big discovery on the horizon?" She smiled winningly. I gestured to the waiter and discreetly ordered another round of the same. *I'll have to mortgage my flat to foot the tab,* I secretly thought, *but it will be worth it.* This woman had poise, humour, and a gorgeous mind.

"Well, I sense an analogy," I continued. "Rummaging through baggies from the scene-of-the-crime is much like looking for the next best read, I'd guess. The lab is mostly workaday. Applied methodology, don't you know."

"I imagine you are being humbly modest," she rejoined, sipping at her drink. "Word is you're rather a brilliant thinker. I'd guess you have an experiment going on the side?" Elizabeth had somehow intuitively struck the right chord in me, and I felt my guard dropping.

"Well, I do have a small lab set-up in a large closet in my flat, but it's quite basic—none of the fancy analytical machines of the company. And there's not much free time to experiment. I have some ideas on the back burner, but of late I'm distracted and preoccupied by matters on the table at work."

"Something other than the polythene bags cropping up? I suspect you must follow where the funding leads. Publishing goes that way, too. We may detest a manuscript at the same time as we know it will sell, and sell big, and we must throw our enthusiasm behind it, great literature be damned. Must put gruel on the table after all."

"Ah, please, sir—may I have some MORE?" Somehow I couldn't resist the line. She'd set me up perfectly for it, and she smiled with satisfaction.

"Seriously . . . what's the current project?"

"Can't actually spill it out—confidentiality and all that. But we do a lot of work carbon dating artifacts and tracing DNA profiles, not always involved with crimes and murders."

"So you're not cloning Dolly the sheep in the back lab? Or perhaps a twenty-first century version of Jack the Ripper, God forbid?"

"Oh, so you heard about our job earlier this year. . . ."

"Difficult not to, my dear boy. It was all over the tabloids. 'Ripper Diary and the Gory Truth' followed by 'Ripper Couple Scam Thwarted by Scientist.' I take it you're the heroic Scientist."

"At your service," I beamed back. I liked the way this woman thought, and the way she could hold her own. Touché and touché.

Elizabeth glanced at her watch and hurriedly said, "Kingsley, I must run. Dinner appointment with a client. Don't give me that look—really nothing glamourous or exciting—just work. A potential new sci-fi book in the offing. It's been such fun chatting."

Chatting? Well, yes, but so much more, I felt. She seemed to see the real me—no posing, no façades. "We've performed our duties to Mum and Tessa, but strangely enough I really would like to see you again. Possible?" I needed to confirm something before she disappeared like a fairy spectre from this enchanted bar.

"Well, everybody needs a friend, and whether or not they realise it, everyone needs a heroic scientist. Here's my card. You can give me a tinkle on the blower, and I hope you will."

She smiled, gave me a quick kiss on the cheek, and wafted away in a cloud of black chiffon and alluring fragrance. Through the sating of my senses with the fullness of her presence and the fog of fine gin in my head, I saw the waiter discreetly approach bearing a small silver tray. "Your check, sir," he said, oh, so softly.

*   *   *

Chapter 9

Two fine martinis hadn't resulted in a hangover, and I arrived at lab next day feeling an elevated sense of anticipation concerning the issue of two women, one from the past and one decidedly of the present and future: Audrey and Elizabeth. All this talk of heroism, tongue-in-cheek though it had been, had permeated my consciousness and my conscience. I knew I must do the right thing regarding the pipe, the scientifically ethical thing. Even though everybody wanted a discovery of some personal artifact we could link to a life otherwise shrouded in mystery, I could report only certainties, scientific certainties. It was tempting to imagine the media splash and the celebrity of reporting "Shakespeare's Pipe." I would go down in the histories as a scientific hero, to be sure, and everyone would discover the consistently stellar work of our lab.

I had refreshed my second cuppa and was staring at Audrey's face in my ruminations when there came a light tap at the door.

"Kingsley? How's it going with the pipe business? Got it all sorted out? Haven't caught a glimpse of you for days."

"Oh, Gordon. Come in, come in. Sight for sore eyes. Tea? I have Earl Grey. . . . Well, pedestrian going, really. ^{14}C on the ash is clear for circa 1600." Gordon's eyebrows raised into arches. He glanced towards the pipe on the examination table with what seemed a new respect.

"My stars. So it is a Tudor relic. You're certain of the reading?"

"Checked and double-checked. I gave the counting a long span for accuracy's sake. Exciting business."

"I guess you know my next question. Any trace of fluid or cells on the stem? Can you put this pipe in a specific person's hand?"

"Gordon. Glad you're sitting down. There were lip cells, and I have a profile." I clicked the screen away from Audrey's face and over to the graphic representation of a human's blueprint. Gordon gazed at it with wonder. Could these bars and blotches be the secret code of the genius of our Bard? The thought was awe-inspiring for any scientist. Just a small hitch, a minor deviation in any of the amino acids, A-C-G-T, could have determined the creative uniqueness of William Shakespeare, to date unrivaled and unduplicated in universal history.

"By gad, whose is it? Any matches?" Without a word, I clicked again, back to Audrey's gentle and steady gaze.

"Meet Audrey Thompson, modern day descendant of the smoker of the pipe."

Gordon's silence was almost palpable; it seemed to fill the lab. I could imagine that I was hearing the wheels of his mind as it assessed the situation, its possible results, and the next steps to be taken. Gordon was assistant director at the lab and wielded a steady hand. His head was always clear—reliable bloke all 'round. I relished sharing my results, and this was the time for corroboration, verification.

"Let's ring her up, then, on the old dog and bone!" Generally lab-rat types faltered when the mechanical tests had run their course and the human element became necessary. I was happy to see Gordon move directly to this uncomfortable recourse. Good man, confirmed again. "We can inquire if her great-greats included the Shakespeare family."

"Can't ring her. Poor dear met an early end, sorry to say."

"Well, that's the last of it then. You report your year and leave the owner a mystery."

"Except. . . . Our Audrey was a genealogy buff." I clicked the screen over to her heavily webbed family tree. Gordon took this in, again with the palpable silence filling the lab.

"She follows it back to the beginning of time, eh? Cain or Seth's side?" Gordon smiled. "Any geniuses hanging in the branches?"

I filled Gordon in on the brief Shakespeare family history I'd been able to sleuth out, and I clicked to the entry of John Hart in both lines, Will's and Audrey's. It was like trying to knot together two stretches of rope that didn't quite reach. "And then there's the bother of the missing daughters. Petering out of the mother's mitochondria."

"Hmmm. Dead end again," Gordon pondered. "But what about following the X chromosome?"

One more click and Audrey again stared at us from the screen. She was our tip of the iceberg, and without some other piece of physical evidence to link the pipe to Shakespeare's lips, we could only surmise if the Bard himself was submerged in the waters of her heritage. She was a prominent iceberg, but she still rested in the murky waters.

"Well, tough luck, old chap." Gordon seemed to have reached the inevitable conclusion. "Still, a Tudor pipe in the walls of the Birthplace—it's going to hit the tabloids.

You'll be on the goggle-box again, old boy. First the Ripper and now the Bard of Avon. What's next? The mastodon of the Scottish Highlands? A Warwickshire man as the missing link?"

"I don't fancy my own face broadcast to all England and the entire Kingdom. We're going to need a media spokesman if this keeps up. Though I'd prefer toiling away in quiet obscurity, this sort of press is always good for business. 'Get your DNA profile. Fill in your family tree' sort of plan. You're spot on, mate. I'll get the paperwork in order and ring up the Stratford blokes: 'circa 1600, smoker inconclusive.' And we'll get the pipe back into their hands. Don't want to harbour a security risk here in the lab."

Gordon downed the last of his Earl Grey and stood with a noticeable awkwardness. He looked me directly in the eye, and I could see an odd watery glaze behind his glasses. What had brought on this unaccustomed surge of emotion? He extended his hand and then pulled me immediately into a brief clumsy embrace.

"Kingsley, I just want to say I'm proud to be part of your team. We stand here together on the verge of glimpsing the secrets of life. There's no other I'd want to share such a moment. You keep us to our professional ethic. You're a prince of a man." Then he turned quickly on his heels and the door of the lab swooshed shut on its automatic hinges, leaving me alone with my pipe, my inconclusive results, and a stash of DNA potentially as powerful as dynamite.

* * *

Chapter 10

I rang up Mum to report dutifully on my date with Elizabeth. Her machine picked up, and I was grateful not to have to submit to her certain interrogation over all the gory details. "Kingsley here. Just calling to say thanks for the intro to Elizabeth. She is indeed a lovely girl, and we had a splendid time. I'm sure to see her again. Love you, Mum! Talk soon." My timing had been lucky, as today was her weekly book club meeting. I'd have to make a mental reminder of that—good way to avoid a long chinwag and the lecture about grandchildren but still keep in touch.

I pulled Elizabeth's card out of my shirt pocket and examined it. The icon was of an open book—I hoped that was a symbol of her personality. Her image flashed into my mind, the way she held herself with composure and confidence but without abrasiveness. The quickness of her mind and the charm of her repartee. Her winning smile. I put the card near my nose and sniffed. Ah, yes, and her provocative perfume. She listed both office number and mobile. I dialed the latter.

"Elizabeth here." Thank God she'd answered in person. I hoped her heart had perhaps skipped a beat at the sight of the lab's caller ID. In my eagerness and distraction I'd forgotten the injunction against private calls on the company phone.

"Have you survived the old gin fog? Kingsley speakin', if you can recall who I am." What a lame opener, I thought with chagrin.

"Oh, yes, no harm done. What a pleasant evening! Thanks for taking it with such grace, being set up and all."

"My dear, **you** are the epitome of grace, and I am completely smitten. There you have it. All said. Heartstrings left dangling."

"What took you so long?" she laughed, responding without a beat. "And where do we go from here?"

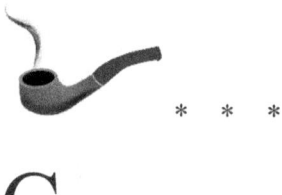 * * *

Chapter 11

Where we went from there was on a whirlwind of a courtship, at least from my admittedly inexperienced point of view. It was almost as if we'd been biding our time through our twenties and well into our thirties simply waiting for our paths to cross. Sometimes in life you feel a sort of kismet at work. Both of us had focused on self-development and fulfilling careers, yet there was a soul-loneliness unfulfilled in us both. We seemed to fit right together like pieces of a jigsaw puzzle.

Occasionally over dinner Elizabeth would fill me in on some of the plots in the manuscripts she was constantly scanning. The special interest of her portion of the press in fantasy, horror, and sci-fi attracted loonies along with bona fide authors. Her job was to sift through the chaff for kernels of grain. She read of aliens infiltrating space ships and of monsters beneath the sea. She told me of mutants and zombies and murderous ghosts, of utopias and dystopias. I wasn't quite clear on how she ever found value in these types of stories, but she explained to me that most of the plots were variations on a few classic themes. What made a work stand out for her was the beauty of the narrative consciousness at work. True literature was a mastery of forms, from sentences to archetypes. She had a discerning eye, and the press valued her for that.

During our conversations I shared a bit more backstory on both the Ripper case and the pipe before us, the only exciting events worthy of note within recent lab history. Against my better judgment I told her about trying to link the pipe cells to our great Bard but with little luck. I think the idea appealed to her imagination. She seemed to be able to sense the magic inherent in the scientific method.

At least my predilections and even my obsessions with scientific truth did not scare her away, and we grew close quickly. I discovered—or should I say revived—a deep sensuality within myself, which was rivaled in her own appetites. Evenings and week ends became glorious explorations into both a new mind and a new body. Mum had called several times to ask why I seemed AWOL, but I felt richly embroiled in life, with maybe even a richer future ahead for the two of us, Elizabeth and myself. We would soon find an opportunity to look eye to eye into the future, which laid itself out like a riddle before us.

*   *   *

Chapter 12

The fog was beginning to gather along the banks of the Thames, but Elizabeth and I had braced ourselves with warm alcoholic libations and bar tidbits and were clearing our heads in the air while enjoying a prolonged chat. Of late our conversations had been one of the few things keeping me grounded in the actual world. Without this warm, vital person to be my tether, my mind and I would be floating off in the ether somewhere like a kite that's lost its string. Elizabeth was well-educated and well-informed with a stunning wit and imagination. Being with her was a comfortable state, like lounging about in flannel pyjamas. She continued to display an uncanny intuition about my own character and bent of mind. As the youngsters say, she completely *got me*. Indeed she had me, and I could not be coy about it. I was an open book to her, like the one she depicted on her business card.

"So the matter of the pipe has been set to rest with no glitches?" Elizabeth inquired. "I was wondering, as you still seem a bit off in another world."

"Yes, my dear. Gordon and I concurred the only thing was to report the date but remain inconclusive on the owner's DNA. We were sure of that descendant Audrey, but we couldn't accurately name the forebear who smoked the pipe. We returned the item to the Stratford authorities along with our results."

"No big media blow-up either, really. They did report a new artifact but no one seems to be pushing the idea that it was Shakespeare's pipe, more's the blessing."

"Blessing indeed, but the lab's a bit of a rut again. I must simply get used to the mundane life. No heroism in my cards—but another fine blessing in you, my dear, my light, my joy." I put my arm around her shoulder and pulled her close.

"So that affair is concluded. But here we both are, grown-ups with our passions decided and the world seemingly pulling us down and holding us back. Kingsley, what would you really like to accomplish? Can't you see your life just ticking away day by day dealing with the mess of evil perpetrated by man against man those baggies represent? I'm almost envious of those writers who do create a best-seller. They are able to influence thousands of readers, to lead them forward, to change their minds forever. Don't you want to leave a legacy, make a mark— make a difference—something positive for this old earth?"

"How well you read my deepest thoughts," I responded after a pause.

"And what shall we do about it?" she asked, rhetorically, I felt.

She did not yet know the horrible fantasy I had begun to harbour in my imagination. I wanted to reveal my hope—which might become my intention—but it felt too potentially explosive to formulate into words. Elizabeth shuddered a bit in the damp chill and drew her collar more snugly about her neck. If I were to put my desire into language, if I spoke my dream, it might become a plan of action. I felt the need to keep it submerged in my thoughts alone, at least for now. The idea of it beamed out so enticingly that I could not be rational or analytical. I could not think it through to its probable consequences. But neither could I erase it from my mind. It seemed like the lighthouse ray that beckoned me to port. Safe harbour or fatal elfin fire? I could not know, unless. . . .

*   *   *

Chapter 13

The gas flame flickered in the click-on hearth of my bedroom, emitting a golden glow and a cosy warmth on this dreary London afternoon. Elizabeth lay beside me dozing, her hair gloriously mussed and haloed out on her pillow. Our relationship had developed without hesitation into a satisfying intimacy. We were as comfortable as two old married folks, willing to give all, eager to share everything. She had quickly become my best friend and confidante. Elizabeth was a perceptive and attentive listener, and I'm afraid I had hogged most of the "confessional" time.

What I did know about her work in a fully successful career endeared her to me. She had an uncanny eye for well-written archetypal stories. The books she sponsored ignited the imagination—while they incorporated predictable gems of underground catacombs, mad women in attics, phantasmagorical creatures both natural and man-made, and the daily practice of magic, the authors she found breathed new life into the old forms. In many ways Elizabeth was making a profound contribution to our heritage, encouraging and supporting visions of possibility that entertained us but kept us all dreaming as well.

She stirred a bit next to me, and I saw her shining eyes with their direct gaze blink and then focus. She smiled her winning smile with a look of comfort that reached into the core of my being.

"Hey, sleepyhead," I said, from my vantage point propped on an elbow above her.

"Ah, it's heaven to be warm here with you," she said, and snuggled close.

"Nothing to compare, my love." I hugged her in return. "You are my other self. I can't breathe without you near me. 'So are you to my thoughts as food to life, or as sweet-season'd showers are to the ground.'"

"Always the romantic hyperbolist," she laughed, pulling out of my embrace. "But in your case it's forgiven."

"From what you've told me about the manuscripts, you appear to share a bit of the same curiosities—driving passions, lust for life, dabbling in the forbidden arts. Would you like some tea to wake you up? Or at this hour, how about a drink?"

"Something light—Lillet?"

When I returned with the aperitif, Elizabeth had propped herself up with the pillow and began to talk more about her theories.

"It's not the conventions or the events that are appealing in a good manuscript," she began to elaborate. "Most readers will respond to these rather intuitively. Set the mood, and the precise effect is bound to follow. Have a remote mansion on the moors or a laboratory with a struggling, thwarted scientist, and you've prepared the ground. You've engaged the senses—what a professor of mine called the 'primitive' response. Then you can employ innovation and stimulate an aesthetic response—make everything old new again—put new wine in old bottles, as they say. I seek out the new wine of literature. What I look for is the same quality I adore in you, coincidentally."

"There's something you actually admire in me?"

"You already know. There must be a spirit of striving for whatever is possible. The character cannot accept apparent human limitations. He will see only the ideal, the best in all of humanity. The character will not be satisfied with mundane existence—simply will not settle for the lowest common denominator. Curiosity and daring, maybe even derring-do, is the only path, and we follow wherever it leads. The genre lives on because it inspires us even while its familiarity of form comforts. Don't you see? It's the best of all stories—a pattern we know with an outcome we may desire and fear. Compellingly told, these stories keep our species alive and well—and evolving."

"My darling, it's too much to suggest that in all of this there is any analogue to my own pedestrian existence, although I *am* flattered. My character is steady and my mind well-trained, but I creep with the snails rather than soaring with the peregrines. *You* are my light, and you lift my spirit to its greatest heights."

"Don't be so sure, Kingsley, or so modest. We are young, as yet, and life can be long, very long."

* * *

C hapter 14

Mum insisted on bringing the entire cast together at her townhouse: Tessa and her mum, and Elizabeth and myself. Good thing I adored women, as I was sure to bear the giant's share of good-humoured ribbing about our new romance. At the last minute I pressed Mum to include another of the male persuasion, and she allowed me to invite Gordon, of whom she'd heard a great deal. He'd been with the lab for a dog's age but was a bit at loose ends now, having lost his wife. While he was not what one would call a sparkling personality, he had a wry Scottish sense of humour and was urbane enough to contribute to just about any conversation. Elizabeth had pronounced him attractive in a serious, tweedy sort of way, and that seemed just fine for Mum, who was vibrant but traditional and not terribly with the times. No one could predict where their meeting might lead, but surely it would at least temporarily assuage each of their loneliness, and take the spotlight off of me alone.

Mum had focused almost exclusively on me and on Renaissance art after we lost Dad. She had bought a yearly pass to the B.M. and dragged me along each week end. She would plant me among the fossils and herself wander rooms of grand classic paintings, exposing her mind and taste to quite an education with the self-guided tour tapes. While she confronted and pondered Christ in many poses of distress, I contemplated trilobites and dragonflies in amber, wondering if their genes might still be accessible for examination and possible revivification. And then there was her bi-weekly book circle to keep her busy—but a romantic interest, even one at arm's length, might bring a surge of activity to her life and, I thought selfishly, take some of the pressure of her attention off of me.

Tessa and her mum, Gladys, were just beginning to sip their glasses of pinot gris when Elizabeth and I arrived with Gordon in tow. Tessa and I had been school chums, and she and Elizabeth were good girlfriends. Gladys was a stylish middle-aged woman, longtime friend of Mum, and member of the book circle.

"Here's the happy couple now," Mum cooed as we came in. Everyone grinned knowingly at us.

"Mum, Tessa, Gladys, I'd like you to meet Gordon, stalwart of the lab. He knows all my secrets at work, so treat him well, would you? Gordon, these are the important women in my life."

"Ladies, a very great pleasure indeed!" Gordon nodded with an old-school air as he gently took each woman's hand. "It will be difficult to keep closed lips in such delightful company, I'm sure."

"Wine, everyone?" Mum poured and passed around the glasses. "Here's to a rosy future for us all!"

"Hear, hear!" "Cheers!" "Cin cin!"

Mum set a beautiful table and was an accomplished cook. She treated us to a carrot and ginger soup followed by short ribs glazed in pomegranate with a Yorkshire pudding. She saved the mixed greens for a palate cleanser and ended with a good old English trifle, layers of lady fingers, cream, and fruit. Each course included more wine to keep the conversation good-humoured and well-oiled. We covered Elizabeth's and my meeting. We reminisced about how things, including ourselves, had changed since our school days. Gordon spoke a bit about his youth in the northern climes. Mum and Gladys shared their latest read and news of the traveling gallery exhibits.

"Quite a splash you fellows made with that recent pipe business," Tessa finally broached. "And before that the Ripper hoax! Who says lab work is boring? Kingsley, you've always let on that it's quite un-glamourous. I think you've been misleading us just to put us off the scent. In reality you're shaking the earth on a daily basis behind closed doors, eh, Gordon? Mysteries of the past, the secret of life, forbidden experiments, that sort of thing?"

Gordon and I exchanged a quick, knowing glance. Gordon had been graciously accepting refills to his wine goblet, and I saw him prepare to take the bait. With a flushed face, he began to outline our methodology in testing the pipe—still, in my mind, *Shakespeare's* pipe.

"Kingsley took the brunt of the responsibility," he said, generously. "Must be oh-so-careful to avoid contamination, preserve the integrity of the artifact. Some of these younger chaps get excited or cavalier and take short-cuts. Step by step the lab CAN unlock mysteries, Tessa, my dear. Just have to be patient and persevere. Kingsley's our man for that, no doubting his results. His testing is correct and his own ethic unquestionable. I've never known him to betray our allegiance to the scientific method and its explicit codes."

"I'm fortunate to have colleagues like Gordon to palaver with on possible findings," I chimed in—as the heat of the limelight was making me uncomfortable. I did not cotton to all this talk of the scientist as contemporary hero and saviour, especially given the thoughts that had occupied me lately.

Gordon had warmed to the subject. "Well, that Ripper diary's over and done with—until the next fame-seeker produces a new artifact—and the pipe's all wrapped up, too. Literally, wrapped up and returned to Stratford, complete with all our findings, right, Kingsley? So I'm afraid it's back to skin cells under fingernails and soil samples in tyre treads, with that creature we've been cooking up relegated to the back burners."

Everyone laughed at Gordon's "confession," and Elizabeth took on the discussion. "Our literature has accomplished keeping all the great myths and stereotypes active in our collective imagination. Every month I see several manuscripts that rework our classics in one way or another. All the patterns pre-exist, and we love to see them applied to updated circumstances—hero with a thousand faces sort of thing."

"Oh, yes, our book circle loves a familiar pattern," remarked Gladys.

"Gordon and Kingsley may not have a creature on the back burner," Elizabeth continued, "but in our fantasy they *could*. We need to keep that possibility open. We feel a need for the doors to magic remaining ajar. Robots, clones, monsters, the insane, creatures and destroyers—combine that cast of characters with the brilliant, the heroic, the tempted, and you have ever-resonant patterns."

"Oh, you've always had such a great imagination," remarked Tessa. "Even when we were kids. You'd be acting out dragons and heroic battles."

"We *want* to imagine secret workings of labs after hours and behind locked doors. That may even have been the allure for our professionals here. Tell us, Kingsley, weren't you drawn to the forbidden potential in the scientific method? Don't you feel that one day you will discover or create something on the cellular level that brings the human race closer to God? We have the desire to know. It's been with us since we stood on two legs and fashioned an axe-head."

"Or when Eve tempted Adam with the apple," said Gordon.

"You can even find that in the B.M. displays," Mum added. I was glad to see her participate. "When the finger of God touches the form of Adam, it's the spark of creation, the spirit of life, He's transferring. When the womanly saint raises her eyes to heaven in ecstasy, she's feeling the power of the Creator within her. Haloes are the glow of that life force. In art we must visualise it, but in the lab you must *render* it visible. The struggle for existence, the battle between good and evil, between creation and destruction, it all happens in actuality on the atomic level, like specks of paint in the pointillist style that come together to create a form."

"What a fascinating connection!" Gladys commented. "I'd never thought of dots of paint as atoms, but of course. Put them together into a conglomeration, and you achieve the visible image." She looked at each person at the table rather conspiratorially. "You can see I chose my colleague carefully. No end to the enrichment, in books and in art."

"Isn't that how a computer screen works, too?" Tessa conjectured. "You have millions of the little dots—what are they called—?"

"Pixels," Gordon and I said in unison. "It's short for 'picture element,'" Gordon explained.

"That's it, pixels. When the image gets blown up you can see the tiny individual pieces that make up the picture. Kind of creepy, really."

This subject interested me, and I couldn't hold back now the conversation was rolling. Usually in social gatherings I tried to steer clear of philosophy and scientific details. Most people did not enjoy conjecture or theory, and it was both safer and more comfortable to stroll gently through inconsequential topics and contemporary events. Wear your learning lightly, we'd been taught. But this group had stridden confidently into some of my favourite terrain, guided by my amazing Elizabeth. "And, perhaps more importantly, you can see the spaces between the dots." My comment landed with a thud, and silence rose around it like a cloud of displaced dust.

"Hmmm," said Elizabeth as the dust settled slightly. "You need to explain this further, Mr. Scientist. I'm thinking you mean that the atoms are rather like the mythic patterns in stories. They comprise a template, a backbone as it were, but the actual materiality of existence contains many variables, like the blank spaces. Am I on the right track at all here?"

"If not the highway, at least the by-way," I responded. "When you and I look at each other, or touch each other"—I gave her an affectionate and intimate glance—"we are interacting more with space than with matter, as strange as that may seem. We appear palpable and whole, but think about those models of atoms you studied in grammar school. Often the impact of the lesson eludes us at that age."

"I confess I don't think much about atoms on a daily basis," Tessa laughed. "Even if we did learn about them with our three R's."

"There is the nucleus, and it's surrounded by orbiting electrons. The whole of the atom is substantially the blank space occupied by those orbits. It's a vibrating matter, cohesive through the gravitational pull, if you will, of the centre, the core—sort of like the earth and the moon, or many moons, if we had them. Do you remember the models made by school children for their science fairs? Put the earth and the moon at its appropriate distance into a very large box, and I think you can see it would be mostly empty space."

"Of course, it would be an outsized box indeed," Gordon commented.

"Or on a larger scale, imagine our sun with its many orbiting planets. Place the solar system into an extremely large box in your imagination and then peer into it, if you would. Primarily you will see light-years of empty space. Yet we do exist, and we seem real and substantial. We can individually think about and consider our own existence. *Cogito ergo sum,* as Descartes observed. *I think, therefore I am.* I am aware of myself thinking about myself. Am I subject or object or both? Where does my self reside? And where do I stand to observe that self regarding itself?"

"Yes, it may seem odd to compare the galactic with the atomic," Gordon confirmed, "but that's one of the great correspondences of order. Our Creator made 'something' out of virtually 'nothing.' And the patterns all fit together."

I picked up where Gordon left off, sort of tag-team philosophy. "So the secret of life we've discovered in our labs, if you want to know all, is something you cannot place under a microscope."

"And you are taking home a fraudulent salary, then?" Tessa asked playfully.

"You might say that," I replied. "What holds everything together is the 'glue' of creation, breath, spirit, that which resides in the 'spaces in between.' Life is a vapour. This is something known by all creative geniuses. It's art that carries the truth."

"Yes, that is what I feel in the great galleries of the B.M.," Mum reaffirmed.

Encouraged by Mum's comment, I continued. "We needed to know, as Elizabeth has said, and then we needed to express. We drew sketches in ochre on cave walls. We left our own palmprints there too as negative images, paint blown around the outline of the hand. We beat on hollow logs to make organised sound. But music is as much in the silence as in the reverberations of the notes. 'For what is your life? It is even a vapour, that appeareth for a little time, and then vanisheth away.' The wonder, the miracle, is that we make any kind of mark at all on this earth, given our insubstantiality."

I gazed at all the faces around the table, and they were wonderfully open to the ideas of this discussion. Those gathered here could not guess, I supposed, how near the topic was to my own thoughts of late. I was indeed close to examining this relationship between matter and spirit on my own.

Gordon added, "The creation stories talk about God as 'breathing life into us.' That animating breath is the glue that makes us cohere."

"In Comparative Religions we had a unit on Asia," Tessa eagerly recalled. "I remember their poets and philosophers talking about the space contained within the vessel to be as important or even more important to its function as the bottom and sides, those parts we consider as material and real. Is that what you're getting at?"

"Oh!" Elizabeth perked up. "I remember hearing somewhere that when you watch a film, for over 50% of the time you're sitting in a dark cinema staring at a blank screen. What you actually have is a series of still shots placed together in a sequence. The human eye will hold onto an image and then connect it with the next one to make the mind think it's perceiving movement. But it's just static images, one after another with darkness between and all around. We are the ones who perceive it and then make the meaning, out of a kind of nothingness."

I continued, amplifying Elizabeth's analogy. "I guess by extension you could say that each person carries the Creator within." This conversation had gotten lively. "The genes are the material blueprint, and that's what we scientists work with. But life resides in the invisible force that animates matter. Life and being—they exist in the spaces in between."

Mum had been silent for a while but suddenly her eyes brightened. "Kingsley, when your father died, I had that experience," she said solemnly. "They brought him to hospital, and I sat by his side. 'He' was there, and then, in an instant, he was no longer there, even though the body remained. When the light drained from his eyes, I felt a waft of breath enter into my own being. I've never said this before, but I think his life force came into me and I carry it as part of myself even to this day."

Everyone was respectfully silent following this confession. "How beautiful," said Gladys, touching Mum's hand. To regain her own composure, Mum offered refills on coffee and brandy.

"That gets us into conservation of spirit, no pun intended," I observed, "and it must be a topic for another day. No more brandy for me, Mum. What a glorious dinner, and what lovely company, all. But I think I'd better get my companions back to their warm beds before dawn arrives 'with her rosy fingers,' as Homer would say."

Gordon, Elizabeth, and I rose from the table, and Elizabeth began helping Mum clear away the dishes. I felt it had been a successful evening, and I was grateful Gordon had been present as intellectual and moral support. This group did seem genuinely interested in our work, and I felt safe and comfortable with them and their good will. Much to be said for family and old friends. But none of them, not Elizabeth, not Mum, not Gordon even, could conceive of the turmoil within my own spirit and the terrible but wonderful secret I harboured in my lab.

 * * *

C hapter 15

The living Shakespeare occupied my mind these days. I was racking my memory by day and scouring the plays by night trying to find counsel to guide me through my ethical dilemma. It was easy enough to pick out a line here and there that sounded sage—yet not terribly helpful. "A wise man knows himself to be a fool." "'Tis one thing to be tempted, another thing to fall." To get at the truth of these statements I had to remember it was not Shakespeare speaking but a character. I saw deep irony embedded in most of these lines, as if Shakespeare were purposely undercutting the inherited wisdom of the ages. It was frustrating not to be able to have direct access to his phenomenal creative mind. Everything left to us as "Shakespeare" was buffered through the medium of drama or the elaborate and artificial conventions of the poetry of his day. I needed to know what he, the author, really thought. I wanted Shakespeare to speak directly to me.

My editions told me little about the man and his life. In a desperate search for facts I left work early on Friday afternoon and jumped on the tube, emerging at the Euston Square stop for University of London. A passing student pointed my way to Humanities, and by reading the board directory I located a resident Shakespeare expert, Trelawny Huddlestone. I found his office door and knocked tentatively. This was unfamiliar territory to me, the literature wing at university. The professor called out "Come," and I pushed open the door.

He was not as old or tweedy as I expected—rather a youthful chap surrounded by piles of books and papers in disarray. His hair was rumpled, and he looked a bit weary.

"Yes?"

"I'm not a student, sir, but I was wondering if I might call on your expertise for a few moments. Kingsley Armstrong."

"Well, what's on your mind?" he asked gruffly then suddenly sat forward in his chair. "Say, aren't you that fellow with the Birthplace pipe? I've been following the story in the press."

"We had it for testing, but it's been returned to its rightful place. It was Tudor all right but otherwise inconclusive. Might have been the Bard's. We can't say for sure."

"Always exciting to think of an authentic artifact. We have such a scarcity of genuine Shakespeareana. Why don't you have a seat?" He rose from his chair and bustled to the front of his desk. "Here, let me move that stack of papers. Endless marking, don't you know, bane of a teacher's life." He cleared off the seat for me, piling the stack onto his already cluttered desk. "So exactly what kinds of tests did you run on the pipe?"

I was taken aback by the specificity of his question. Surely he was unfamiliar with laboratory processes. "We followed our usual protocols in cases like this. Physical description, locale found, carbon-14 dating, and of course, DNA profiling."

"You mean there was actually 400-year-old DNA on the pipe?" He seemed more than casually interested.

"The carbon dating placed the artifact at circa 1600, yes. And we were able to scrape some lip cells from the stem." I tried to be careful not to give away any confidential information.

"Oh, my! That puts the pipe from Shakespeare's house in somebody's mouth, doesn't it? Do you realise what an extraordinary find Bard DNA would be? You might almost say that discovery would change the world. We'd all have to agree to what use it might be applied."

"Well, no worries," I quickly backstepped. "We were unable to make an accurate identification. As you probably know, the Bard's line died out within a few generations."

Dr. Huddlestone sighed. "Another dead end, alas."

"That's actually what brought me here to you. Working with the pipe got me curious about Shakespeare the man. I was hoping you could help fill in some of the blanks."

His body relaxed as he settled back in his chair. "Blanks are all we have, dear fellow. The facts you can enumerate on the fingers of both hands, all from public entries about his estate and possessions—except for these grand praises of his genius by his fellow actors John Heminge and Henry Condel. Here, look at the Preface to the First Folio." He took a gigantic tome from his shelf and opened it to the front pages. "These friends called him 'a happie imitator of Nature, [and] a most gentle expresser of it,' and added that 'His mind and hand went together: and what he thought, he uttered with that easinesse, that wee have scarse received from him a blot in his papers.'" He traced his finger along lines in a large, old-fashioned print.

"It's clear they admired his talent, even considered him a natural genius. And look, here's the famous dedication, a sweet poem by his friend Ben Jonson, saying that Shakespeare, 'star of poets,' 'was not of an age, but for all time.' We have these testimonials, and we have inherited a body of work called 'Shakespeare,' but we do not know, we cannot know, the man himself except through a glimpse here and there. He exists for us as a cipher, an image we need to create for ourselves."

"But I have so many questions." I sat forward in my chair. "Is there nothing else to give us insight into what he thought, what he was like? Is there any point at which you experts think he speaks to us directly? I want to know how the synapses of his brain fired to make poetic connections, the eye that 'glanced from heaven to earth,' 'in a fine frenzy rolling,' as he says in one of his comedies."

"Sounds rather mystical, doesn't it?"

"I want to unravel the chemistry of that mystery."

"Ah, you and all the world through the ages. All we can do is attempt to reconstruct."

I reached into my coat pocket for a list of ideas I'd been assembling during my reading. "What a fabulous memory he must have had, to know thousands of lines by heart. And what a sense of rhythm to produce what seems like impromptu speaking all clothed in blank verse."

"Yes, Jonson notes this as effortless iambic pentameter that must have peppered even his daily conversation. He seemed to be intimate with the heart of mankind at the same time as he was a master of mythic stories—struggle of the sexes, urge for revenge, push through ambition for power and position. He probably carried a sense of his own excellence, as his contemporary Robert Greene called him an 'upstart crow' and a 'Shake-scene.'"

"So was he himself a role-player, a chameleon?"

"Well, you know he was an actor. His work assents to the power of love, yet he left his own wife and family in pursuit of . . . what? We can only conjecture—a livelihood, fame, the glamour of London city life, a private passion."

I consulted my list. "But was he present when his children were born? Was he a proud papa?"

"We know that his only son, Hamnet, departed this earth at age eleven."

We were interrupted by a knock at the door, and a young face peered in. "Professor, can I see you about my essay?"

"Will you return in—say—thirty minutes?" The professor gave me an inquiring look, and I nodded. The door closed.

"So what would Hamnet's father have wanted to teach him; what heritage did he desire as a personal bequest to the future?" I continued.

"He had a grandchild, Elizabeth Hall, he may have spent time with."

"Did he teach her to angle or to hunt? Had he realised he was becoming legendary? Did he recite to Elizabeth lines from his own great writings? Was he a storyteller? Was he an antic clown?" My list seemed endless, my curiosity unsated.

"I like to think he was a man of humour and of heart."

Not much help there. I continued to read from my list. "Did he whisper love sonnets to his own wife Anne? Was he a sober and sombre personage? Or was he gregarious? Had he planned to retire from the world of letters? Was he optimistic about the human race?"

"Whoa! Slow down there. All we know is that in his will he left Anne 'the second-best bed.' You may interpret that as you like it. As your questions indicate, so much yet to discover about our genius and not much hope of new evidence from his life. Most of us scholars have given up hope for new discoveries in bardology and in fact have taken to reinventing Shakespeare constantly through modernised versions of his works. We call it 'presentism,' *Julius Caesar* set in a Nazi Germany, *Romeo and Juliet* as gang wars, Hamlet as a thwarted action hero. There is still lots of interest in—and profit from—Shakespeare, but whose Shakespeare? He has become a lucrative trademark rather than a literary giant."

The professor concluded his lecture without really answering any of my questions. I decided to turn to a slightly different topic. During the past weeks after returning the pipe, I had scanned the shelves at Foyle's to find the contemporary Shakespeare news, and I had these books spread out on the desk back at the lab along with my copy of the *Arden Complete Works* from my Cambridge days. I had noticed that even the visual images presented to us blurred into confusion, and the professor had a poster of some of these portraits on the wall behind his desk. They were arranged in rows like Andy Warhol's soup cans.

"I've seen different portraits of him, too, beginning with that familiar Puritanical-looking wood carving from your First Folio of 1623." I pointed to the first picture on his poster. "The basics give us that primitive, plain-looking balding man in a square collar, and at the other extreme that fully-recognisable squiggle portrait by Picasso, again a balding head and roundish face."

"Oh, yes, the centuries have offered us romantic gypsy-like portraits and noble Grecian classic portraits." He turned and pointed at each one in turn. "We have pale-skinned bards and swarthy bards. Here in one portrait he wears a single earring. These images do not form into a consistent composite—instead they speak of predilections of the viewer and the culture. Whatever we need in our bard, that's what we envision as 'Shakespeare.'"

Ah, I thought to myself, as my mind jumped back to our dinner party conversation. We have, as with DNA, a blueprint or a template of the man, but he lives for us in the darkness of the blank spaces left in his biography.

"May I ask where you acquired that poster? I love the way it illustrates our varying visions of the man."

"I picked up several copies at a specialty store during my travels. Here, because I'm afraid I've been of little help to you, why not take this as a memento of our conversation?" He reached into a bin and handed over the cluttered desk a roll in cellophane.

"I'd love it! And at least, sir, you've verified my suspicions. Most things about the man we'll just never know." I rose and put the rolled poster under my arm. "I'd like to thank you for your time."

"Thanks for stopping by. Fun to meet someone who's handled the Birthplace pipe. We don't often get public interest in our subject."

"Grateful for the chat," I said, as I opened the door. The anxious student was waiting just outside, and he replaced me in Professor Huddlestone's office.

I returned home, and, stimulated by this conversation, secretly threw myself into Bard research. I hung the professor's gift on the wall in my home lab. Gordon had been correct in saying that the matter of the pipe had been wrapped up and laid to rest. There was a pipe, it was from Shakespeare's days on earth, it had been returned to the Birthplace, and that was that, owner and smoker unknown.

But, as my heart pounded out in a kind of daily mantra, *not unknowable, not unknowable, not unknowable.*

In the moments between forensics jobs at work I pondered my Bard books. My head was filled with speculation and conjecture—and lines and lines of wonderful poetry. The dinner party conversation haunted me. What is a man? Once the body has been interred, what happens to the essence? There were traces of this man, no doubt, in the writings rescued for posterity by his compadres. Aside from us now digging up the bones and extracting the marrow's DNA, all else was lost—except for perhaps that sample we'd garnered from the Birthplace pipe. Strange that a rhyme on the Bard's gravestone specifically warned against exhumation—"Cursed be he that moves my bones."

I knew theoretically, and my imagination could visualize dramatically, that everywhere people went throughout life they left traces of themselves. We shed cells and hairs and droplets of sweat and spit and blood and pus and phlegm and—yes, tears—continuously. Plants, sea creatures, dinosaurs, and every species of man, all left microscopic traces piled 'round us and under us. This old earth was more than knee-deep in DNA; it was strata-deep in traces of life, traces of unique individual lives. The rub was in separating and isolating an individual trace. But that problem was solved for us with this enticing pipe artifact. The DNA—if it was Shakespeare's—was there, in a vial in my lab, real, separate, and all replicated out, ready for whatever came next. Was it Shakespeare the man I had in my possession?

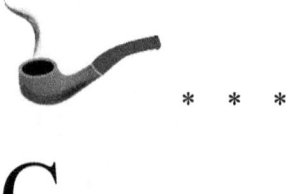

* * *

C hapter 16

After a light tap on the lab door, Gordon came in carrying two steaming polystyrene cups. "Well met, old man!" I greeted him.

"Aye, long time, do you have a minute? Brought you in a wee cuppa." I swiveled my chair away from the table filled with Bard books, and Gordon sat across from me, handing me the tea. "What a charming girlfriend you've found in that lass Elizabeth!" he said. "I wanted to thank you for tagging me along for dinner. Some conversation, eh what? The secret of life and all that."

"Some fascinating perspectives on what we do, I agree. That group made interesting connections, especially with how we find meaning and truth. To tell all, the ideas have been playing around in my mind ever since."

"Same here, old chap. Makes me consider the microscope work with a renewed sense of purpose and importance. Anything to perk up the hum-drum. Maybe I'll come across that creative spark. Curious what sort of artifact might pop up next. You'll have to let me have a go at it next time, now the pipe business is well behind us. Too bad we couldn't make a certain trace on that DNA. Our own faces would be on every newsstand and goggle-box, probably brandishing the old pipe itself. What a relief to get the thing back to its home, out of our hands and our responsibility."

"Ah, yes, yes," I responded sort of absent-mindedly. Gordon glanced at the lab table behind me, spread with books.

"What's this? Still looking into our absent subject's life? Isn't that Will's portrait you're pondering? Do you think Audrey bears a resemblance?" he asked, surmising my purpose.

"Oh, no, I've pretty much let that go. You can just get curious, you know, and I was filling in some of the gaps in my spare time."

"That's a heap o' books for idle curiosity. But I know you, Kingsley, and you're not a man to take things lightly. Any mention in those books about smoking?"

"Not a whiff," I smiled back, and Gordon dropped the subject.

"I must say, that Mum of yours is quite a gal," he broached suddenly, and I realised this topic was the true purpose of his visit. "I wonder, have I your permission to pursue the acquaintance further?"

My smile turned into a hearty, delighted laugh. "What a role reversal, old friend! I feel like the proverbial father granting a suitor permission to woo his daughter. I must warn you, her dowry consists solely of her charm and intelligence! Of course, you have my permission—and my good wishes and blessings. A little fun will be just the tonic for both of you. Man is a social creature. We are not meant to dwell alone. 'Every Jack must have his Gill,' as our Bard might say. Now the pipe is gone, let his spirit guide you."

Gordon rose and as once before here in the lab he offered me a warm embrace. "Thanks, old boy! It sets my mind at ease." And I found I was beginning to enjoy this sense of extended family, as odd a lot as we might seem.

* * *

Chapter 17

After inadvertently rousing Gordon's curiosity when he spotted my Bard library in active use, I decided to keep any activities feeding my present passion—really, obsession—clandestine. I bundled up my tomes, loading them into tote bags for easy transport each day out of the lab and back to my flat. Within a fortnight, they were nicely situated on the table in my small home lab. I had constructed a rudimentary work space with materials gathered over a life-time of scientific puttering. When equipment was ready for replacement at work, I often salvaged it for my home lab, and now I had a modest and compact but respectable research and experimentation set-up right there beyond my lounge. Friends and relatives knew to steer clear of the mad scientist's private realm, so any project I dabbled in remained undisturbed for as long as it lasted.

The rotation at work was bringing 'round a three-week vacation for me. I welcomed the notion of some time off. Usually I would have added "to myself," but recently I could hardly conceive of leisure without putting Elizabeth into the picture. She'd been busy of late and just might go for some time away together, the two of us. London was, as usual in heading towards winter, drab, drippy, and gloomy. A week on the sand of a sunny beach might warm our bones and reanimate our spirits.

We were to meet for dinner at J. Sheekey, and I hoped to surprise her with the getaway proposal. I contacted an old acquaintance of Mum's who ran a travel agency, and she located a holiday package deal for Marbella in the south of Spain near Gibraltar. Five days away would be a delight and still give me a fortnight to work on my home project.

I was first to arrive at the restaurant and they'd seated me at a nice table. "My darling, there you are," I said as I looked up to see Elizabeth rushing towards me, and I stood to give her a hug and help remove the misty coat. I shook it off and draped it over a chair. I had already ordered her a glass of a fine Languedoc, and she sat and immediately sipped.

"Mmmm. You always know just what I need."

"Bit of a damp chill out there tonight. These dark winter days deflate the spirit despite ourselves. Glad I'm with you, my dear, and you are my ray of sunshine in any clime." She always took my compliments, which were genuine but sounded extravagant, I'm sure, with a kind of humble skepticism, and she gave me a crooked smile in response. "There's bound to be a lull at the publishers this time of year, yes? So why don't we seek the actual sun, take a few days in the south? That might help us endure 'til first cuckoo."

"Seriously, Kingsley? What were you thinking?"

"Can you spring a few days away? We can avoid all the holiday obligations and just focus on ourselves. I've found an all-inclusive resort in Marbella in the south of Spain. Swim-up bar and the lot. We can become scantily-clad beacons of paleness sporting straw boaters and clutching tumblers of sangria."

"Speak for yourself! I'll have you know I do visit the tanning bed, and I'm prepared to reveal—well, most. A few relaxing days in the sun sounds like just the prescription to cure the drippy drearies. You are a saviour, my love."

"Being your slave, what should I do but tend upon the hours and times of your desire?"

Our salads arrived, to be followed by brook trout, and we finalised details. Luckily Elizabeth could get time off, although I was sure she would tuck a ms. or two into her carry-on bag. Part of what I adored about her was her complete independence from me and her separate passions, yet still we drew together like magnets. Socrates's friend Aristophanes had recounted a myth about jealous gods separating the rotund human race into halves, which then spent all their time rolling lopsidedly around seeking to be reunited. She and I made a complete circle, or nearly so, augmented by family and friends. As a formerly inveterate loner, I found this to be a new sensation. I'd always had Mum, but now I had opened up to allow the circle to expand. And my spirit itself felt warmed, nourished, by these new connections.

*   *   *

C hapter 18

Marbella had proved a glorious refresher for the two of us, much like a pre-honeymoon. Elizabeth never failed in compatibility, cheerfulness, and stimulating company, and I tried my best to keep with the pace. Five days had whizzed by, yet in memory it seemed a leisurely blur of azure seas, warm sun on bare skin, exquisite cuisine, and nothing to do but be idle and enjoy sensation. All this seemed just opposite to my usual routine of a chilly commute with bag lunch in hand to a sterile lab where the wheels of my mind were all that heated up.

I was not expected back at work for ten days, and Elizabeth had thrown herself into waiting projects instantly upon our return. Mum, bless her heart, had her usual daily occupations, but now her evenings and week ends were taken up by Gordon, who accompanied her tirelessly to galleries and the B.M., followed often by an extravagant late lunch or high tea. They were both as giddy as teenagers.

While I'd tried to avoid pondering my dilemma while in the south, the idea and its potential had incubated despite myself. This was my secret alone, and somehow it seemed what I was born for. It beckoned me, whispering me on like destiny.

That whisper ironically drowned out—and silenced— my inner voice of conscience. On some level I knew all these things: that cloning a human was a scientific taboo, that I would in doing the deed violate a professional code of ethics and trust the lab had placed in me, and that I had little actual knowledge or experience in possible outcomes, other than that I would be supplying a new body to our Bard's genetic make-up. But the whisper hissed on, and its constancy emboldened me. It hinted at the grandeur of recreating our greatest poet; it stressed the urgency of opportunity, the DNA there and the rest of the requisites readily available to me had I the nerve.

Carefully preserved alongside my books was the blueprint of our literary hero, for while I had dutifully returned the pipe, I had slipped aside some of those lip cell scrapings—and here they sat, in my lab, like an undiscovered country. Three vials there were, and they drew my gaze as well as my imagination as I tried to focus on my reading.

My "Bard library" was arranged on my small lab table as it had been when I left on vacation, and I continued to scan the pages looking for insights into the poet, the man, with nothing new to be discovered. My now extensive research kept running into blind alleys. If only we could speak with him! Perhaps the secret of his genius would be immediately apparent. The gaps in our knowledge were entirely frustrating, with no hope of news, unless. . . .

If I were to move ahead, I would need an egg cell from which I could extract and discard the nucleus containing the donor's genes and then insert the "Bard's" DNA to fuse both into a viable egg that could be stimulated to begin division. A blastocyst would form, and that could be incubated, developed into a foetus that would be the twin of the source DNA. I wasn't actually thinking that far ahead at the time, but one of the items I had salvaged was a twentieth -century incubation machine. It sat at the ready next to me, and it would create the perfect environment for blastocyst development if supplied proper nutrients by the experimenter.

At work we had never been involved in cloning, but as a matter of course the lab had perfected the DNA replication process, and cadaver parts had been harvested by the forensic morgue in the event of some experimental necessity for a certain kind of tissue. A brief visit to the lab downtown would set me up perfectly for my little trial.

I cut an unlikely figure, here at the new year bundled up in a Scottish overcoat and cap with a healthy tanned face the only part of me that remained uncovered. The clerk at the tea stand greeted me with "G'day, gov'nor! You're looking quite the toff these days! New lease on life with the new year, eh?" as he handed over a steaming polystyrene cup.

I wandered into the lab with everyone saying "Kingsley! You look great! Get back to your gaff! You're on holiday!" I waved at Gordon as I passed his lab, and he jumped up to waylay me. Pausing, I pushed open the door.

"Back from the tropics, eh, lad? How brown you are! Good time and all?"

"Yes, splendid, thank you. Just popping in to pick up something from the lab. A little 'homework,' don't you know."

"Well, I do hope you'll try to enjoy some down time, and I trust you'll settle your mind on that Bard affair once and for all." After a slight pause, Gordon's eyes began to twinkle. "I've taken care of your family in your absence."

"Many thanks, old man. Gordon, you are a true gem. I've never seen Mum so glowing as she's been of late. Ta, now. See you in a fortnight."

I meandered towards my lab, scoping out the whereabouts of my co-workers. There was no big case on our tables just now, so most were tidying up or working through some of our backlog. Nothing at all happening in the morgue as I passed, so I gently pushed in through the door, moving directly to cold storage. All samples were perfectly categorised, and it took only ten seconds to locate "ova, human," pocket three specimens, and exit as silently as I had entered. Heart pounding, I continued to my lab, kept on my coat, turned on the light for show, waved through the window at a passer-by, shuffled through a few papers, and made my way back down the corridor to the door.

The only apt metaphor for how I felt on the ride back to my flat was "with child." This must be how pregnant women felt, a sort of holy importance, a warm glow extending only into the future. I was carrying an incipient, potential person in my pocket—and that person could be a new incarnation of England's greatest writer and mind. While my feeling was real and palpable, the idea was still premature and ghostly. All I could do was try my hand at the cloning process, and with my rudimentary equipment and my own inexperience, I was unsure of any chance at success. Somehow I felt obligated to try.

The DNA blueprint sat temptingly in my home lab. Over the weeks I had convinced myself that it would be a crime against both posterity and the past *not* to use it. All our questions could be answered with a simple process and some patience. I had not meticulously thought through the details of possible consequences; but the idea of the miracle compelled me forward. At this point I no longer had a choice. Wheels had been set into motion. While I looked innocent to my fellow commuters, in my pocket I had dynamite for the world of science, for the world of letters, for history, for England . . . and for my own private life, if I thought far enough ahead.

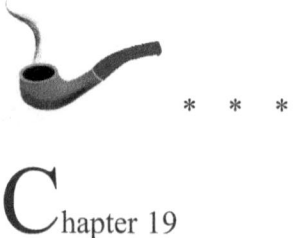

*   *   *

Chapter 19

Often I'd performed my weekly calls to Mum as a kind of dutiful obligation, but of late I longed as a son for a simple chat with his mother.

"Hullo, dear, how's the holiday going?" she said when she picked up my call. Gordon had convinced Mum to upgrade to caller ID.

"Hi, Mum. Oh, Marbella was simply divine. Nothing but sun, sea, warm sands, and potent potables. Elizabeth and I are both aglow with golden tans. Do tell Daisy she did well by us, won't you?"

"Of course I will. She'll be pleased. So glad you were basking while London remained its drear and drippy self. Now what's afoot for the rest of your holiday?"

"Nothing special, Mum. Elizabeth's hard at work, and I hear your time is productively taken up as well. With you both abandoning me, I plan on tidying up and puttering around in my lab here in the flat."

"Oh, such a martyr. But all work and no fun . . . well, you know what they say."

"My entire life is fun, with my family and friends around me and my work—my work—so compelling—and my passion."

"Oh, poor Kingsley, such a plodder. . . . When will you be finding room in your workaholic life to begin a new family? It's only grandchildren that will make our circle entirely complete."

"Ah, I seem to recognise that tune. Only time will tell, dear Mum. Elizabeth and I are certainly on the right path, and I'm so grateful to Tessa for insisting we meet. I could not have created a more perfect woman for myself. Elizabeth is simply a love. And speaking of which, I need to ring her up now. When shall we three meet again?—or four if Gordon tags along."

"Let's have lunch on the week end before you return to work, what say you?"

"Right-o, dear girl. Ta for now."

I immediately dialed Elizabeth's number but got her recording. These days, since our return from the south, she was deeply immersed in several book projects. Her passion for bringing science fiction visions to life drove her as my passion for the secrets of cellular life urged me on. We were both in our own worlds, now plunging forward in parallel. It was something of a miracle. I simply left a greeting on the machine to let her know she was on my mind, and then I turned to the urgent matter at hand.

Moving the Bard library to a side shelf, I cleared and prepped my work area. Ever since the news of Dolly the sheep, those of us in the scientific community had followed every nuance and development in cloning experimentation. The process was no longer a fiction or a fantasy, and I easily could get down to its brass tacks. The layman could even find step-by-step instructions on the internet. One only needed the right equipment and a bit of luck, although the process itself was universally forbidden. The experimenter in me moved deliberately ahead, closing his ears to rising whispers of ethics. There seemed to be only this very moment and precise procedures.

I carefully used the autoclave to sterilise my materials and laid out rubber gloves and slides, petri dishes, pipettes, and probes. My scope was at the ready, and I ran a quick cycle on the hand-me-down incubator. Check—operable. My three ova were preserved in the cooler, and I had the separated pipe DNA close to hand. I was methodical, and my mind moved forward with a singular clarity. The possibility had obsessed me for weeks, and now I must follow it through. It seemed an imperative. I could do it, and I was doing it. *I failed to wonder if I should.*

I extracted the parent DNA from a single ovum and then inserted my pipe DNA into it. This would erase any contribution to the organism from the original egg donor. All traits that developed in the ovum and—can I think it?— embryo would be determined solely from the genes of the pipe DNA. This was a relatively easy procedure, and it went smoothly, although my hands shook. I had that poster from the professor that compiled several Bard portraits in rows, and I had placed it on the wall above my desk. All those faces were like possible outcomes of my little experiment, all beaming down on me in blessing. The effect on my emotions was profoundly circular. While some might interpret the scene as outlandish and unspeakable, rather like bringing a long-dead corpse to life, it was sacred and holy to me, the fruition of my decades of research and dedication to science—maybe even my reason for being.

I was participating in—actually creating—the moment of human inception. I might be able to fashion a human being through science. But I had not considered what soul might appear to animate this body. Could the Bard's spirit, floating somewhere in the cosmos, sense the reincarnation of its old body and find it again? At base, that was the desideratum, the entire point: to bring our Bard to life once more and to experience the essence of his genius. Would the configuration of his brain and its chemistry manifest identically to the original in this copy? Again, there was that matter of his soul. What if the genetic genius received a criminal spirit as its life force, an Iago, as it were? What would determine the character of this genetic potential? I had not bothered to consider factors like context or the nurture part of a person's existence. These thoughts flitted through my mind as I inserted the pipe DNA into the egg, but my driving passion pushed them aside, and I proceeded as planned, in a sense consequences be damned. As in my life to this point, I would deal with problems as they arose.

With the insertion completed, I placed the zygote into an incubation environment. It appeared unremarkable, similar to other lab specimens in processes I'd performed countless times, and I was glad I had two spare eggs and plenty of pipe DNA if this attempt failed. My mind wandered through conflicting thoughts crowding into my head as I gazed through the scope at my little egg. Then, detecting movement, I blinked, and blinked again. *Consumatum est*; the deed was done. My zygote had begun visibly to duplicate and divide. A baby was on the way, and I was its parent, was I not?

* * *

C hapter 20

For the next several days I alternated between states of ecstasy and numbness, and time passed in a blur. The zygote demanded my attention like a pot coming to the boil. Whatever else I tried to do in my flat, the egg called to me, and I had to check on its progress. Cellular division was well underway, and I could detect lines and ridges on the surface as the structure became more complex and sophisticated. For just one moment my mind connected to a possible future, and I wondered . . . at what I had done, at what I was doing, at what might come next. At that instant I thought to destroy the egg. Part of the impetus for the experiment had been simply a self-test, a challenge: could I instigate a cloning? Yes, I could; I had. Let that be enough, test passed. But the root of my desire was much more, and that reached deep into dangerous ethical ground.

The dark mystery surrounding our Bard's creative genius drew me on—so many questions to ask him, so many observations to make about his perceptions of humanity and his poetic expression. All those answers resided in the material of my experiment, here before me, rapidly following nature's blueprint and bringing itself full-blown into our modern world. I did not allow myself to say that I was creating life in my makeshift lab in my flat.

Right now my zygote was to me cells under a microscope, excitingly dividing and reproducing. While I could not project into "what next"—the consequences—I also could not bring myself to end the experiment. My mind did not envision an actual corporeal person at that point. I was working with nature and the impelling imperative for life. It was not a creation, I told myself, so much as a *re*-creation.

The universe had presented me with opportunity, and it was my duty to use my skill to follow through. I could not bear to destroy the creation of which I was the sole parent. As I glanced up at my series of Bard portraits, it seemed that each of them was smiling in approval.

 *   *   *

C hapter 21

The remaining days of my work holiday continued to pass by in a fog. My machine had several messages from Elizabeth, but I was locked in a solitary state, rapt in my zygote and its process of division. I could hardly admit to myself the task I was engaged in, the course I'd set into motion, and I certainly could not be trusted in conversation with another. How would I even find language that could express my mental condition, let alone my spiritual state? And how could I explain my obsessed action?—not at all precipitous, but carefully planned and executed, even if without foresight. I stared at my zygote, ticking away with life, unassumingly following its cellular imperative for cleavage. Its motions of augmentation began to seem to me like the pulsations of a beating heart.

And that beating seemed to synchronise with my own heart, harmonise with my own pulse of life. I felt linked to this thriving organism, and with that symbiosis I neared a moment of no return. Almost against my will I had made a commitment, or a series of commitments—first to the pipe DNA as that of the Bard, then to preserving it for posterity. Next to the cloning attempt itself with the purloined eggs, and now, in spite of myself and my mounting fears of the unknown, to gestating and bringing birth to a human life, most likely the exact genetic replica of England's greatest mind.

When I had failed to destroy the zygote, I had crossed a threshold. My zygote was quickly becoming an embryo, and would grow into a foetus. Minuscule cells came and went in our lab. I had destroyed myriads of them over half a lifetime of experimentation. I could also have quashed this teeming life at an early stage, but I did not. The longer I waited, the grander loomed the ethics of the matter. In my soul, however, I knew I could not murder this creature I had conceived. Now I must turn to planning for its next few months of incubation and its debut into our twenty-first century world. Although variations of these genes lived on in others on earth, this was the precise genetic configuration that had resulted in literary genius.

At once the details of the future which I had instigated began to clarify and take shape in my imagination. Of necessity, I was to become a parent in perhaps the strangest circumstances the world had ever known. This pulsating compound cellular mass was to become my own child. Instinctively I bowed my head and said a silent prayer to our Creator, beginning with an Our Father and moving into a fervent confession followed by a plea for blessing and guidance. This must not be an unholy birth, no matter its conditions of inception.

My heart hoped beyond all hoping that the mysterious force of the universe would send a benevolent soul into my baby's body, one that would be fertile ground for full flowering of this miraculous DNA. And my future would now be dedicated to fostering this child so that the genius of our Bard could once again shine its light upon England.

* * *

Chapter 22

Calmed by my meditative prayer and steeled to my destiny, I turned my mind to present action. In my current situation, how is it that I could rather suddenly become a father? Mum had been pressing for grandchildren, true, but that implied a logical series of prior events. The days of foundlings left on the doorstep were long past. My child would not be of fairie magic, but of scientific magic. Of course, adoption was a possible "story." I visualised single parenthood, and it simply seemed unlikely, unlike me.

If my life were to be turned on its ear, and if I were to perform due justice to my child, a family unit seemed mandatory. The timing of it all was uncanny, seemingly predestined: Mum hounding me for a grandchild, and

Elizabeth, the perfect Elizabeth, walking straight into my life. I allowed these thoughts to gather and then settle into my consciousness, and then I inhaled deeply with a new sense of resolution. Glancing at my developing child, still a pulsating mass of vibrant cellular life, I knew what must be done. I hoped to become a husband as well as a father, and the sooner the better.

I had few qualms about confiding in Elizabeth. She believed in scientific miracles, and she knew my character. My situation might seem an event from one of the novels she sponsored, come to life literally here in modern-day England. And it occurred to me that might excite and delight her. She too was an adventurer. Together we would be a new version of Adam and Eve, a young middle-aged couple embarking on partnership and parenthood with a child of the past and for the future.

Suddenly my path loomed distinctly before me and my head was clear. Feeling much calmed, I surveyed the clutter that had accumulated in my flat and set out to tidy and clean. The sink was filled with teacups and crusty plates. I put them to soak and cleared and wiped the worktops. Moving through the lounge, I picked up stray papers and pieces of clothing. Walking towards the bedroom, I paused in the door of the guest room, picturing it in my mind redecorated as a nursery. Splendid! And there was a small bonus room that could serve as Elizabeth's home study, with a Murphy bed for overnight guests.

I arranged my closet, noting that I could easily compact the contents, clearing half the space for another's needs. I refreshed the bed muslins and towels, also running an antiseptic wipe over all the bathroom surfaces. Locating the Windolene beneath the sink, I began to polish the glass, but my eye became arrested by my own image. I was absolutely stunned by the vision of this man apparently so sure of his course. As I had analytically observed my zygote creation, I now surveyed myself with an objective eye, the eye of a scientist. What I perceived both excited and appalled me.

Step by step I had forged ahead. My intentions all along had been relatively innocent, fueled at first by curiosity and then by desire, which grew into a kind of obsession for knowledge. Elizabeth always cast me as a scientific hero, but at some point in this journey I had crossed the fine line of ethics into forbidden territory, and now I was beyond the point of no return and committed to, bound to, my own creation. While my plan was to bring this baby into our world and rear it as normally as possible, I was certain that others, if they found out my scheme, would accuse me of playing God.

I was not an over-reacher, and I did believe firmly in our Creator. Was it not our human imperative to let our talents shine? Were we not obliged to develop our potential to its fullest and put it to use in the world? Perhaps the Creator was actually working through me. In some way, according to some grand plan, maybe I was to be a pivot in linking the past and the present. Shakespeare himself had proposed a teleological view of human progress. The hand of God guided us all towards a benevolent conclusion—that was true grace. Perhaps I was meant to reveal this oneness of time, its purposeful flow—and its conservation of spirit. Our Bard already "lived on"; his writing bore a kind of immortality. My experiment was merely an extension of that immortal mind into a corporeal presence. I felt the enormity of the task ahead, to nurture this being back into the world. And I prayed that I would be equal to the endeavour.

Part II: The Birth

* * * Elizabeth Montague

C hapter 23

Since returning from winter holiday in Spain with Kingsley, I'd been under water at work. Writing had become a popular pastime, and everyone wanted to be a best-selling author, it seemed. Part of my job was to cull through the submissions, panning for gold. And I had endless meetings with agents who pitched their clients' plots to me. My mind was a-swim with tales of fantastic creatures and journeys through outer space.

I settled into my recliner with a hefty box of manuscript pages before me and a steaming mug of Lapsang Souchon by my side. Although my job consumed most of my energies and much of my free time—reading—it fulfilled me. In university I had specialised in literature, and this was an extension of my passion. Reading, not just for fun but for actual monetary profit. Until lately this work had been enough for me, as it fed and fueled my active imagination. Ideas filled my head and meetings, drinks, dinners my hours.

Most of my school chums had married by now, and they thought my single life glamourous. They alternately envied me and encouraged me to join their lot. Frankly, I was beginning to see the appeal of nesting. An empty flat was cold comfort even after drinks at a posh bar—or perhaps especially then.

Reading was a solitary activity—and ironically, most of the plots I read carefully placed the aspiring hero into a buzzing social context. Actions performed in a vacuum had no significant consequences. It was the effect of an individual's choices on society that was the stuff of narrative. I was, as they say, not getting any younger, and it would be well for me to apply the lessons of literature to my own life. What consequences lay ahead for me? Without some drastic changes, I could foresee only a bleak and solitary sameness.

My mind wandered away from the plot laid out on my lap. Kingsley was a blessing. I had long resisted Tessa's urgings for a romantic meet-up with any of her prospects for me. Through the years I'd found blind dates to be horrendous ordeals, awkwardness of introductions, search for something held in common, posturing of egos, push for instant intimacy. With Kingsley it was different, comfortable from the first moment as if we were meant to be together. He had a bumbling manner that was disarming. Yet his wit and humour shone through, and he was in many ways a naïf with an idealist's outlook, smart but vulnerable, sophisticated yet unmoored, anchored in his lab work yet adrift in the flow of his own life story. Rather like myself.

I don't think he was aware of how he was lending a sense of plot and sequence to my life, which now moved forward with a larger, expanded purpose. He was supplying a structure and perhaps a happy ending to my own personal narrative. I sipped my tea and felt content, washed in the warm glow of memories of the Spanish sun and my new sense of the security of a loving man and our circle of family and friends.

The buzz of the phone interrupted my reverie. I saw by the caller ID it was Kingsley, from his home number.

"Kingsley? I was just thinking about you!"

"Elizabeth, my dove. You are *never* out of my thoughts. Are you awfully busy, my dear?"

"Just settled in with a manuscript about an Irish bloke who runs across leprechauns in the Tara mining project. Were you aware how malicious those magical fellows can be? Evil to the core."

"Or at least cheeky, I hear. Well, sorry to interrupt your fun, but I'm rather urgently in need of your presence."

"I've missed you, too. I can visualise your tan fading already. How's your holiday home-work getting on? You've seemed the recluse these past few days."

"That, among other intimacies, is the present subject of concern. I need your excellent good counsel."

"I can tear myself away from the wee evil folk, I think. Shall we meet for a drink? Replay the original scene?"

"That would bankrupt me, I'm afraid, and, um, the subject is rather confidential and private. Could you come to my flat? We can cosy up to the hearth—and maybe you could bring along an overnight bag? In addition to mind-time I'd like some skin-time if you're game."

"You do know how to entice a girl. You make me feel desired. And important. And completed. Count me in. I'll be there with my bag and my still-vivid tan—and perhaps little else by way of clothing."

"Ah, I enjoy a good flirt! I'll be ready by half-six, my love." I could hear the smile in his voice.

* * *

C hapter 24

I felt equally at home in Kingsley's flat as in my own, although he lacked my reading recliner. And I adored his company. We shared similar values and dreamed like dreams—and we loved to laugh. Hours sailed by when we were in conversation, and there was also our physical compatibility. Single independence and freedom be damned—there was nothing like love-making when you were *in love*.

Kingsley and I were both what might be called "mature," no longer part of the young dating scene. Through our twenties and into our thirties we had put our heads down to study and then build careers. We'd each had the occasional fling, but our goals and energies lay elsewhere. Now we were both highly "evolved," both a bit lonely, both ready for a new stage of life. At first I resisted thinking of my identity as part of a pair, coupled up, but now it felt safe, nurturing, and comfortable. I was still completely myself but even more fulfilled, sharing with another.

I scanned my closet for a ravishing outfit, as Kingsley was always appreciative. Choosing and donning my laciest underwear, a snug pair of jeans, and a sequined top revealing décolleté, I packed my overnight bag. At the last minute I resisted stuffing the latest manuscript on top. I didn't mind leaving the leprechauns behind. This night we would remain undistracted, focusing only on each other. It was a quick tube ride from my place to his, and I knocked precisely at 6:30. Kingsley met me at the door holding a small bouquet of red roses. He looked quite the schoolboy, a tentative hopefulness in his gaze.

"Roses for the flower of my life," he said, as he embraced me with his free arm. "Smell! 'The rose looks fair, but fairer we it deem for that sweet odour, which doth in it live.'" There was a youthful vulnerability to this man that attracted me, like iron to a lodestone. His facial features were elongated and his eyes a clear and steady grey-blue, his head topped by sandy hair slightly receding near the temples. He kept it groomed but often neglected a regular trim, so that it mussed easily and lent him a distracted air that suited his mad-scientist demeanour. His Spanish tan was holding on, and he seemed aglow with vitality.

When I returned from settling my bag in the bedroom, he handed me a small glass of Amontillado, and we sat, sipping, and nibbling on smoked almonds.

"I sense a continuation of the Spanish theme," I remarked. "Mmm . . . this takes me back a fortnight. I can almost feel the balmy breeze from the Alboran."

"Ah, London's version, a roaring fire. You are simply captivating bathed in the flickering light, my love. Just as glorious as in the tropical sunlight."

I smiled in reply. I'd come to enjoy and even half believe his extravagant compliments. They seemed from the heart, although I suspected he'd picked up love-language from the old sonnet sequences. That was fine by me, much preferable to comments about my "booty" or other specific body parts.

"You seem in fine form tonight. I think holiday is good for you, Kingsley. Relax, enjoy life, calm the mind—all that recreation routine."

"Well . . . I must say actually my mind is far from calm. More accurately, in a turmoil." I raised my eyebrows in a sort of query. "This is what I need to discuss with you, and it's a complicated saga." I rearranged the sofa cushions and snuggled down to listen.

"First things first. Elizabeth, I love you to my heart of hearts. I can't be without you, and I'd like you to consider moving in here permanently. Quite a life-change for us both, I know, but I think it's right, and I will devote myself to your happiness." I swallowed hard as my eyes teared over. I was quite gobsmacked. "Do you think we could make a go of it—together?" He moved next to me and put his arm around my shoulder, pulling me closer. I gazed up at his sincere face and could not find my voice. This came as a surprise—not entirely unexpected but a little premature, I felt.

"I am committed to you completely. I was hoping you felt the same," he added after my pause.

"I . . . I do!" I managed to gulp out.

"Those are the very words I wanted to hear," he laughed, and he smothered my face with small kisses. He paused and held my hand tenderly. "Now, will you repeat those same words in the church?"

For a moment I felt weak and rather dizzy, a combination of fine dry sherry and a jolt of overwhelming emotions. Kingsley looked at me expectantly, as my mind tried to process the enormity of this moment. How would marrying—and marrying *him*—change my immediate future? My eyes scanned the flat, assessing its potential to accommodate my own furnishings, seeking verification of ample private space, a room of my own so to speak. Scenarios of daily life flashed through my mind's eye: both of us going off to work, relaxing later in this spacious flat, stimulating and compatible conversations . . . a mother-in-law!

Sure, I had forged a comfortable life for myself as an independent working woman. But where was the pleasure beyond intellectual achievement, and where was the fun? A middle-aged woman finds fewer and fewer chances for a genuine love-match, I feared. And would I allow my fear of commitment—really my fear of change and of giving up full control of my own solitary life—to hold me back again and again? Other chaps just hadn't seemed worth the risk, but with Kingsley somehow my fears had shriveled. Debating if I was fully ready for this leap, I allowed my eyes to return to his familiar gaze awaiting a reply. Heeding my intuition, I found my body soften and relax as if flooded with a soothing, warm oil, and a quavering sound came from my lips, "What day, then, did you have in mind?"

*   *   *

C hapter 25

Kingsley and I toasted the beauty and solemnity of our joyful promises with more fine sherry. My emotions were flying high, and both of us were giddy. All my nervousness was gone. This decision and this man felt absolutely right.

In choosing the next best seller I often had to follow a combination of analysis and emotional insight, but in life sometimes the heart may know better than the head. My own heart was throbbing warmly, contentedly.

I anticipated that Kingsley might want to discuss some wedding plans, at least in a sort of tentative manner. He cleared his throat and moved closer to me on the couch.

"Now for part two," he announced.

"How many parts can there be?" I answered laughingly. "The opener was a smash."

"Well, actually, three, and it's the last that will blow you away. Elizabeth, to make our lives together we will have many decisions that follow rather like dominos in a file. Can you give up your flat? Shall we pool our finances? Will you keep your name or take mine? Or shall we hyphenate? And, to the point, what do you think of starting a family right away?"

"You absolutely amaze me. You have never seemed much like the family man. Are you trying to tell me you're already pregnant?" Kingsley smiled wanly, and it was clear he intended a serious discussion.

"Think about the facts of our situation. We are both well into adulthood and settled into our careers. Mum presses for grandchildren on a weekly basis. We have the means to provide amply for a child—we even have room for a nursery here in the flat—and we're sure to be exemplary parents. Consider the joy we would share tending to a wee one. Much laughter in store for all."

"All right, sure, I'd like to be a mum someday. My clock is tick-tick-ticking. And a child of ours can be nothing other than handsome and extraordinary." I caressed his cheek with my hand.

"I concur—your looks . . ."

"And your brains! The wonder of genetics! How can we lose?" I beamed at him, thinking he'd enjoy my reference to science.

"Okay, now for part three, and to turn this theoretical discussion quite specific. What would you think of starting a family within the year?"

I grinned broadly. "Well, we can certainly give it the old college try, and if we fail, it won't be for lack of effort. Our success will lie in our stars, not in our selves." I was enjoying the intimacy of such talk, as it presupposed a future for the two of us as one, no secrets, a single path. I was sure, as an expectant mother, to be the centre of attention among my friends, some of whom would harbour the green-eyed monster of envy.

"Part three coming at you now in earnest. My darling, I have begun something I cannot now put to an end. Please . . . hear me out. I need your approval, and I need your partnership."

My warmly throbbing heart cooled instantly and dropped into my stomach. Something seemed wrong. What could spoil the happy intimacy of this moment of planning our future together? Was another woman carrying his child? I could barely allow my mind to conceive the thought. Was he asking me to take another's child as my own?

"You have always supported my dreams of taking a leap forward—or perhaps more accurately backwards—with cellular research. You know the potential for science to gesture towards mystical truth, and you have encouraged my idealistic quest. We speak of 'making a baby' between us, but I have to confess that . . . I've begun to make one on my own."

A wave of shock and fear tingled my entire being. And then I felt the rise of a hysterical giggle that grew into gasping laughter. I choked, and Kingsley firmly patted my back.

"My love! Breathe! Slowly!" My gasping slowed then stopped. He handed me a tissue, and I dabbed at my tearing eyes.

My mind clutched at the only plausible possibility. "Is this really the time for an outlandish jest?" I chastised. "You had me there for a moment. Well played! You looked quite serious."

Kingsley gulped audibly, then rose and took my hand, pulling me to my feet. "Come with me."

He seemed to be leading me into the bedroom, and perhaps he would try to atone for his bad joke with some earnest baby-making on both our parts. But he veered towards the closed door of his home lab. Pausing, he retrieved a key from his pocket and turned it in the lock. The door swung open to a small closet-sized room crammed with two tables placed in an L-shape and some mechanical equipment, with shelves above filled with books and, strangely, a large poster with several portraits of William Shakespeare peering benevolently down on the whole enterprise.

He removed a shallow glass container from an environment-controlled cabinet and placed it under the viewing scope. Staring through the lenses, he positioned the container then gestured me to look for myself. A fateful premonition had begun to germinate just below my throbbing heart, and it grew exponentially as I approached the scope with dread. Blinking, then focusing, I saw—by microscopic standards—a rather large biological mass scored with several road-like lines across its surface. It looked like a small brain to me. Then I was sure I saw it move. I flinched in surprise and refocused. Again it moved, and this time I noticed a slight augmentation in size. The thing seemed to be growing.

Straightening my back, I confronted Kingsley directly. "What **IS** it?"

"That, my darling, is our baby, if you will have us."

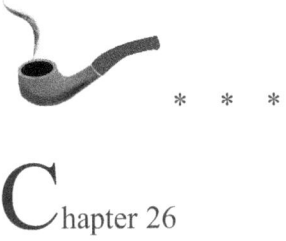

* * *

Chapter 26

I must have swooned. When I opened my eyes I was lying on the couch with a cold flannel on my forehead. Kingsley was hovering above me with a concerned look.

"Did I have too much to drink?"

"No, you are dead sober now," Kingsley replied. "You fainted in the lab and I carried you back out here."

"My hero! I must have been quite the dead weight."

"I will carry you through any hardships, as long as we both shall live. Your swoon has not blacked out our promise to one another, I hope . . . and the other events of our evening?"

I paused to try to clear my mind. The scene came back to me like a light on a dimmer turning to full illumination, slowly, but brightly. "You, you . . . asked me to move in with you. And to be husband and wife. And to start a family. Right away. Now."

Kingsley beamed. "You pass the quiz, darling. Parts one and two, perfectly recalled. Now, anything else come to mind? What about part three of our conversation, complete with illustration?"

My eyes widened as the scene in the lab crept back into my consciousness. Something shocking and unspeakable was taking shape, and it was of Kingsley's invention. "Wha . . . what have you cooked up in there? That . . . that *thing* under the scope. It was pulsating!"

Kingsley stood and walked into the kitchen. "Let me bring you a nice mug of green tea, and then we'll sort this out."

I rose with some difficulty, a bit woozy and unsteady on my feet, and made my way towards the loo. My eye caught the lab door, and on impulse I tried the handle. Latched and locked! Had I truly been in there and seen . . . some throbbing mass of protoplasm? And what had Kingsley called it? I shook my head vigourously.

At the basin I ran cool water and filled a tumbler, drinking it all down in large gulps. Must clear my mind. Tendrils of my hair were damp from the wet cloth Kingsley had applied to my brow. I looked no different from usual. But I sensed a strangeness in my new fiancé that was difficult to put into words. He seemed . . . calmly . . . crazed.

I was—fairly—certain we could ride this out, whatever it was. I thought I knew him well. I had so trusted his character until now, and I felt it was still intact, full of integrity at his core. I admired the passion of his scientist's curiosity and dedication, but tonight it had manifest itself in a frightening way. That gleam in his eye—combined with an ultra-calm and rational façade. I was seeing him in a new light, and this was unknown territory.

Out in the lounge Kingsley had placed my steaming mug on the end table and situated himself in a comfortable chair. I reclaimed my spot on the sofa and warmed my hands with the hot teacup. He looked at me steadily and directly. And then, with a slight tremor in his voice, he began.

 *   *   *

Chapter 27

"Oh, Elizabeth. I can't really find the logical thread that justifies what I've been through, and what I've done. All I can say in retrospect is that each step of the way has seemed ordinary and even inevitable. I'm asking only that you hear out my story at first. And then I'm hoping you will still consent to join me for the subsequent episodes— help me turn this into a tale with a happy ending."

I nodded silently. He seemed to have regained a tone of sanity. I curled my legs beneath me, settling in for a narrative—my specialty—but this one had real-life consequences for me and for my future.

"I think the idea began growing at Mum's dinner party. We were all talking about scientific magic and the mysterious essence of human life. Then later you and I discussed an imperative for each individual to be the hero of his own life, to make a lasting difference in the world. My head was full of hifalutin notions, I guess, and then the pipe business had landed in my lap. I started to wonder about those gaps in Shakespeare's creative life. We'd all like to hear more from that incredible talent, and I had that DNA from the pipe. An inner voice assured me it was truly that of our Bard, and I was tempted—tempted to see if maybe we could bring him back to life, or to start life over, with us.

"The DNA sat there in the lab, small as it is, like an invitation to life. It seemed to me a golden egg, a gift from the gods, and it called to me. I had the means, and I began tinkering, and everything fell into place. What you saw in the lab, Elizabeth, is Baby Shakespeare, a true clone of our Bard, swiftly developing into a human foetus."

"Unbelievable" was all I managed to utter. And then, "But why? Why didn't you talk it over with someone? Me, or Gordon, or someone else at the lab? Or the professional organisation? And how can you be sure it's Shakespeare's DNA?"

"They had all seemed to lose interest at that point, and everyone thought we'd returned the pipe with all its evidence back to the Birthplace. I told no one I'd secreted away the DNA, and I admit, that was an unethical step for me. It seemed such a powerful and perhaps fleeting opportunity, and I guess I became obsessed. I searched the archives to assuage my curiosity, but we know damn little about the man himself. He's nearly a cipher. Everything is conjecture and reconstruction—'Shakespeare' is a constant re-creation. It seemed so logical—create him again, give him a second chance, and all our questions will be answered. The circumstances were too compelling. I just knew the pipe was his own."

"So you bore the burden of choice on your own back. I see that now." I paused. "And I think I can see that your intentions were honourable. But you failed to follow through to the consequences. *If* you allow this mass to grow, what kind of creature will it be? It will always know it had an unnatural beginning. How will it legally enter our world as a true human baby? And how did some spare DNA turn into an embryo anyway? Don't you need a fertile egg to make a baby?"

"That was my second sin. I absconded with a human ovum from the morgue parts storage at the lab."

"Kingsley, worse and worse! This is several steps over the line, can't you see? Did you sign out an egg, or what?"

"No—much more cloak and dagger, I'm embarrassed to say. I nicked it on a trumped-up visit to the lab to pick up some 'papers.' In and out, none the wiser."

"And took it home in your pocket, I suppose! Illegally kept DNA combined with a stolen egg. All cooked up into a baby at your home lab. And you want this to be *our child*? Whose egg was it? Won't her genes pollute the purity of your pipe sample?"

"You remove the egg's source DNA before implanting it with your target sample. What we have is pure Shakespeare gestating in the back room, luv." He looked at me with pride.

I rose, stepped towards Kingsley, and slapped him hard. He rocked backward with the blow, put his hand to his cheek, and gave me a stunned, questioning look. "You are mad, and you are anthropomorphising to rationalise your crimes. I don't care what your scientific manipulations have accomplished! That thing is nothing but a soul-less monster, your own creation! The only recourse now is for the two of us to march in there and destroy it—and never speak of the matter again!" I took his hand and tried to drag him to his feet. Instead, he pulled me onto his lap. He placed both hands on my shoulders so he had me locked tightly in a kind of trap.

"I'm disappointed in you, my wife-to-be." His eyes were glittering strangely. "I hoped you would see that this was an opportunity handed to me on a silver platter. This embryo is the culmination of all my research and all my humanitarian desires in one small package. You must think calmly about the potential benefit to British culture in the birth of a second Shakespeare. This baby—and yes, let's call it that, not a monster at all, but a fertilised human egg developing according to nature's mandates—this baby harms no one by its existence. Our great Creator was its creator too, one step removed, through me as His—or Her—agent. The heart is already beating as it were, in a life force that is pulsating with vitality, with the will to live.

"You witnessed it yourself. It is *my* baby just as surely as if I had donated semen to its inception, for that embryo is the product of my own genes in their highest manifestation. It came to being through my mind, my hands, and my will. I refuse even for a moment to consider squelching its natural development. Don't you see? The very fact that it sits in our lab pulsing with being is a miracle! To kill it would add sin on top of sin." He continued to keep my eyes riveted to his.

"And our cosmic mandate now, you *and* I, since we have promised to cast our lots together, is to foster and rear this baby. What an incredible opportunity, Elizabeth! What a first for history and for the world! Although we will—we must—let this beginning be our secret, the child will be a prodigy like no other, except the original from the sixteenth century. We shall spare no opportunity, no enrichment, for his education. He will be like Mozart, given early training in all the arts. We will teach him to read at three, and we will recite all the writings of his predecessor, his genetic parent and twin, to him constantly.

"Nature and nurture, past and present, all will meet in this, our baby, our Baby Shakespeare. And now what I ask of you is a heroic act of acceptance. If you can accept me in my greatest accomplishment, then you can accept my baby as well. Not a monster, Elizabeth. A gift from the gods. A product of my own being. A baby. *Our* baby."

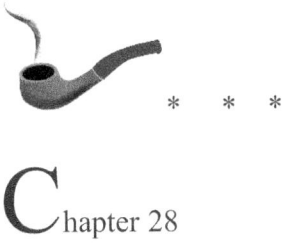   *   *   *

Chapter 28

As he spoke, the old Kingsley had seemed to return. I saw the daft gleam in his eyes soften to an intense and sincere passion. As he spoke, he also loosened his grip on my shoulders and I remained as a prisoner of his logic rather than of his force. He sat silently, allowing me to let his reasoning roil in my mind.

In a way all my being down to my very spirit recoiled against the idea of that thing in the lab. A scientist could create a human body, perhaps, but whence the soul? That was the secret we had not and could not decode. But if the source truly was William Shakespeare's DNA, surely a like soul would follow. Kingsley was right in saying that would be a miracle for England, for the English-speaking world and beyond. And he wanted me to participate in rearing this extraordinary being, as my own, as *our* own.

My mind searched for any kind of precedent. How would it be any different from raising an adopted child? I clung to that thought. A baby, born healthy and intact, was in many ways a blank slate. We, in our parenting, would give the child direction and instil in it values so that it would develop a fine character. Scenes from such a life materialised in my imagination. I could visualise Kingsley and myself as happy, successful parents, pushing our child on a swing in the park, walking hand-in-hand, a three-some, through museums, playing Punch-and-Judy with hand puppets in a playhouse, enduring splashes from the tub as we bathed our child. Add to this mix an extraordinary inherited genetic talent, and the picture seemed nothing but idyllic. Sure, the actuality was rather like the story-line from one of my manuscripts, but it was beginning to seem plausible.

Over these past months I had come to know Kingsley's character intimately. He was—excepting in the case of our hasty courtship—not a rash or impetuous person. The lab knew him as staunchly ethical, and that was the theme of his entire life. He was deliberate and methodical. But he was not cold, either. I saw the private Kingsley as warmly humanistic with a vast store of empathy. His intentions, regardless of his actions, were honourable. And I harboured not a scintilla of doubt about his affection and devotion to me. Our love was deep and would be lasting.

This baby was not a product of a diabolical plot. It was a sort of accident, really, as if two people had neglected birth control. Every baby was born innocent, even, or perhaps especially, in the details of its inception. I could see how the baby in the lab deserved its chance—its second chance—and it could not have chosen better parents. I thought of Kingsley's Mum and realised there might be the prospect of grandchildren of our own through this child, a gift for posterity. Only we two would have the satisfaction of seeing a continuation of the truncated Shakespeare lineage, in our very own family tree, and that was a gift that would bear returns into perpetuity.

Kingsley was sitting quietly and regarding me calmly. Although a dark feeling still lurked at the base of my reasoning, there was my man, and he needed a response. There was no leisure for further dallying, no time for thought.

"All right," I said simply.

"That's my girl!" He gave me a bear hug and held me long. It was almost as if our souls were trying to merge through the closeness of our bodies. "Elizabeth, I love you beyond what words can say. I open my self, and my destiny, completely to you. Whatever may transpire, *you* are my first treasure, and I will never let you down. 'And when I love thee not, chaos is come again.'"

Overcome by warmth and emotion, I could only murmur assent into his ear despite that inner darkness of doubt, and we held onto that moment of pure intimacy until our arms ached.

* * *

C hapter 29

"So, we will plan a festive wedding?" Kingsley pried us apart and broke the silence.

"Oh, yes! Small and beautiful, in a chapel. Mirth and dancing to follow."

"And you will move in here? And become Mrs. Armstrong?"

"How about both of us being the Armstrong-Montagues? Would you share my name as your own?"

"Of course I will, my love." We both beamed in satisfaction.

This had been a long and emotionally-trying night, and we'd eaten nothing but the smoked almonds early in the evening.

"Let me whip us up a nice avocado-and-cheese omelet," Kingsley proposed as he rose and walked to the kitchen. He saw cooking as a sort of extension of lab processes, basically combining chemicals in a palatable way. I followed, and he put on the kettle to refresh my now-cold cup of tea. He assembled his ingredients and began chopping and mixing. The aroma of onions sweating in butter made me realise I was famished. Kingsley hummed as he worked, but each of us remained otherwise silent, lost in the enormity of the decisions we'd agreed upon and the uncertainty of the new chapters to our individual lives.

"Now, just a couple more details about the rest of our little family," Kingsley commenced as he whipped the eggs with a fork. "How exactly shall we grow the embryo?"

My heart jolted again and my emotions retracted slightly. "What do you mean? It grows, we take it as ours, and the journey begins."

"Elizabeth, secrecy is essential, as you know, and I do *not* have an adequate incubator here in our lab. Before too long that embryo is going to need a host—sorry, a *mother*." He slid the egg mixture into the pan with the onions and began grating cheese.

"I've already said I will be its mother, with you as the father."

"Are you prepared to accept that role immediately? It's done routinely with surrogates. A brief procedure, out-patient, and the embryo is implanted into your uterus."

My eyes grew round and I swallowed hard. I had not even begun to consider the harsh reality of the mechanics of this adoption. Of course Kingsley was right. If we were to build our family with as normal-looking a sequence as possible, this was the best way. We would be married, and then we would be 'expecting,' one announcement following in the footsteps of the other.

I knew women with fertility problems, and they had used *in vitro* fertilisation. This process Kingsley suggested seemed much the same: I'd be receiving a fertilised egg, already dividing and developing, which would settle into my uterus for nurturing during gestation, and to which I would eventually give normal birth.

Looking at it as objectively as I could, I found the sequence almost appealing. In some way the baby would be part of me. I would have participated in everything but the absolute beginning. The idea of carrying a foetus from the Renaissance seemed fantastic, like something out of one of our manuscripts. I alone would be the maternal link between Shakespeare's time and ours.

I tried to view assent as courageous rather than outlandish. In the same way as Kingsley had risen to his highest potential in taking a risk, if I were to throw in my lot with him as I had already promised, then it seemed I must also accept the logic of his destiny and myself become heroic. Concentrate as I might, I could not see the harm in saying yes.

Kingsley was busily chopping a ripe avocado. Seeking his direct gaze, I asked, "Won't the doctor question us about the fertilised egg?"

He sighed with relief and reached over to stroke my arm affectionately. "Oh, my darling. You will be a luminous mother. No, I can bring the embryo to him in a vial marked with the lab ID. We've performed fertilisations in the past, applying sperm to ova, so he will suspect nothing out of the ordinary. But we must move with haste. Can you set up an appointment for next week?" He placed the steaming omelet on the counter in front of me and poured water from the whistling kettle into my cup.

"Will you be there with me?" I stared with a kind of horrible irony at the egg dish laid out before me.

"How could I miss witnessing the union of my beautiful wife and my precious baby? 'What's begun cannot be undone. We shall be partners in greatness,' my love. Now let's eat."

*   *   *

Chapter 30

"Kingsley, what are you going to order?"

Gordon, Kingsley, his mother Violet, and I had gathered at The Castle on Cowcross Street to catch up over lunch. This pub had been a favourite of George IV, and the menu was fairly upscale. We had not all spoken since the Marbella vacation and certainly not since the events of the momentous evening and the procedure that followed. Today we planned to make our announcement to them—but only the marriage part to begin. News of expectancy would follow later, in good time, although I was already feeling quite the pregnant lady with Baby Shakespeare the size of a lima bean resting snugly in my belly. The implant had gone off without a hitch. Entirely painless if a bit of an awkward position.

"Mum, I've not eaten here before, but the onion tart looks good. Waiter, what do you recommend for the ladies?" Kingsley said.

"Our wild salmon fish cakes are very well received, sir. And might I suggest rib eye with watercress for the gentlemen? May I get anyone a drink from the bar? Perhaps some wine?" He presented a leather-bound book, a list outlining their cellars and their boutique brews.

"Nothing for me but iced tea," I quickly replied. I vowed to treat this child inside me with care and respect.

"Hot tea for the other lady, and a pint of your best bitters for the men. And we shall follow your recommendations, eh Gordon?" Gordon nodded enthusiastically.

"Tell us all about Spain—and the remainder of your holiday. You both look the image of health," Violet said. She smiled at me warmly.

"Oh, the resort was luxurious," I replied. "These all-inclusive spas make a vacation easy. Simply arrive and you're taken care of. The sea is nearly aqua there, and it's quite tropical—the ocean like a calm, tepid bathtub. Very bright, nicely warming to the bones and to the spirit."

"We simply lounged about, not much more to tell," Kingsley added. "Guests from all countries, but it's typical Spain with a Moorish flavour—just across from Africa there—so lots of ornate tiling and open courtyards. Exotic to the English eye. And flamenco entertainment after dinner—quite stirring. Aside from our dear Elizabeth riffling through a few pages she brought along, it was total indolence. I'd recommend it to anyone needing a warm-up getaway."

"Here, Violet, I got a passerby to take a few shots of us by the pool." I held up my mobile, which included a camera, and she and Gordon both gazed intently at the small screen.

"Oh, you look so happy! As if you're on honeymoon or something!"

Our drinks arrived and Gordon raised his pint, saying "Cheers!"

Kingsley cleared his throat. "Well, you asked about the rest of our holiday. I tinkered about at home, but one chilly night I proposed marriage to this beautiful woman, and she has agreed to be my wife. A bit unorthodox, honeymoon then wedding, but so be it." He put his arm around my shoulders.

Gordon and Violet smiled conspiratorially and then offered lavish congratulations. We were grateful to receive their approval and their blessing. Personally, I felt that their warm reception eased the strangeness underlying our situation a bit. I hoped we could present a face of normalcy even as we pursued our mad project.

The waiter brought a large tray bearing our four lunch plates and, without that annoying "who gets what?" you so often hear, placed each dish in front of the appropriate person. The food was aromatic and savoury, and we ate with quiet pleasure. Kingsley and I fielded a couple of questions about wedding plans. "The sooner the better" we both responded.

"No need to dally once the mind is made up," Kingsley added. "Get a nice new dress, Mum. There'll be a small ceremony, and within the month if we can secure the chapel. I'm hoping Gordon here will stand with me on the gentlemen's side."

"My pleasure, old man. Happy to oblige."

"Well," Violet began. "Didn't Hamlet say something about weddings and thrift?"

"Yes . . . ?" said Kingsley.

"I was thinking if I found a suitable dress I could wear it for both your wedding—and my own." She and Gordon beamed at us like Cheshire cats.

"You sly dog!" Kingsley exclaimed to Gordon.

"Oh, Violet! How wonderful for you. And at the same time as your son!" I chimed in.

"You might as well stand up just the once," Gordon said. "Thrift all 'round." And he raised his glass once more. "Here's to a blessed future for us all."

* * *

C hapter 31

"Bethy, I adore that lacy neckline, but you need something a bit less fitted. You're actually beginning to *show*." Tessa added the last in a loud whisper from her plush armchair near the dressing area in Bridie's Elegant Gowns.

I twirled in front of the three-way glass, feeling like the proverbial cinder-maid-turned-princess. What woman does not adore trying on fabulous gowns? If all went well, this was a once-in-a-lifetime event, and I meant to enjoy each sensation. But Tessa was right. I scrutinised my mid-section, which was bulging out ever so slightly.

I turned to the matron. "What do you have in an empire waistline?" She furrowed her brow, and I read her look as disapproval.

"Keeping with the Chantilly lace? And the mid-length train?" she inquired. "I shall search the racks," she sighed as if the request were highly unreasonable. I refused to let her attitude throw a damper on my day. Over the years we'd all become accustomed to the haughtiness of London shopkeepers. They acted as if we were putting them out by giving them our patronage.

Tessa and I continued to admire the current gown I wore while we waited. "Bethy, all of these are simply stunning. If we could nip this one in a little under the bust, it would be perfect. Kingsley's jaw is sure to drop—you are a vision from a dream."

"My head is in sort of a fog, I think. So glad you're here to help guide my choice. All these changes so quickly—and between the two of us, I'm rather hormonal these days. I feel like crying, but it's from absolute happiness."

Tessa had risen and located a stand with several tiaras to which veils of various lengths were attached. She picked one up and tried it on. It suited her—instant glamour and romance. She adjusted the short veil over her face and then mugged lifting it and kissing me. We broke into giggles, and she said, "C'mon. Try this one with the seed pearls."

By the time the matron returned we had sorted through the entire inventory and chosen one with a longish veil. We liked the drama of lifting it at ceremony's end. With an apparent enormous effort the matron held up her new selection and spread out the skirts for my perusal.

"What do you think, Tessa? To me the skirt is too bouffant, and I don't care for the tiers." The matron frowned.

"Oh, yes, I agree. Something a little less fairy princess, more streamlined and slimming. But the high waist is just right."

"Do you have one with a less extensive skirt? And not sleeveless, please, although a revealing neckline is fine." I winked at Tessa. The matron sighed heavily.

"Yes, miss," she said and disappeared into the back rooms again. Tessa and I giggled.

"If you've got it, flaunt it," I laughed. We were alone in the front of the shop.

Tessa drew closer to me and whispered, "You know, I was shocked that you would be starting a family so soon, hun. Result of a rash unprotected moment, I'm assuming . . . ?"

"Things sometimes just happen." I covered the truth in a general comment that bore little resemblance to the series of events that had changed my entire outlook, all in a single night, and made me the bearer of a secret I was forbidden to share, forever. "After all, Tessa, we both know about ticking biological clocks. I want to be a mum, and pregnancy feels divine. I have new purpose, a trust to nurture another life, inside me. Kingsley's aglow with attentiveness, now that I'm to be a bride and a mother, all in one."

"I've known him for a dog's age, honey. You have brought him out of middle-age doldrums and back to life. If he fails to treat you as you deserve, he'll have to answer to me. After all, I'm responsible for a little matchmaking that started the whole shebang, and I'm still hoping my instincts were right."

"All's well, but I do appreciate your concern. We girls need to stick together. He's a good man to the core and will be a splendid father. Can't you just see him talking about the structure of atoms to our little Armstrong-Montague? He'll be building models and pointing to the empty spaces between the nucleus and the electrons, God knows."

"He's always been a bit of the mad scientist, but you will keep him grounded." She rolled her eyes up into her head and placed her fingertips to her temples. "I see nothing but bliss in your future."

We were giggling again when the matron returned. She glared at us disapprovingly while holding out the perfect dress. "If miss concurs . . ." she sniffed.

When I emerged from the dressing room in the new dress, Tessa gasped and nodded.

"Please be so kind as to wrap it up for me." I told the matron, trying to answer her scorn with politeness. I flashed her my most winning smile, and again she sniffed back.

"Miss will be a radiant bride."

I beamed at her with warmth and satisfaction. If I could win over the curmudgeon, I felt I could conquer any challenge that might lie ahead.

 *   *   *

Chapter 32

"I don't think anyone is harbouring any suspicious thoughts," Kingsley said as he and I took time for a quiet moment before gathering our wedding garb and motoring to the chapel.

"I had to confide in Tessa about the pregnancy," I responded, "and the rest of them will know soon enough, as my small bulge will reveal our little secret."

"Well, just one aspect of it, that is," Kingsley clarified as he gently stroked my belly. "No one must have an inkling of the baby's origin. I'm not even sure what the penalty would be—whether the law would come after us or we would simply face widespread moral outrage and censure." His face drew a blank.

"How *could* anyone know? Even Dr. Knowles is in the dark. I think, my love, that your project will move ahead safely. And today we accomplish part two, as you so aptly called it, although parts one and three are already well under way. And how amazing that it will be a double ceremony. Mother and son together, both embarking on new beginnings. It can only be a good omen."

"And take some of the scrutiny of the spotlight off of us!" Kingsley exclaimed. "If we could have gotten away with it, I wish we could have eloped, just the two—er, three—of us. We are all that matters."

"Ah, but how sweet to include the rest of the family. I'm so pleased for Violet and Gordon. It's a day of reversals—pregnancy then marriage, honeymoon then wedding, son's ceremony then the mother's."

Kingsley laughed. "And don't forget the fertilised egg that was seeking a hospitable womb."

I frowned. "Well that definitely takes the rosy romantic glow away."

He pulled me close. "Elizabeth, do forgive my point of view. I realise the sacrifice you're making for me, and there is no better way that you could demonstrate your deep commitment to me—as I am, complete with my outlandish science project. I'm the most fortunate fellow on this earth, if at times clunky in my expression. 'Doubt thou the stars are fire; Doubt that the sun doth move; Doubt truth to be a liar; But never doubt I love.'"

* * *

Tessa and her mum Gladys joined Violet and me in a dressing room at the chapel and helped us prepare to walk down the aisle. My dress truly was out of a fantasy; it transformed me into a bride like no other, yet like *all* others. It was a perfection of the convention. Violet had found a street-length brocade dress in silver-grey, modest yet elegant, and Tessa and Gladys as our attendants wore variations of a deep blue silk with straight skirts and an overblouse. Violet and Gladys were obviously mature women, but both were petite and had glorious well-coifed hair styles that rendered them "silver foxes." We made a striking foursome.

"Elizabeth, my daughter . . . how good it feels to say that! And you look radiant, my darling!" Violet's eyes filled with tears.

"Oh, Violet . . . Mum. You yourself look stunning. The dress is a dream, and there's no better groom than Gordon. I'm so pleased we're sharing today's happiness." We embraced carefully, so as not to muss our dresses.

"He seems a bit of a blusterer, I know," Violet said as she wiped her tears, "but he's a gentle man at heart and steady as granite. I think the future paints us as two doting grandparents if your union is so blessed."

"Time will tell, dear. Let us now be happy brides—I hear the organ, and that's our cue." Arm in arm we stepped forward into our futures.

* * *

Chapter 33

I was reclining uncomfortably in my reading chair, long since relocated to Kingsley's flat, rehearsing in my mind the swift and unusual events of the last half-year. The double wedding had been a fine affair, and my new husband and I had announced my pregnancy within the month. My physical discomfort had grown in concert with the foetus, it seemed. The more the baby developed, the more I experienced sharp pains and acute emotional distress. Kingsley's behaviour was certainly a factor. He had become overly attentive to the point of possessiveness and even more reclusive than usual. I was beginning to feel a prisoner in my new flat when the phone rang.

I heard the voice of Kingsley's Mum. "Elizabeth, just checking in on my daughter and grandbaby. How are you feeling, my dear?"

"Oh, Violet, hi. I'm holding up, I guess."

"My darling, is something the matter?"

"I don't want to complain, but this is all such a new experience for me. There's a heaviness to moving about, and the baby just seems contrary. When I want to sleep, he's jumping hurdles in there, and sometimes I almost feel as if he's kicking to punish me—or to try to escape. I know it all sounds silly."

"Well, dear, it's been a long while since I carried Kingsley, but there are simply rough days, and the closer you get to term, the more will be the discomfort. You must focus on the result. Soon we'll all have a brand-new addition to the family. Gordon and I are keen to see if the baby will resemble his father and what kind of aptitudes he will display—will we have another scientist in the family, I wonder?"

"Violet, you know we'll support this child, whatever direction he wants to go."

"Of course, my dear. But I can hardly wait to see what develops. The family has seemed so incomplete since we lost Kingsley's father. This birth completes our circle again. I can't fully explain what it means to me—and now for Gordon too, who never had a son. Kingsley's been kind of a substitute son for him, and now a grandson in addition! The beat goes on, as they say. So sorry your own parents aren't here to share in the joy."

"You are my own dear mum now, Violet."

"I wouldn't have it any other way. You've been much at home these past weeks, my dear. Have you given up work completely?"

"No, not at all. But Kingsley has wanted to keep an eye on me in my condition, so the office has been messengering me over the manuscripts. I can send back my evaluation and recommendation by e-mail, so mostly I'm working from my easy chair."

"Ah, easy chair, but not an easy time. What about meetings?"

"I've had to cut back temporarily on all the deal-making over dinners, I'm afraid. It may be for the best. I'm not drinking at all on account of the baby, and even the aroma of rich foods makes me feel ill. I do hope motherhood itself is less an ordeal than this pregnancy has been."

"Do try to stay calm, my dear."

"Thanks, Mum, and I'll call with any news. Cheerio for now."

I rose with some difficulty—too front-heavy for good balance and leverage—and waddled towards the kitchen to make some tea. Passing the door to the nursery, I stopped to assess the progress of our redecorating project. Baby Shakespeare began moving around vigourously as if to help with evaluating his future bedroom. After some preliminary discussions, Kingsley had thrown himself into creating this room, the perfect nursery. In a way it was a sweet gesture. He had generously found space for me in the flat, and now more of his territory would be given over to the baby.

But these last months my new husband had seemed to undergo a change. He was less laid-back than before and exhibited almost obsessive behaviours at times. He was focused on me and the baby, of course, but sometimes I felt he regarded my belly above all, and that I myself was simply the convenient vessel to play out his science experiment. I had agreed to the plan not only to support

Kingsley's genius, but also to be a full participant. I felt that carrying the baby would make me a partner in the project. But the baby had not ever felt mine or even part of me. It seemed uncomfortable and out of place from the moment of implantation. I felt like the temporary hostel for an alien. There, I had admitted it. Baby Shakespeare seemed to me an unnatural being, and I was serving as the human incubator.

We had been meticulous to veneer our plan with normalcy. To all outsiders, everyone we knew, we were a blissful newly-married couple with successful careers now happily starting a family. All interested parties awaited the arrival of a son in the Armstrong line. More often now I returned to my first instinct, that the baby—the creature really—was a sort of monster cobbled together by science, not by nature, not by our Creator. And instrumental as I was in this plan, I could not now say *No thanks* and excuse myself. I had made my choice, supporting this man I'd fallen for like never before, and now I must abide the consequences.

Hormonal changes could wreak havoc with an expectant mother's judgment, I knew, so I could not completely trust my feelings on this. I shook my head to clear my thoughts, and my eyes lit upon a framed print Kingsley had placed just athwart the crib so it would be in the baby's line of vision. My stomach dropped in a sort of horror, for it was the poster of many portraits of Shakespeare I'd seen before in the lab. All these faces seemed to be smiling gently at me in a mocking triumph.

* * *

Chapter 34

Kingsley had granted me permission to meet Tessa for lunch. As I showered I examined the changes my body had undergone. I looked like a normal gestating mother, but my bulge seemed from my point of view a tumour. I can't say when my attitude had altered, from hopeful acceptance of the foetus to a niggling and foreboding abhorrence of the life inside of me.

I was hoping I would be able to love the baby when he arrived. The first scan had determined the sex as male. I was hoping my natural maternal instinct would kick in when I laid eyes on the newborn son. Babies are all helpless and adorable, no matter their genesis. When our strange symbiosis was ended, perhaps I would feel more loving towards and protective of the vulnerable being inside me.

I could share my feelings of doubt and fear with no one. Kingsley was my sole confidant in this matter, and for him the baby was a holy topic. I had attempted to explain my doubts—even my fears—on several occasions, but his ears were closed. No complaints to be allowed; sacrifices to be made to further science and for the betterment of the world. That generality was easy to argue when you were not the one whose body had been colonised.

Staring at the abrupt movements churning just under my own skin, I knew I had begun to regret agreeing to be a party to this bizarre and unsanctified experiment, but who could I tell, and what could I do now? I had hoped to share in Kingsley's passion by participating. But now I was both too much involved and not enough involved. I carried the baby, the product of the experiment, but the passion, to obsession, involved me not at all. I was like a piece of lab equipment, completely depersonalised, dehumanised, defined by my function. I was ancillary—necessary but, in the end, I feared, disposable, dispensable. The baby was all that mattered, and I felt trapped by my circumstances.

It would be good for me to get out in the spring air and have inconsequential conversation with someone uninvolved in this plot, someone who loved me for myself.

Tessa was already seated at Soupe du Jour on Houndsditch when I arrived. She waved then stood and hugged me hard.

"Oh, Bethy, forgive me, but you look quite drawn. Is everything all right?"

"Tessa, pregnancy is no picnic after all, especially at our age—so take note. Nothing out of the ordinary Dr. Knowles says. But I simply don't feel the picture of health. Thanks for getting me out of the flat. I've become a prisoner of my condition, it seems."

"How's the hubs reacting to the pregnancy?"

"Well . . . Kingsley is super attentive . . . perhaps overly so."

"Honey, what are you saying?"

"Oh, Tessa, sometimes I feel the baby has taken precedence over me and my life. It's hard to play second fiddle after being the blushing bride, the complete centre of everyone's attention."

"We need to find a way to remedy that. I want to throw you a proper baby shower, luv, where you will once again be the star. What do you say to Saturday fortnight? It'll be at my flat. We need to equip you with all the latest baby gear to make your life easier. And the doting father-to-be will not be welcome. Women only."

"Thank you, thank you! It sounds like such fun—silly games and jokes and prizes. I wouldn't miss it for anything. But . . . I will have to clear it with Kingsley."

"Girl, what's happened to you? Surely you've not given up independent choice."

"I'm sure it will be all right. As I said, he's been overly attentive. Maybe he's just being protective. I don't see how he can deny the baby his shower."

"*His?*"

"Oh, yes—we did have a scan, and the jutting out bit is definitely present."

"How exciting! Now we all know how to tailor our gifts to the little gentleman. I'm sure Kingsley is overjoyed."

"Everything pertaining to the baby pleases him."

"Well, really, isn't that what every expectant mother hopes for? You are still central to him, surely. Without you, there is no baby after all."

Little did Tessa realise how untrue that was. And that got to the crux of our situation. The baby was entirely of Kingsley's instigation, a relic from the past transported genetically into our generation. He alone begat it, bringing it to life in his lab. I had not doubted his love for me, but now that the baby represented the culmination of his scientific career, his obsession had overtaken his affection.

That much was clear to me. The changes I'd noticed in him had to do at bottom with his focus, and that was based on his priorities. Personal attachments paled in light of scientific advancement. I was important—and bore watching over—because I was the vessel for cooking up the experiment. When I had said yes to marriage and to a family and ultimately to Kingsley's plot already underway, I had assented to a role I was now uncomfortable playing. No more were we to be "partners in greatness." Kingsley was traveling a solitary road, and he would soon be joined by a small companion he would lead by the hand. Who could know where their path would wander?—except somewhere without me. And the path is smooth that leadeth on to danger.

* * *

Chapter 35

"Why must all these women insist on sharing in our project?" Kingsley grumbled when I told him about the shower.

"Darling, they don't know the baby is a science project. They think we've done it the old-fashioned way and they are participating in our joy. A baby is always a community event—as they say in America, 'it takes a village.'"

"I'd like to keep you here in the flat where I can watch . . . *tend* to you. I don't like your being out and about where anything might happen."

"Kingsley, I am a perfectly sound thirty-six-year-old woman who happens to be pregnant. Women from the beginning of time have kept on with their daily lives while expecting a baby—even while tending to their other children. I am not an invalid. And I am not a thrall. We've been much too isolated since the wedding. I'd like to get out; I *need* to get out. You're making me gloomy by keeping me in the flat twenty-four/seven—and that can't be good for the baby. His health and welfare depend on my own."

"If you go, I think I'll just tag along to keep an eye on you."

"No, you won't. Women only. Tessa's explicit instructions. Plus you'd be chagrined—or bored to tears—by the shower ritual. Silly games, lots of teasing. I need a few moments of girly lightheartedness—*without* you."

"What if something happens with the baby while you're there? Have you thought of that?"

"I have my mobile, Kingsley. I can ring you up on the instant. Plus it will be fun for both of us to look at the gifts when I come home. That nursery can use a bit more colour, more whimsy."

"What do you mean? I've outfitted it perfectly for our baby bard. He won't need infantile distractions. He has the mind of a genius, after all."

"Well, yes, but he does need a childhood, and despite his genetics, *we* will serve as his parents. He *will* be a child of the twenty-first century in all ways but the one."

Kingsley grasped both my arms and looked at me hard.

"Elizabeth, I thought you were with me on this project."

"Kingsley. . . I . . . I am. I mean, look at me. Part three, just as you outlined. I am carrying this alien baby at your behest, at your desire. But the baby will be his own thing, not a simple replay of the past. We will nurture him and shape him. As you said, it would have been a sin to destroy a growing life. We've made the best of your experiment."

"You just don't get it!" He shook me slightly. "My experiment is to bring Shakespeare back to life. You are chosen—much like Mary before you—as the crucible of this miracle, *my* miracle. We must do everything to recreate an environment that will duplicate yet improve conditions for the flourishing of his talent."

"Kingsley, let me go! You're hurting me!"

He loosened his grip, and the warmth visibly returned to his eyes as if the demon possessing him had left. His clench became an embrace.

"Oh, my darling, do forgive me. Of course, of course you are the mother of the baby. I just have such a passion for his potential. I can't let go of the idea of his creation and how ground-breaking it will be to have recreated Shakespeare. I get lost in that idea sometimes and forget how intimately you are involved."

The embrace warmed me and softened me to the Kingsley I knew and loved, but a part of me held back in a kind of fear and wonder. This was not the first time his "passion" had changed him into a fiend. I felt his assault on my individuality at the same time as the baby inside me seemed foreign and hostile. Attacked from both sides, I was losing my real contact to humanity, and I felt stunningly alone.

"Go. Go to your little party," he managed to squeeze out. And then he said more gently, "But ring me up every hour just to ease my mind, won't you, luv?"

And where is the joy? I wondered. How could I ever reclaim a life of innocence, before Baby Shakespeare?

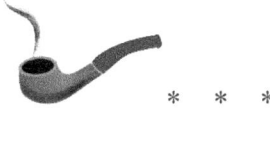

* * *

Chapter 36

The jelly felt cold as the technician prepared my belly for the ultrasonic scanner. Thankfully, Kingsley was at work, and I had been able to get away for this appointment by myself. The initial scan had reported the sex of the baby, and everything else was normal. But now, approaching term, I felt uneasy and actually pained. I wanted to know what was happening, and it was news I didn't want to share.

"Oooh, you're getting quite the baby bump now," said the technician. "Won't be too much longer. Any problems?" Her dreadlocks were trying to escape from the nurse's cap plunked down on her head.

"Um. Well, yes. It's difficult to explain. Something doesn't feel right. The baby doesn't seem part of me. Sometimes there's a great deal of pain and . . . almost like an attack on me from the inside."

"Ah, missy," the technician replied in her Jamaican accent, laughing. "There's going to be kicking and turning. The little fellow is practicing to join us in our world."

"It's not just the movement. I can sense a sort of hostility, and there are kicks and punches that seem like a punishing assault."

"Sometimes the mind can make strange interpretations of perfectly normal events, dearie. Is this your first?"

"Well, yes, but I know and believe what I feel."

"Let's get Dr. Knowles in here and take a look around, shall we?" She pulled on a cord and pushed open the curtain around the table on which I reclined. While we waited, she adjusted the monitor so that I could have a clear view as the scanner revealed shadowy shapes of the inside of my uterus. After a light tap on the door, the doctor entered, brisk, perky, and smiling. His prematurely bald head, which he had shaved clean to his skull, had a shiny glow to it.

"How's our little mother today? Nearly to term, I see. Now don't be calling me in the middle of the night! Let's plan for a daytime birth." He and the technician laughed. "Let's see how the little chap is doing."

After flipping through my file, he pulled on rubber gloves and began to move the sensor slowly in a circular pattern over my swollen belly. Occasionally I would flinch as I saw—and felt—my skin jut out from an inner poke.

"Ah, yes, he's stimulated by our actions. He can feel the pressure of the sensor," the doctor said. "Mmm-hmm. Mmm-hmm. Good position. Head downward. Legs tucked in. . . . There's a foot, right there . . . genital area, decidedly male . . . here are the hands, clenched in towards the chest. Oh, look! He punched out with a tiny fist! We don't often see that during the scan." Dr. Knowles chuckled; I cringed.

"You say you're having some pain?" he asked, not really listening for an answer.

"Well, yes, as I was telling the nurse . . ."

"Ah, there's the head—can you see the monitor all right?"

I saw the creature as a dark shadow and his movements as malice towards me. How could I explain?

"See how mature and nicely formed the head looks? Quite a large cranium . . ."

"Doctor, nothing feels right. The baby is hurting me . . . I think on purpose."

"There, there. Sometimes expectant mothers get crazy notions in their heads. Babies are innocent, my dear. Just look closely at this well-developed little boy! His movements indicate he's restless and getting ready for his exit. I see nothing out of the ordinary. He's already grown toenails and fingernails and . . . well, they are a bit long. Unusual. When he jabs out, that may be what you feel. But I discern no perforations in the amniotic sac."

I could see the tiny nails on his hands and toes. They seemed to me sword-like weapons. I felt that he knew how it hurt me when he kicked and he punched. Surely he could feel me flinch with the pain each time.

"Back to this lovely large head now. See, eye, nose, chin—he's much less a polliwog than before, eh?—and there's the mouth in a happy smile! Let's get a snapshot of that for you to take home."

What I saw was not a smile but a smirk. The one eye stared out at me in a kind of defiance. The fist shot out again. I flinched in pain.

"I see no indication at all of anything that would be causing unusual discomfort, my dear. This is a very healthy baby, well on its way to respond to labour. I must caution you about letting alarming thoughts overtake your mind. Hormones sometimes cause odd sensations—run rampant with the emotions. Just hang in with us, think good thoughts, and soon you'll be cradling this lovely boy. Have you and your husband decided on a name?"

I paused, then blurted out, "It's William Shakespeare!"

"Old Will, eh? Nice homage to our great bard. Sometimes children do grow into the names they are given."

"No! You don't understand! It's William Shakespeare!" What was I thinking? I had sworn never to reveal the secret of this baby's origin, and here I was blabbing. I dreaded to think what Kingsley would do to me if he'd heard my thoughtless disclosure. "Oh, just wishful thinking on my part, doctor," I said to cover my error. "You see, I work as a literary editor, and it would be my dream for the child to become a great writer. Sort of silly of me . . . magical thinking and all that."

"As I was saying, high hormone levels, volatile emotions. With the size of this baby's cranium, I'd say he has a good chance of being the genius you so desire." The technician began to wipe my belly clean and the doctor removed his rubber gloves and wrote something in my file. He turned back to me, pulled the gown over my bump, and offered a hand to help me sit up. I took it, as my agility was hindered by my girth.

"I'm going to prescribe a mild anti-anxiety medication for you, dear. You need to try to remain calm, especially now as we near the onset of labour. There will be acute pains with that, you know, and they will radiate from the centre of your back 'round to the front of the pelvic girdle. Be still and breathe deeply when they strike, and when they are ten minutes apart give us a call—but do make sure it's between nine and five." He patted my hand and smiled at his own joke.

I smiled wanly—and sanely—back at him, thinking about those fingernails and toenails on the little creature from the past who would soon tear his way out into the twenty-first century.

* * *

C hapter 37

I was waiting outside the flat when Violet's car pulled alongside the kerb. The sooner I could avoid Kingsley's involvement in the shower, the better. All morning I'd been having stronger pains than usual, and I was not in a mood to have to coddle or mollify my husband's misgivings. I'd assured him that the scan had gone perfectly, but he continued to hover over me and fret—about the baby.

"Hello, darling! Just climb in if you can," Violet said through the open window. A large gaily-wrapped bundle sat on the back seat of the Vauxhall. I clambered in and stretched the seatbelt to its full length to snap it into the hasp, which I could not even see beyond my own belly. "My, you look just ready to pop!" she added.

"I *will* be relieved when this part is over."

She began to steer the car expertly through light London traffic.

"May I inquire about your appointment with Dr. Knowles? How was the scan?"

"He says everything is A-OK," I said, trying to add a note of brightness to my voice. I felt put upon by how everyone seemed to want to appropriate my pregnancy in one way or another. *They* should have to feel the jabs of the stranger within as I was.

"Does he predict when the baby will be born?"

"Any day now, any time. The baby and I are both fully ready."

"I'm just beside myself with excitement, my dear. Both Gordon and I can hardly wait to lay eyes on our beautiful grandson. How is Kingsley doing? He hasn't rung us up lately."

"Oh, Mum. He's quite concerned about the child's birth. Anxious for it to come off without a hitch. I guess you could say he's 'expecting' as well. He's constantly in that nursery putting the finishing touches on one thing or another."

"Well, I do hope he's saved space for some of the gifts you'll receive today. Always room for something more to brighten and enrich the baby's environment. Stimulation is the way to go with an infant. Ah, here we are, and someone leaving a space just in front. We must be living righteously."

Violet pulled adeptly into the parking space and retrieved the bundle from the back seat, then we climbed the steps to Tessa's townhouse. I cringed with another sharp pain as we ascended, and I instinctively clutched my side. I was hoping Violet had not noticed. The door opened to colour and the noise of festive female voices. Tessa had put up streamers everywhere, and brightly-wrapped presents crowded a table. All our old school chums were chattering away, and they whooped at my entrance. One by one they hugged me, patted my belly, remarked on how wonderful or how strained I looked, and how I'd changed since the wedding. Tessa took my arm and led me to the refreshments table.

"Nothing alcoholic for me, of course," I told her, "but I'm keen for a stiff one as soon as labour's over and done with. Oh, Tessa, what an amazing cake!" In spite of my mood, and my pains, I began to feel the joyous spirit of the gathering. The cake was in the shape of a bushy tree with a large cradle nesting in its branches, a baby within. Brightly coloured birds perched on other branches, and down the tree trunk ran the words "Rock-a-bye-baby."

"Well, I know the baby has been restless. I thought maybe we could persuade him into some quietude, at least through suggestion," she replied. I hugged her as well as I could, my protruding belly hindering a close embrace.

"Thank you, my friend, so much for staging this gathering. My heart is lighter already." She returned my steady gaze, and each of us had to brush away a tear. The party began in earnest.

First we sat in a circle and played a game of predicting the birth weight of the baby and how long labour would last. Each person jotted down a number to fill in the gaps in a fictional narrative about the birth. As I read the narrative aloud, each woman in line filled in the number she'd written down, to much hilarity.

"When the labour pains began, Elizabeth breathed hard for ----- hours until Kingsley agreed to call the doctor. She stayed in hospital for ----- days, with pains occurring every ----- minutes. When the bouncing baby popped out, he weighed in at ----- pounds and ----- ounces. After giving birth, Elizabeth immediately lost ----- stone," and so on, with each woman laughing out the number she had written down. This story made for a gruesome-sounding labour, and I hoped it was not prophetic.

The next game focused on the women's purses. Tessa had a long list of items one might need in tending to a baby, and she called them out one by one. We all scrounged through our bags, and whoever found the item first got a prize. Those who didn't have the item had to drop out, and the items became more and more unusual. "Safety pins.

Moist wipes. Mobile phone to ring up the father. Vaseline—or as a substitute, lip gloss. Teddy bear. Pacifier. Extra diaper. Bib. Onesie." By this point even those who had children came up empty, and Gemma was proclaimed the winner and received the grand prize, a packet of bath salts from the Dead Sea.

This got us into the mood for baby items, and Gladys said, "Oh, let's open the gifts now." Tessa and Gemma began resituating the pile from the table to just at my feet. After I opened each card, we passed it around the circle, and each woman ooh-ed or smiled at the sentiment or sheer cuteness. Tessa kept a registry of the gifts and giver, and Gemma fashioned a long necklace for me out of the bows and ribbons. My function was to open each gift, admire it, thank the giver, and pass the gift around the circle.

The women had been generous and full of ingenuity, as the gifts included both the practical and the whimsical: books, blankets, clothes, stuffed animals, toys, a diaper bag, a hanging mobile, skin care products, a mum care package full of various teas, and other baby adjuncts and appurtenances. With nearly every gift I opened I felt a stab of THE PAIN, as I had come to call it. I had to swallow it down and offer only a beaming smile to the group. We came at last to the large box from Violet's back seat.

"Oh, I do hope you like it," she proclaimed.

"I'm sure I will! Let's see," I said, gulping back yet another stab of THE PAIN. I handed the bow and ribbon to Gemma and carefully untaped the paper. The box read "Perfect Pram." It was an old-fashioned carriage perambulator in a deep blue with an adjustable sun roof, some assembly required. THE PAIN stabbed again. "Oh, Violet, it's brilliant!" I managed, and stood—with difficulty—to hug her.

"While the hippo is risen, let's cut the cake!" said Tessa.

"Everyone—thank you so much. Baby Sh . . . Our child will be the most stylin' baby on the block, thanks to your good taste and good wishes. I feel honoured and blessed. Thank you, thank you. I love you all."

The women gathered around the refreshments table and Tessa portioned out pieces of the tree-cake to admiring oohs and aahs. I reclaimed my chair, but as I sat THE PAIN shot through me again. Gathering some calm to myself, I tasted the cake, vanilla and cinnamon with a cream cheese frosting.

"Mmm, Tessa, yummy," I managed, just as a burst of water gushed down my thighs and pooled near my feet.

"My God, she's in labour!" Gemma announced. "Her water has broken! Call for the ambulance."

"Oh, no. Just let me dry off here." Tessa brought me a towel.

"I'll get the car running." Violet jumped up and headed for the door. "Do ring up Dr. Knowles—and Kingsley!" she added. "Tessa, help her down the porch, won't you?"

"I'm coming with you," Tessa replied.

"Don't you worry, dear," Gladys said. "I'll clean up here and arrange the gifts for transport to the flat."

Tessa and I got into the back seat of the Vauxhall, and Tessa kept her arm around me. "Breathe, honey. One– two, one– two. Deeply. Innnn. Ouuut. That's it."

THE PAIN abated for a moment, and Violet adeptly steered through a maze of streets towards hospital.

"Ahhhh!" THE PAIN returned with a vengeance and pulsed through my torso, circling forward from my back. Tessa gripped my hand tightly.

"Nearly there," announced Violet as the contraction subsided. Very soon we were to look Baby Shakespeare in the eye and see what he was made of. I hoped I would survive the ordeal.

 * * *

C hapter 38

"I told you not to go to that damned shower! And you didn't ring me on the hour!" Kingsley, his face behind a white mask, was louring above me as I lay on the uncomfortable birthing bed.

As it was a hiatus between the bouts of pain, I croaked back at him, "Labour would have begun whether I was at the shower or not. When it's your time, it happens." This was not a good moment to fall under one of his fanatical verbal attacks.

"How is the baby? Is the baby all right?" he asked quickly.

"Yes, yes. And I'm just fine too, although riddled with pain at the moment. Aaagh! Please, call in the doctor." Kingsley pulled on a cord, and people dressed in white bustled in. "Can you do something for the pain? It's sending me through the roof!"

Dr. Knowles came hastily through the door. "Usually it's best for the baby if you can weather it out," he instructed.

"But I'm literally being stabbed! Those nails!" I cried out.

"Would you please wait outside?" the doctor said to Kingsley, who backed reluctantly towards the door.

"What does she mean, nails?" he called as they pushed him the last steps out of the room.

"We'll administer a partial pain block through the spine," Dr. Knowles said as they rolled me onto my side. After some cold touches of instruments on my lower back, I began to feel relief. In gratitude for a respite from the stabbing, I dozed, then woke to cries of "Push!" For what seemed like endless tries, we went through a cycle: Push, breathe hard, rest. Repeat. I was exhausted by the effort, and by the cycle, when Dr. Knowles said from beyond the sheet tented over my knees, "All right, I have that lovely large head, and this one could do it. Give us one last push—hard!"

I felt a great purging and fell back completely spent. In the distance I heard the cry of a newborn. "When we are born, we cry that we are come to this great stage of fools" echoed through my mind. I could feel nurses around me cleaning me up, but I simply wanted to rest. My part—or my largest part—of the project had been completed. Surely Kingsley could find no fault with me now.

Some time later I opened my eyes to a vision of Kingsley sitting by my bed with an intensely loving gaze. For a moment I was transported back to our days of courtship, our nights of new love, when I seemed the centre of his universe. I was about to speak to him when he dropped his eyes to the bundle on his lap, and I refocused the whole picture. His adoring gaze was not for me. Baby

Shakespeare lay cuddled against Kingsley's chest, and it was ever so clear that together *they* formed a complete universe—without me, the mere functionary.

Kingsley looked up again, his eyes gleaming. "We did it!" he said. "Part three of the experiment a resounding success. And oh, Elizabeth, what a specimen he is! Don't you want to hold him?"

My feelings were conflicted. Through these nine months I had come to resent this alien inside me, and I had sensed his hostility towards me. But now he was simply a human baby, regardless of his genetic origin, and I had given him birth. As the bard himself had said, "One touch of nature makes the whole world kin." Perhaps this baby could become the agent to bring Kingsley and myself back together, joined and united in parenthood.

"All right, sure thing," I said, and Kingsley rose carefully and gently placed the bundle in my arms. The baby's eyes glittered up at me; he was taking stock of me, I was certain of it. There was no recognition that we had been "together" for nine months. He did not smile or coo. He simply regarded me.

"What do you say, luv? Isn't he a beauty and a marvel?"

"Yes, an adorable baby," I replied. I was unable to feel maternal towards him, even though he was tiny and vulnerable. To me he seemed strong—strong-willed, powerful. The consciousness I sensed in him seemed fully developed and, as I had thought all along, malicious.

"I examined him thoroughly with the nurse," Kingsley went on. "All fingers and toes intact. A quite large and well-developed head—so handsome! One slight anomaly— it seems his nails are extraordinarily long and durable. We tried to trim them, but they seem impenetrable. Couldn't get much of a purchase on them."

"Yes, I know about the nails." Kingsley let my comment pass him by without notice.

"Mum and Tessa waited for a long while, but then they went home for a rest. I've rung them up, and they're mad to see the baby. Oh, they're glad you came through all right, too. I think we can expect 'em shortly. Here, let me take the baby if you're done meeting him."

"Oh, we've been acquainted for several months." Again Kingsley seemed oblivious to my innuendo. "And now, look, he has wet all over me!" I exclaimed. Kingsley tenderly took the baby, sat down, placed a towel between the baby and his own trousers, and turned his attention to me.

"Darling, do you know how happy you've made me? Look at what I hold in my arms. This is a first, a breakthrough in scientific history. And what a coup! *You* completed the experiment. *You* nurtured him and carried him. Without *you*, my creation would not have survived. And," he dropped his voice, "it is the exact genetic copy of England's Bard of Avon!" He gave the baby another lingering, admiring glance. "But to all the world he is," Kingsley consulted the plastic wristband on the infant, "Baby Boy Armstrong-Montague! 'It's a wise father who knows his own child,'" he chuckled. "Shall we name him formally now, my dear?"

"All right, if you like. I was thinking of Christopher. Then we can call him Kit, short and sweet. Perhaps an allusion to the Bard's nearest rival, Marlowe." Kingsley's eyes widened in a sort of shocked horror.

"What are you thinking? There can be no other name for him than his own. He must be first name William, second name Shakespeare."

"Don't you think that might lead someone to uncover our secret rather handily? After all, it's not even a year since the lab had the pipe. It would not be difficult to add two and two, as they say."

"Oh, don't worry. I've thought about that, and my accomplishment is so outlandish that no one would even consider it as a possibility. And we can simply cite your admiration for England's greatest literary hero."

"So it's on me? But I want to name him Kit!"

"There's no sense in arguing, Elizabeth. It was determined at the moment of his genesis. The letters even spell it out, Will-I-am. And Will he must and shall be."

Again I silently acquiesced, and again I realised that I was not an equal partner in this project. I tried to imagine my own days stretched out ahead, "tomorrow, and tomorrow, and tomorrow," now for a lifetime irrevocably tied to this alien creature brought to life by my husband, this creature I would now have to address with a constant reminder of his unholy beginnings as William Shakespeare.

 * * *

C hapter 39

Violet, Tessa, Gladys, and Gordon burst into the hospital room in a wave of noisy glee. One by one they approached the bed and hugged me. Gordon carried a bouquet of mixed posies in a vase, and Tessa a handful of gas balloons. Gladys hugged a large teddy bear.

"Oh, darling, we've just come from the viewing window!" Violet exclaimed.

"Handsome wee gent you have there." Gordon took my hand. "He's the spit 'n' image of his old man, if I do say so."

"He's beautiful and you are brilliant, Elizabeth," Tessa cooed. "How do you feel, honey? Terribly sore? Much relieved it's over, I imagine."

"Many congratulations to the new mum," said Gladys.

The surge of their good will bathed me in a feeling of normalcy I tended to lose when around Kingsley. I'd given birth to a fine son, and now our lives as parents, surrounded and supported by interested family and friends, would begin. I smiled as they chattered energetically around me, like comical birds.

"Yes, I'm all right. It seemed a long ordeal, but the staff helped me along, and we survived. The baby *is* cute, isn't he? Tessa, sorry if I damaged your floor with that gush of water."

"Don't give it a second thought. All in good cause."

"We gazed at him for some time," Violet offered. "He has such serious and penetrating eyes to him. I guess he'll be a sombre, thoughtful boy, like his father."

"Have you and Kingsley decided on a name?" Gladys asked.

I gulped, wondering how this might be received. "Well, yes, and this may surprise you. Because his spirit has crossed both our lives, mine through literature and Kingsley's through lab work, we've followed that venerable tradition of honouring England's greatest writer in our own child. He will be William Shakespeare Armstrong-Montague."

"That's a mouthful!" Tessa responded.

"A large name for a wee lad," said Gordon.

"A lovely gesture," commented Gladys. "A true English name, carrying on a stellar tradition."

Violet looked thoughtful. "Elizabeth, you never knew Kingsley's father, my first husband, whom we lost now over thirty years past. Did you realise that his name was William? What a nice tribute." She was visibly moved.

"I'm sure Kingsley had that in his mind all along," I answered her. Lies and more lies. I hoped this did not become a way of life.

The door opened and a nurse pushed in a rolling bassinette containing the young master, who was just waking from a nap. "Feeding time!" she called out. "Everyone wait outside, please!"

"Might I stay?" Tessa asked. "Close friend and supporter, you know."

"If the mother agrees," the nurse replied.

"Of course, do stay." I was actually grateful not to have to face the child alone. His gaze unnerved me. The others bustled out after peeking inside the crib once more with appreciative noises.

The nurse picked up the baby and held him towards me, saying, "Let's try nursing. Can you drop your gown?"

I'd been aware of the fullness of my breasts, but I had not consciously envisioned nursing the creature. An involuntary shudder overcame me, but I swallowed hard and prepared to act the loving mother. He nestled right in. His eyes were closed. He began nursing, but I felt a sharp pain. "Ouch!" escaped my lips, and the nurse looked concerned.

"There should not be pain," she said. "You will get used to the sensation."

"Ouch!" There it was again, a sharp pain in my breast.

The nurse frowned and removed the baby to examine him. Then she pronounced "Enough for now" and quickly wheeled him from the room.

"Oh, dear," I said to Tessa. "Evidently I'm already a failure as a mother."

"Some women don't nurse at all, Bethy. Some babies don't take to mother's milk, and sometimes the arrangement just doesn't work out. It's still completely natural. Whole generations have been bottle-fed, so don't fret."

Dr. Knowles knocked lightly and entered the room. "Hello, ladies," he said. "May I speak to the mother alone?"

Tessa and I exchanged glances, and she rose quickly and left the room. I looked at the doctor inquiringly.

"Nothing to be concerned about, but I'm going to recommend bottle-feeding for you and the baby. It's quite unusual for a new-born, but he has buds of small teeth quite present. I'm sure that's what you felt when you cried out. Nothing volitional on the baby's part. He's simply doing what comes naturally, and he's an early developer, it seems. But we don't want blood mixing in with the milk."

"Doctor, are there any other abnormalities I should know about?" Nothing about this baby could surprise me. I still thought of him as a science experiment, and I was remarkably aloof.

"Not that we can see now, except for his large and well-developed head. I'm sure you'll want to fill in your husband on the matter, and we'll keep an eye out as he grows. With these early developers, surprising things can in fact happen, and no one is quite sure why. We'll bring him back in with a bottle so you can have some bonding time."

Tessa returned along with the bassinette, and we tried a second time, with a small change, the bottle. The baby drank hungrily, and happily enough, it seemed.

"Tessa, he tried to bite me!"

"Don't be silly. Babies don't have teeth."

"This one does. Tiny buds of sharp teeth. And razor-sharp nails. He's a living attack arsenal."

"Oh, for Pete's sake. Get a grip, Elizabeth. He's a living *doll*."

And I knew in my heart that the baby hated me but I would now have to assume the hypocritical role of loving mother. I lifted him to put him against my shoulder to burp him. He was remarkably pliant and soft, and when I didn't look in his eyes I could almost love him.

 * * *

Chapter 40

When the baby and I came home to the flat from hospital, Kingsley seemed completely fulfilled. It wasn't that I or our marriage made him happy, but the fruitful result of his experiment, which I had delivered. So I was a link in the chain but more or less irrelevant now my function had been completed. All of Kingsley's energy and attention were directed towards Will. We hardly spoke except to make arrangements for tending to the baby, whom I still feared— with an indelible memory of his assault on my own body and a knowledge of his unnatural origin. Frankly, I was glad Kingsley took over most of the baby chores, but I suffered from my own trepidation with Will and the loss of my loving partner.

Where had our passion gone? It had been that passion for each other—body and soul—that had bonded us, and that passion that had affected my own decision to start a family with the Kingsley I so love, even if that family would begin in an unconventional manner. We were an extraordinary couple, and at first I'd been seduced by our secret of scientific magic. But now we were a trio.

I wondered if we might rekindle our spark, especially now that we had the result of our experiment in living and breathing form. And I set out to hatch a plan of my own. Violet gladly offered babysitting services for an evening out. I lit upon Friday next and made a reservation at the Dorchester, the posh bar where we'd had that first blind date. The circularity of it seemed pleasing, and I hoped it would renew the romantic feelings.

My figure had come back nicely, and I dug around in my closet to find the brilliant dress I'd worn that night. Slipping it over my head to try out the effect, I zipped it easily and was shocked by the image of the woman who regarded me in my reflection. While she still looked slim and cut an attractive figure, her entire demeanour was . . . worn. She looked knockered and beaten down, like those women who've been at the same service job for decades. No wonder Kingsley turns away from me, I thought, and I resolved to curl my hair and use make-up to perk up my face.

I conspired with Gordon to have the company car fetch Kingsley and carry him directly to the Dorchester with no fore-knowledge of destination—only that he was meeting me—and my spirits lifted all week in anticipation. I gave Will a wide berth in the flat when not feeding him or handing him his toys and books. Violet fetched the boy after lunch on Friday, and I took a slow luxurious soak in the tub before tending to my preparations. The warm bubbly water relaxed me, and my mind wandered to our days of courtship, when Kingsley was nothing but charming. He enjoyed the romance of our early days together, and he was an attentive and appreciative lover. With him I'd felt a refuge I'd been missing from my daily life and an excitement about our future together. That excitement culminated in our partnership to incubate the created foetus. And now this creation was part of our family.

When at last I dried off and pulled on the dress, I did bear some resemblance to the woman I once was, the woman Kingsley had courted so well. I took the lift down to the garage and drove to the Dorchester, letting the valet park the car.

Kingsley was already settled at a small table—I spotted him from the door. Luckily his head was down and he was lost in private thoughts. I rummaged around in my bag for a small atomiser and refreshed my perfume, just behind my ears and on my wrists. A passing gentleman smiled at me appreciatively.

I flounced towards Kingsley's table, and he saw me coming. I tried to look confident and sexy. He smiled as if in memory.

"Buy a lady a drink?" I asked, sitting delicately in the chair across from him.

"Ah, yes, what was it . . . gin and forbidden fruit?" He inhaled deeply as if the perfume transported him to an earlier, happier time. My God, he did remember. Yet his expression changed almost instantly and he failed to continue the playful flirtation. "Elizabeth, you look lovely—but what have you done with Will? You're not going to want to become tipsy what with mothering yet to do tonight."

"One drink, Kingsley, please, for ourselves. I know I am a mother and will be unto death, but I had hoped tonight to do some wifing instead. You and I still matter as a couple, and we're letting parenthood dampen our spark. Can't we try to re-ignite it, at least for tonight? I want the Kingsley who charmed me back again."

The waiter took our drink order and silence descended on our table.

"What are your thoughts?" I asked.

"That this is a bloody silly extravagance," he said matter-of-factly.

"Why can't we just talk like we used to?" I asked. "You never talk to me anymore. I feel invisible and irrelevant."

"This is not the place for such a discussion." He looked around embarrassedly.

"We're paying for the luxury of staff discretion in all matters," I replied.

"What do you want me to say?" he asked.

"Something genuine. Something about ideas. Something affectionate. Something not about the baby. You once considered me your best friend."

Our drinks arrived and we both sipped. Kingsley made no move to offer a toast.

He broke the silence at last. "You have been my partner, and you know how grateful I am for your part in the project. And what a success, eh? Our boy is a miracle, thanks to the magic of science." He glowed with self-congratulatory pride and touched my hand.

"Sometimes he frightens me to death," I ventured.

"What rot! That, my dear, is all in your head." He removed his hand.

"Why don't my feelings matter?" I protested.

"Because they pale in light of the larger enterprise," he said, sipping. "Our entire focus must now be on rearing our prodigy. Who knows what he'll bring to the world—this second time around."

"Kingsley, I miss our closeness. I miss our love. Will seems to have gotten in the way of our . . . partnership, as you term it."

"What greater love could there be than joining together in an experiment like no other? You must let feelings give way to commitment to our project, now that it's begun as such a great success. We must follow it through," he replied. "No turning back now."

"Is he a success?" I submitted.

"What do you mean? Look at him, he's perfect."

"A perfect what? Sometimes I wonder if he's really a human," I responded.

Kingsley slapped the table, causing both our drinks to spill. The waiter quietly glided up and removed the drink glasses, discreetly sopping up the mess with a pristinely white tea towel. Kingsley glared at me during this operation. "You're embarrassing me," he said when the waiter glided away again.

Having begun, I felt I must elaborate. "His body is not natural, I'm sure you've noted. Those nails, torturing me, and then the teeth. And the enormous head. And there's something not right with his attitude towards people. He doesn't want human contact. It seems my task is to fetch and carry, whatever baby demands. I'm a prisoner of his desires. He only has eyes for you."

"What a cruel interpretation of our incredible creation," Kingsley replied. "Shame on you, Elizabeth. Will is one of the greatest humans ever to have been on earth. Surely you can't resent tending to his needs."

"You're wrong, Kingsley, so very wrong. Will is NOT," and I dropped my voice to a whisper, "the Bard of Avon. That's where your error lies. He is something else, something new—or rather old *and* new. We can't know how the Bard's DNA might have been tainted or altered in the process. And we can't know what kind of man the original was, both at his species' moment and in his own character. Perhaps he was like all those villains he created. He'd have to think and know those thoughts to put words to them, can't you see? Our Will is manifesting the dark side of your great bard."

The waiter reappeared with the check. Kingsley stood slowly, gathering himself as if after a blow to the stomach.

"You will *not* betray me and our project now," he spat out deliberately. "We are both in service to the greater good. Now let's get home and tend to our son." He turned on his heel and left.

I sat for a moment alone before calling for the car. I had not betrayed anyone, except perhaps myself. I had never meant to sign away my own life when I agreed to be the baby's mother. I thought that would make Kingsley happy and bring us even closer together. As he had said, "partners." But now it was the two of them, father and son, who were partnered, and I was left to float on my solitary sea of despair.

The marriage was gone except in name only, and except for rearing the child. The love might still linger on some level, but the passion was dead—as I wished the clone were too. I wished he had never been born, or re-born. Even polite concern had disappeared from our little family. I could no longer confide in Kingsley, and I had to live up to his expectations. I could see no plausible escape now the wheels had been set in motion.

I started from my reverie to find the waiter at my elbow.

"Is there anything I can do for you, *madame*?" he inquired quietly.

I smiled up at him with weak resignation. "No, no, nothing at all. Thank you. Nothing to be done."

Part III: Childhood

* * * Violet Armstrong-McLeod

Chapter 41

My concerns about Kingsley and William Shakespeare Armstrong-Montague began a couple of days after his birth. Gordon and I had decided to run by Kingsley's flat on the way home from meeting our new grandson. The first-time father was sure to be exhilarated but exhausted. This had been a trying year, what with the two marriages and then the nearly immediate announcement of pregnancy. It all had seemed to make Kingsley a bit frazzled.

"I do wonder that Kingsley isn't at hospital with his wife," I said to Gordon. "You'd think he would want to be more involved. I heard he missed the actual birth, too, although he was there to receive the child as soon as he was cleaned up."

"Timing on these matters can be dicey," Gordon replied. "All his talk at the lab these months has been about the child. He'll sort out his proper role all right, don't you fret about it."

"Well, I just want to make sure he's right as rain. Elizabeth and the baby will come home tomorrow. I hope everything is prepared for them. The baby is simply a dream, isn't he, Gordon?"

"A wee darlin' he is, indeed."

Kingsley buzzed us in, and we found the entire lounge cluttered with the gifts from the shower.

"My darling son, the new father! How are you holding up?" We embraced warmly.

"Hullo, Mum. Oh, just trying to tidy up and get organised here. Gladys brought by the shower gifts. Quite a haul! Greetings, old man . . . Grandpa!" he said to Gordon.

"I guess we all have new titles and new roles now," I said. "Kingsley, you look a bit distracted. Are you taking time to care for yourself?"

"I'm fine, Mum. Couldn't be happier, actually. Just want all to be shipshape when the baby comes home." Kingsley began moving items into the nursery, and I followed. I hadn't seen it since its transformation. The room was painted a cheery blue, with a handsome rocker near the antique-looking crib. The crib, however, sat directly across from an unusual framed poster, a large print with several different portraits of the Bard of Avon. I found all these faces, all those eyes, a bit unnerving.

"Kingsley, couldn't you find a poster of clowns—or animals? This Shakespeare art is out of the ordinary for a nursery, wouldn't you say?"

"Facial recognition, Mum, one of a baby's first tasks. He'll have us to look at as members of his species, but these images will reinforce his sense of human features, always there before him. And then there's the tie-in with his name, of course."

"Oh, yes, again rather unusual, but I was quite moved that you had selected the name of your own father, as little as you remember him."

Kingsley stopped bustling for a moment and looked at me blankly, then said "Oh, yes, well, I hoped you would approve. Elizabeth wanted to call him Kit, I'm afraid. Just too ghastly—and undignified." We returned to the parlour, where Gordon was riffling through the paper.

"So what time will you collect them?" I asked.

"The hospital will give us a ring when they're ready. They've been keeping in touch." Oddly, the phone rang at that moment. Kingsley had one of those incomprehensible, indecipherable one-sided conversations, but his tone seemed a bit dark.

"Darling, is something wrong?"

"Oh, not really. Just Elizabeth with a new wrinkle. I don't know if you noticed William's nails. They were quite well developed *in utero*—very long and strong. It turns out there's a similar trend with his teeth, another durable body substance. He already has buds pushing through the gums. An early developer he is, quite the go-getter. At any rate, this makes nursing out of the question, so we'll need to get in a store of bottles and nipples and sterilisers, all that paraphernalia."

"Oh, poor Elizabeth! How is she handling the situation? That must have been surprising—and painful—for her!"

"Um, right. I do guess so. She didn't actually say. Just focused on the baby, don't you know."

"And you didn't ask. . . . She is such a radiant mother. You're a fortunate man, Kingsley, lovely, talented wife and handsome, healthy son. You are set up for good now. She was just glowing all through the pregnancy, even more beautiful now, wouldn't you agree, Gordon?"

"Never a more ravishing new mum."

"I feel all my wishes have been granted. And here we are, two happy new families." Gordon looked up from the paper and winked at me, and Kingsley began putting on his coat.

"I hate to rush you out, but must run to the chemist for baby supplies now," he said. "We'll want to be ready for the little man."

"And his mum," I added as Kingsley hurried us out the door.

"Oh, yes. And his mum."

   *   *   *

Chapter 42

My son had been distant and preoccupied after his marriage. I had thought he would find deep happiness and self-completion in Elizabeth, who seemed the perfect woman for him. At first I read his distance as marital bliss, and then as the distraction of impending parenthood. He'd always been a sort of loner, although we'd of necessity been best friends, and we'd always remained in at least weekly contact.

But Gordon and I both noticed his apparent lack of concern for Elizabeth as the new mother, and an inordinate focus on everything concerning the baby. We'd visited shortly after their arrival home, and the aloofness seemed also to have infected Elizabeth. She appeared to shrink from contact with the baby, and Kingsley had assumed most of the nurturing chores. He happily fussed over preparing bottles and sat for hours feeding the baby, gazing down lovingly at the infant. Perhaps Elizabeth suffered from post-partum depression. This was more common and serious than society acknowledged. We hoped our mere supportive presence would help to cheer her up.

The baby himself was as unusual as my own son. He had an oblong face, an elegant nose, arched eyebrows, and a high hair line, which looked comically like premature balding. Most remarkable was his aura of calm seriousness. He was not a giggly baby. He had large eyes, with which he constantly scrutinised his world. If I held him, he stared at my face, but not affectionately. He almost seemed to be calculating for some kind of advantage, although he was lovingly supplied with all his needs, all his desires.

He cried and fussed very little, as if he were mature beyond his—I almost said years. And he seemed to prefer being held by men. He was happiest in the arms of Kingsley or Gordon. When he was fussy, it was when Elizabeth or I tried to snuggle him. He was not a baby to warm up to, and it was even difficult to think of him as part of the family. Although he was adorable, there was something off-putting and unsettling, almost judgmental, in his calculating, unflinching gaze. This was not a baby one would think to tickle, or to kiss playfully along the brow, or to play Peek-a-Boo with. He did not coo or babble. Every move seemed completely premeditated.

Elizabeth and I were left alone one day in the nursery with the dozing baby, and I tried to broach my observations tactfully. I did not want to become an interfering mother and grandmother—or even to be perceived as intruding in private matters.

"Such a sweet, peaceful darling he is," I began in quiet tones as we folded some of his clothes. "Now the routine is settling down, you must be quite pleased. And Kingsley is such a help with the baby."

"Yes, isn't he."

"Darling, are you getting enough time with the child? We've been passing him around so much, we don't mean to neglect you."

"The bottle feeding is actually sort of a relief. There was that intense pain from his nails, and I did not need to get bitten on a daily basis."

"Maybe he feels the reluctance. He does seem to prefer the men—and then there's that poster he constantly stares at. Ugh."

"Every baby is different, Dr. Knowles says. As long as he's getting his intimate, nurturing contact, it need not always be from me—or from you, dear. You know that I am with Will most of the day—still reading manuscripts from my easy chair. So I tend to him while Kingsley's at lab. He likes to bathe the baby when he gets home, and after a simple supper he reads to Will and plays with him here in the nursery. The baby sleeps well through most of the night. We're easing into a comfortable routine."

"And do you have quality time alone with Kingsley?"

"Ay, there's the rub. We are very focused on the baby. Not much together time."

"I don't mean to intrude, but are you happy, dear? You appear rather worn down and Kingsley seems almost in another world. I had envisioned you more as a joyous family."

"Well, every unhappy family is unhappy in its own way. The baby himself is a sombre creature, and that rather sets the tone, I'd say. They talk about the luck of the draw with babies and their temperaments, you know. The most laid-back parents can end up with a colicky infant, and party animals with a bookworm."

"Kingsley was always an introvert, Elizabeth, and when his father died in the accident he turned even more inward. I had hopes that being with you—delightful person that you are—and a new baby would liberate him from his personal prison."

"He's always been wrapped up in his lab work, Violet, and I don't mind, as I spend so much time riffling through the latest fantasy stories. We've forged a comfortable symbiosis, and Will hasn't been too much of a disruption. We're managing."

"Ahem. Ladies, I hope I'm not interrupting something important here. Ah, how's my little Bard?" Kingsley appeared in the nursery doorway and then walked over to the crib. At first I thought he had said "bird," but it was indeed "bard." Will's eyes were open and staring at that confounded poster. Kingsley picked the baby up and took him to the changing table. "Mum, would you mind handing me the outfit on top in the tallboy? I'll just give him a change, and then we'll have some reading time."

Elizabeth and I watched as Kingsley put a black, white, and brown outfit on Will, consisting of snap-on tights and a loose shirt with a long vest over it all. The finishing touch was a strange-looking ruffle, and Kingsley laboured a bit to get it snapped just right around the baby's neck. I wondered if it was some kind of modern bib-device, crinkled to catch bits of food. But then, as he sat the baby up on his lap, it hit me—hard. This was a Puritan doublet and hose, complete with ruffled collar. He'd dressed the baby like Shakespeare!

"Mum, could you hand me a book from the shelf there?" Kingsley asked.

The bookcase was sparsely populated, and not with the slim and brightly-coloured picture books most nurseries were stocked with. There were a few dun-coloured larger volumes, all parts of the *Complete Works of William Shakespeare*. I picked one up that was on the end.

"Yes, that's the one. We've begun with the comedies, and we're just onto *The Taming of the Shrew*."

"Kingsley, are you off your head?" I thought he must be pulling an elaborate joke on me. "First of all, where did you find that outlandish outfit? It's just not right for a baby, unless he's attending a Halloween party."

"I had some of these made up at Brown & Brown, specially to go with his name, Mum. I think they are masculine, and serious, like Will here."

"And reading Shakespeare to a baby?! What about fairy tales and Mother Goose? You'll be teaching him to plot and murder in spite of himself. Elizabeth, surely you do not support such nonsense!"

"Violet," she sighed, "I have no say in the matter."

Kingsley reached for the book in my hand, and a defeated Elizabeth and I retreated to the doorway, turning to see my contented son reading to my beruffled grandson, who gazed up at him with round eyes, "'Tis hatch'd and shall be so."

* * *

Chapter 43

As the months wore on, peer pressure prevailed upon Kingsley and he abandoned the Tudor outfits for Will. One day I'd been tending to the baby and he was fussy. He seemed absolutely stifled by that collar, tight around the neck. On an impulse I reached down and removed it, and the baby gave me an unusual smile, which I took as gratitude. At that moment I went to the chest and removed all the bibs. I shouldered Will and strode quickly to the rubbish drop. No more ruffled bibs, ever. Kingsley got the message and disposed of the vests himself, and the baby quickly outgrew the rest of the antiquated get-up.

Will grew quickly into a robust armful, and he seemed always to be thinking about something. That child never acted like a normal baby . . . but then, he had emanated from my son, who continued to read Shakespeare's plays to him each evening. What a ghastly practice, I thought, and tactfully brought over little surprise gifts of coloured picture books about trains and fairies and dragons. But these sat forlornly in the parlour, and Kingsley stuck with the plays. Several times Gordon and I offered to babysit in our own flat so that the new parents could have a night out—or a night at home alone—but Kingsley would have none of it after Elizabeth took us up on it that one time. He loved nothing more than being with that baby.

Elizabeth, on the other hand, seemed despondent and even trapped by motherhood. She seldom left the flat.

Days, while Kingsley was at work, she fed and tended to the baby. At first I visited often to try to help out. She was attentive to Will and adept in feeding him his bottle—and later soft foods—but there was little joyful interaction between them. Of course, his disposition did not invite playfulness. I had never seen such a sombre, steady, focused baby. He was always calm, always watching with those large eyes, and he seldom responded to any adult but Kingsley. He accepted ministrations with equanimity. But any attempt at lightheartedness or triviality he met with his judgmental gaze.

Gordon had scaled down to half time at the lab, and one day he and I stopped by the flat with adorable plush dolls, keeping with the Tudor theme, in the personae of young crowned princes. The baby seemed to have few actual toys. While Elizabeth and I chatted, Gordon sat on the floor with Will and, with pretended voices, acted out a scene with the dolls. Gordon moved the dolls around as if they were walking, and he had them in conversation. The dolls had come with swords attached around their waists, and Gordon mocked them in a duel.

It was a precious and touching scene, the older Scotsman with the rosy baby, both with heads bowed, intent on the dolls. Occasionally Will looked up at Gordon, but he did not reach for the dolls. He watched his grandpa move the arms and legs of the figures, and yet he did not smile.

Elizabeth and I had begun to discuss Kingsley. I no longer tried to hide my alarm at the changes I'd seen in him since Will's birth. Elizabeth talked tactfully about his devotion as a father, and I queried her about his attentions to her as the new mother, which had quite fallen off from an observer's perspective. I asked how his work was going, and we decided to consult Gordon on the topic.

"My dear, have you noticed any changes in Kingsley at the lab in recent months?" I called down to Gordon on the floor. "We're trying to make sure he's not somehow gone bonkers."

Gordon stopped manipulating the dolls and looked up. "Violet, I do think you're overanalysing. Kingsley's been at lab regularly and performs his careful work as always. If anything, he seems even more dedicated to the cause of science."

"Has he said anything out of the ordinary?" Elizabeth looked on with interest, and Gordon laid down the dolls to turn and address us both.

"Out of the ordinary? Not really much time for conversation during work hours, ladies. When we've shared a cuppa, he has mostly gone on about the little lad here and the pleasures of parenthood. He has great plans for the lad's education—a genius in the making, according to his design. Perfectly understandable. Looking to the future."

"All right, then. But I still think he's a bit too involved with the child," I rejoined. "It's often tempting to over-egg the pudding."

Gordon turned back to the doll scenario, but something had changed. Will was sitting still, placid and wide-eyed as before, but the dolls were in disarray.

"Did you see the lad pick up the dolls?" said Gordon.

"No, we were looking at you," I replied.

"What's happened?" Elizabeth asked.

We all looked down to see two small figures, one poised above the other. The one lying prone had a small sword thrust through his chest and his crown flung off his head.

* * *

Chapter 44

It became clear that Will would not be welcome at daycare. It's not that he was a trouble to tend to, but there was something askew about his interaction with the world. Elizabeth continued to be an attentive mother, but she was as undoting as Kingsley was obsessed. Will persisted as an unaffectionate observer, and he continued to develop quickly. He sat, he crawled, he toddled, all to Kingsley's great delight. Both parents spoke to him and encouraged him to respond, and he learned to speak, but he was not a babbler. It surprised none of us that his first word was "Father." His first sentences were a combination of declaration and command—mostly nouns. He would simply state the name of what he wanted, and he had no trouble with pronouncing consonants and complete words: biscuit, blanket, book.

The book he wanted was, of course, his Shakespeare. The complete works contained watercolour illustrations of visions of some scenes from the plays, and to Will these were old familiar friends. Somehow this baby had been able to absorb the sense of the Bard's Early Modern English that Kingsley read to him each night, and he seemed to have internalised that language. After the doll incident, Gordon and I feared that he might also have appropriated the meaner values of some of the plays' villains. If this was the case, it astounded us. Yet, how many children believe in ogres and trolls and fairies, because those inhabit their first stories. The power of literature is strong on the imagination.

It was, however, worrisome that the child had little interaction with others, beyond his father, and with no children his own age. Elizabeth had attempted some play-dates with other toddlers, but Will did not engage with them. As at home, he sat, observing, taking it all in, occupied by the world in his own mind. Whatever characters, whatever thoughts, peopled that world he did not reveal, either through word or action.

The same held true outside the flat. Sometimes I would recruit Elizabeth and the baby for a stroll through the park. She would nestle him into the Perfect Pram, and we would expose him to sun, fresh air, and the colours and movements of the Commons. Even if we pushed him in a swing, he remained calm and sombre as in the flat. He did not protest, but neither did he relish. All around, I worried continuously about all three of them, mother, father, child. On the surface all might seem normal, but something deep and profound was not right, and they seemed to be either ignoring it or, even more alarming, covering it up.

On one of our walks I tried to discuss my perceptions with Elizabeth. I decided that tact had perhaps been too oblique a strategy, so I went straight to the heart of my concerns.

"Elizabeth, my dear, surely you've noticed what an unusual baby Will is."

"What do you mean, Violet?"

"Well, where do I begin? I can't say if it's the chicken or the egg, but the baby is too closely tied to the whims of his father, and that has made him—well, un-baby-like. Kingsley was in some ways an odd duck even as a child, but Will trumps that in spades."

"From the beginning Kingsley wanted to be involved. It's been a help to me, so I can continue with my work."

"Are you blind, Elizabeth? The baby has not warmed to you, or to me, or to anyone really but Kingsley. He does not laugh. He does not fuss. He does not coo or giggle. He does not explore his environment. He does not try to please. He's like a machine."

"Ah, so negative, Violet. High expectations from a grandmother, I assume. He does prefer his father. But he is an early developer and a quick learner. All the tests show him as entirely normal."

"There's more to normalcy than test results, my dear. Aren't you concerned about his emotional development? My son's actions with the baby have been outrageous—the poster, the outfits, the Shakespeare-this and Shakespeare-that. Will's had little opportunity to learn about people and life in the twenty-first century. It's no longer the Tudor world, and we are not all plotting for the throne."

"I don't think there's any damage in the child hearing some of our greatest English poetry, Violet. If it will settle your mind, you and I can also begin taking him to the B.M. and let him absorb some of those wonderful paintings of the old masters. I think he's just a learner. He has a mind that takes in all things, and what eventually will come back out may be a surprise and a wonder to us all."

"I think you're missing some of my point, honey. Does the baby have a chance to develop what they call affect—a connection to and empathy for others? As you note, he seems so much in his own mind. He never seems happy to see me, or Gordon, or even you! His eyes are for Kingsley alone. How will he develop social skills—how to get on with others when things do not go his way?"

"Don't expect too much of him too soon, Violet. He's just a baby. All in good time."

I sighed deeply. I was getting nowhere on the subject of Will, and I had not even begun the subject of changes in both Elizabeth and Kingsley and in their relationship. A strange idea flitted through my mind, and I blurted it out without mediation.

"Darling, perhaps it's time for a second child." I heard Elizabeth gasp, but I blundered on. "Yes, you recovered nicely from this first birth, and it's good to get the family going all in a lump. Will might just turn out to be a splendid elder brother, and having another child around would of necessity take the spotlight off him alone. It would also disperse Kingsley's attentions a bit, and that would be healthy all 'round." As I talked, it sounded more and more like a good idea.

Elizabeth stopped the pram and looked at me as if she'd seen a ghost. She herself was pale. "Never, never, never again," she muttered. "Nought's had, all's spent, where our desire is got without content."

* * *

C hapter 45

Elizabeth continued to turn a deaf ear to my concerns about the entire family. Will was now walking and talking, but his demeanour had not changed. He was still impenetrable and just plain eerie. Elizabeth wore the face of a weary mother, but in the odd moment a sigh or word mumbled under her breath betrayed her inner distress. Kingsley had become a Will fanatic. True, he arrived at work each day, but his entire being focused on his son and immersion into days of yore through Shakespeare's plays.

Their strangeness affected us all—that was the flip side of "it takes a village"—and it consumed my waking life. But even in my dreams the drama stretched its tentacles about my imagination. Will's blank placidity invited projection and interpretation. In my dreams he was a quiet force of malice and even evil. His mind whirred with machinations to debase those he came into contact with. He unsettled people; he brought out their worst desires and fears and set them into motion. When he studied others he saw clear through to their hearts. But instead of identifying with compassion, he saw only opportunity for manipulation. In my dreams he was like a mad puppeteer, yet there was not even mad laughter, no delight even in his evil.

I woke from one of these dreams with a startled cry, sweat and tears covering my face. Gordon roused and held me as I calmed from my quavering.

"Shh, shh, all will be well, my lass," he whispered.

"Oh, Gordon, it was so terribly bleak and frightening."

"Just a nightmare, luv, nothing more." He stroked my brow.

"It seemed so real, and so close to home. It was about Will—and he was a monster! He was fussing in his crib, and I went over to comfort him. I turned his face towards me, and it was wearing one of those blank masks like the Greeks had, with the big eyes. This one was the mask of tragedy. Who would play such a horrible trick on a baby, I thought, and I put out my hand and removed the mask. Underneath was another mask, this one the blank grinning face of comedy. I tore that mask away too, and beneath it was just flesh, no features of any kind! His own face was a nothing, not human at all!"

Gordon paused thoughtfully. "Violet, my darling wife. You are the kindest person I know. You reared a brilliant son on your own, and you are a devoted grandmother. But you take the situation too much to heart."

"I'm evidently at my wits' end about that child and the unfathomable behaviour of his father. This is such a formative time for him, Gordon, and I'm afraid that Kingsley will ruin him for life. They have already ostracised Elizabeth from their little cabal. She tries not to let on, but she is a deeply changed woman, sad to the core—even slightly afraid, I think. And she won't come clean to me. I've tried talking to her on several occasions. But in her denial is a kind of enabling martyrdom. I can't get through to her, and for me Kingsley is beyond the pale."

"I know their domestic life upsets you, but is it our place to interfere? It's a new world, Violet, not like our own childhood days. If they want to bring up a child prodigy, perhaps Kingsley's plan is a sound one. And as for Elizabeth, she's a resilient woman. I think she'll come out of her funk as the child grows older, and she'll return to the sparkling lass she's always been."

"You are the voice of reason, Gordon, and I appreciate that and love you for it. You are my rock. But when the issue invades my very dreams, I must find out the truth. Elizabeth says the child has tested normal, but I think he would benefit from therapy—just to learn to act more like a human being! No one but Kingsley can touch him, haven't you noticed? And otherwise he simply demands and commands. Maybe both he and his father should seek professional help. There must be specialists who can advise on raising a prodigy, help set out a more balanced programme."

"That would be a good plan, my darling. Maybe we can do some research and find some books to pass on to them, or slip a couple of names to Elizabeth, all for the good of the child, don't you know. It couldn't hurt. We all want what's best for little Will."

"Do you think you might speak directly to Kingsley? He always takes his mum's advice with a grain of salt. But you, you're a father-figure for him. I know he values your solid judgment."

"Speak to him and say what, exactly? We do not often engage in idle chatter. Mostly we consider science and its matters."

"Well, there's your opening! Broach the education of a child as a scientific experiment. Kingsley's apt to love the challenge of that topic. Keeping it theoretical removes it from the realm of personal criticism. Then you can bring in other factors—the necessity of warmth and of social skills, of affection along with rigour. It's actually a question of moral education, and he's always been a stickler for ethics."

"I can try, see how he responds, I guess, for you, my lass. Will's a blank slate, like a clean petri dish, and Kingsley will want to run a meticulous experiment. What does the poet say? 'The child is father of the man.' The challenge is to prepare the ground for a beneficent future."

* * *

Chapter 46

Gordon had scaled back on his hours at the lab since the wedding. He was trying to ease into retirement, and the plan was working. He enjoyed his time at home or about town with me and then relished his days at work, as science had been his livelihood, his life. We had indefinitely postponed a honeymoon. We'd been considering Marbella, but matters concerning the baby had kept us in London, and now these matters were approaching dire in my estimation. Today was the day Gordon would take Kingsley aside and discuss Will.

I was involved in my own activities throughout the day, but the outcome of the conversation hovered on the edges of my concentration. Gladys and I were to choose the reading list for book circle for six months ahead, and I was studying, too. I had taken a volunteer position at the Lightfoot, a smaller art gallery. Serving as docent, I led viewers through the gallery and encouraged their interest in acquiring pieces from the non-permanent collection. This meant I needed to bone up on each artist's biography, method, and stylistic periods as well as develop an aesthetic analysis of each work in the collection. My days wandering the halls of the B.M. were serving me well, and I was enjoying learning about new artists.

Gladys came by for tea, armed with her list of titles gleaned from members' suggestions and her own internet research on other book clubs. Over Assam and shortbread we brainstormed over each title, trying to choose the most timely and accessible. After a bit we laid down our lists and just began catching up.

"I suppose you've been spending much of your free time with the new grandchild. How he's growing! Nearly a year already."

"Yes, I visit often and help out as I can."

"Kingsley and Elizabeth have all but disappeared, Tessa tells me. I do imagine today's parenting is completely absorbing—and what with them both working as well."

"Elizabeth does her manuscript selections from home now."

"Well, that's the word—she gets out not at all."

"Truth be told, Gladys, that worries me. Everything in that family revolves around the child—yet it has not been a combined effort. Elizabeth seems withdrawn and exhausted, and Kingsley just the opposite. He is fanatical about being with Will—and he's pushed the Shakespeare theme to an absurdity."

"I did hear something about a doublet and hose."

"For the baby!—can you imagine? But it's not just Kingsley's odd bent with the child. Will himself is . . . disturbingly strange."

"Violet, I've kept this from you out of kindness, to spare your feelings. But I think I should tell you, Tessa and I made a visit last week to the flat. It was just after mid-day, and Kingsley was at work. Elizabeth came to the door looking rather like a mad housewife. We gathered in the lounge, and Will was installed on the floor. There were some soldier dolls nearby, but he did not move around, and he did not play. He looked quite alert and healthy. He has those big eyes, always watching everything."

"Oh, yes, don't I know those eyes."

"Well, he regarded us as we talked, and then he began making demands, just one-or-two-word statements—and Elizabeth would leap up to serve his every desire. He did not cry or fuss or scream. He just calmly demanded, and for Elizabeth these seemed commands. No wonder she's exhausted. Is that what parenting manuals are recommending?"

"I don't think so, Gladys. The baby can crawl and walk. He should be fending a bit for himself."

"Well, worse and worse, I fear. He's awfully adorable, with that little-old-man look he has, and Tessa wanted to snuggle him. She stood and approached him with her arms out, and he simply stared at her. Wouldn't most babies reach out, too?"

"Will is not a cuddler, that's clear."

"But then she reached down to pick him up anyway, and he slapped her hands away. And he looked her in the eye with a haughtiness that sent a chill down our spines. Violet, that child is beyond unusual, and I don't think Elizabeth has a coping strategy except to give in."

"What can I do to intervene, Gladys? As you say, the child is healthy and both parents are attentive—Kingsley overly so. They are both defensive about Will and claim he's simply a prodigy but otherwise completely normal."

"Well, he gives me the creeps—and no one should say that about a baby. I'm so sorry, my dear."

Such an irony that I had pressed and pressed Kingsley for a grandchild so hard that it became a running joke between us. Now the child was with us, and what was to be made of him? His entire being was odd, off. I had kept a stiff upper lip and soldiered on, but now even friends and acquaintances were taking notice and making comment. I was embarrassed for our family and felt powerless to make the situation better.

Gladys regarded me with pity in her eye, and despite our customary genteel manners, we two old friends hugged long, and tears streamed down my cheeks.

   *   *   *

C hapter 47

I had recomposed myself by the time Gordon returned home from lab and greeted him at the door. He was an unusually steady man in temperament and demeanour, but tonight he looked visibly shaken.

"Ah, you're lying in wait for me," he said, attempting a light tone. "How was your day, my dear?" He hung up his coat and gave me a quick kiss on the cheek.

I sighed. "Is there any other subject? A chat with Gladys about this and that over tea. It turns out she and Tessa had an eyebrow-raising experience with Elizabeth and Will last week, only to add to my concern. And yesterday when I dropped in on my way home from the gallery, Will and Kingsley were on the floor playing with that puppet theatre. At one point Will seemed to tire of the game and went into his room. He came back with a book, and it was not from the Collected Works. Kingsley frowned, then snatched the volume away from the child.

'Let's finish with our staging, Will,' he said. 'Shakespeare always comes first—that's our motto.' And Will reluctantly obeyed. Does Kingsley realise what he's done to that boy? Were you able to talk to him?"

Gordon echoed my own sigh. "Violet, might I have a wee glass of Laphroaig? Just to steady my nerves." I did not take this as a good sign. I brought him the whisky and we arranged ourselves in our comfortable chairs. Gordon sipped his drink.

"Well, yes, I was able to have a few moments with your son over tea. I'm at a loss about his state of mind."

"What did he have to say?"

"I tried to broach the subject of Will in a positive manner. That was easy, since Kingsley talks of little else. I mentioned his apt mind and the importance of a variety of stimuli in developing a complete human being."

"How did he take to that notion? Was he able to apply it to Will?"

"At first he was defensive. Will is tickety-boo, Kingsley's doing the best thing for him, end of story."

"I thought as much."

"But then I hit upon the child's effect on others. I mentioned your worries and Elizabeth's apparent weariness. His mind seemed to open up a bit at that. I continued on with a larger circle of experience for the child: other children, close relationships with adults beyond just his father."

"And . . . ?"

"He sees Will as superior to other children and thus in no need of their company. When I mentioned his . . . aloofness, I think I called it, Kingsley said he gets ample affection just at home, and that the child is by nature an observer."

"Ah, so there's no leverage gained there."

"I tried to make an analogy to the full range of input in an experimental situation—the child as a blank slate, the fullest result occurring under a bombardment of options. He smiled and said Will truly was 'a grand experiment.'"

"That may be where some of the child's analytical coolness comes from. He sees it in his own father."

"But then I chanced to mention the Shakespeare ridiculousness, and a transformation came over him. Violet, in all these years I've seen nothing like it in your son and my friend." Gordon sipped at his Scotch again. "It was almost as if a storm cloud took over his entire demeanour. He became dark and glowering." I took Gordon's hand. "'What do you mean, ridiculousness?' Kingsley raged. He claimed that the spirit of Shakespeare had inspired him when he was testing the pipe, and he wants to impart that inspiration into the child. It sounds like an insane connection to make—that somehow the child was born with a link to Shakespeare because of the pipe. *Post hoc ergo propter hoc*, we call it as a thinking fallacy, 'after this, therefore because of this,' and Kingsley as a scientist should know better. There is no logical association between Will and the Bard of Avon, except in Kingsley's mind. And I fear his mind is coming unhinged."

"Oh, my darling. I too feared as much. What can we do? How can we help—and save the child?"

"It's odd, Violet, that this madness seems focused only on the child and perhaps peripherally on the mother. He is still doing sound work at the lab—comes on time, works through his cases, takes care with his procedures."

"But at home it's a different matter. Unless we can break into that circle, Elizabeth is lost, Kingsley is off the edge, and Will will be a misfit. It seems a tragedy in the making," I responded.

"We've offered our love and support," Gordon continued with his analysis. "We've offered our assistance. You've suggested counseling. How much more can we intrude? No one is under threat of physical harm. It boils down to a disagreement about how to rear a child at core, and there are no laws dictating that, so long as the child is safe."

"It's almost a case of too much attention, so the baby dangerously considers himself the centre of the universe," I conjectured.

"We can only bide our time and help as we have opportunity, Violet. But in the final analysis, 'it is not nor it cannot come to good.'"

* * *

Chapter 48

I had learned through an early science experiment of Kingsley's that earth's creatures can adapt slowly to what may actually be drastic changes in their environment. As a frog immersed in water adjusts as the water heats to the boiling point, the larger circle surrounding Kingsley, Elizabeth, and Will altered its expectations for behaviour and interaction. We no longer counted on daily or weekly phone calls. We knew if we visited that Will would be cool, aloof, indifferent. And we found that Elizabeth would be distracted and Kingsley fanatical about his son and immersing him in all things Shakespearean. Over time we accepted this state of affairs as normal.

They kept young Will inside and provided home education. Kingsley outlined a plan for genius-lessons that recreated the Tudor world. His curriculum resembled something out of *The Courtier*, with a balanced system of Renaissance cultural immersion. He taught Will to sing and play instruments; he taught him fencing and daggers. Will learned about ancient history, about politics and power plays. He scrutinised portraits of great men. And above all, he knew and recited by rote the literature of the classic world. At the base of it all was the entire Shakespeare canon, which Will also knew by heart. Kingsley had read aloud to him from the plays every night for more than a decade.

Early on Kingsley had fashioned a small puppet theatre for the child, and together they would act out scenes from the plays and then improvise their own actions. On the one hand it was remarkable to behold, the two of them completely engaged in a world constructed from poetic language, both of them equally adept. On the other hand, this arena became their entire universe, to the exclusion of all others and of any matters of the twenty-first century. Will was entering our world just after we crossed the millennium, but what Kingsley revealed to him was nearly 500-year-old lore, and Will absorbed it to his core. It was his reality. Notably, while he was rapt with this process, Will took little visible delight in such play. This was all serious business, often cruel business. While human nature remains steady, it's true, the dramas seemed not to prepare Will adequately for modern living. His experience of human beings was second-hand, and it was constructed entirely of words.

It was a novelty to hear the child speak, and if we laughed at his quaint constructions, he never shared our mirth. Will seemed to have a quotation for every situation, and as he delivered these adages we all became acutely aware of how thoroughly Shakespeare's phrases had infiltrated our own consciousness. When overdone, however, it was alarming and sounded trite. He almost seemed a small Bard impersonator, and he even came to resemble those portraits he'd stared at from infancy, though Kingsley no longer provided him with doublet and hose. Will did, however, fancy black.

I began collecting my grandson on Saturdays and walking him through the galleries of the B.M. as I'd done with Kingsley in his youth. Will was primarily interested in Renaissance portraiture. People were his genre—but only people rendered as art, caught in amber—not real, live, breathing company. We generally boarded a double-decker to Bloomsbury, and the journey was often a challenge. Will would not take my hand or even hug close to my body. On the coach he would plunk down as he pleased, oblivious to the elderly or the infirm. Everyone gave him a wide berth. His entire demeanour was eerie, off-putting.

He and I had evolved a stilted mode of communication. Generally he would obey my wishes and behave, but he never initiated a conversation, indicated much about his personal interests or observations, or asked questions. He never giggled or laughed. At times I perceived he did play small tricks on me, and they felt mocking, superior, almost malicious. Once in the gallery he wandered away from me, and for a few moments I was frantic. Recalling his love for portraits, I traced him down in Room 46 and watched him unobserved from a distance.

He had spotted an elderly man resting on the bench with his booklet, gloves, and umbrella beside him. The gentleman had dozed off, and Will casually joined him on the bench. Then, glancing around, he surreptitiously grasped the umbrella and slowly moved it under the bench and back just far enough that someone with limited motion might tip over trying to retrieve it. Having placed the umbrella, he gave the world—in an otherwise empty room—a smile that curdled my blood. This read as self-satisfied malice—for its own sake.

From this prank Will meandered through the portraits until he came to a depiction of Thomas Howard, Earl of Arundel by Nicholas Hilliard, where he paused and stared as if mesmerised. I thought he might be recalling his own infant garb, which this gentleman wore in earnest, notably the large collar. Will studied all human faces with the same kind of detached analytical gaze, but he almost seemed more at home with the static old portraits. And he always preferred men. Near Arundel was a glorious depiction of Queen Elizabeth I with all the symbols of authority surrounding her. This earned only a passing glance as Will moved on to linger by James I nearby.

I strode into the chamber and addressed Will. "Ah, there you are, my child. You mustn't wander off on your own in such a large place."

"Well here you found me after all, Grandmum, where I myself am master of my self, and I have always known just where I am."

The child always seemed surprised by the assumption of human connection, and he lacked the imaginative power of true empathy. Kingsley brushed this aside, saying, "He's off in his own little world." None of us except perhaps Kingsley had the key to enter that world bounded by a nutshell where Will himself reigned supreme, king over all he surveyed.

*   *   *

C hapter 49

I had heard through the grapevine that Elizabeth was giving up her position at Medusa's Hair. Through the last decade or so she had continued to juggle motherhood and work, squeezing in time for sorting through manuscripts in lulls from Will's need of her attention. In this technological age she seldom even made an appearance in her office, handling most transactions by video conferencing. Gordon and I were relieved that she retained at least an arm's length connection with the outside world.

I told Gordon the gossip over drinks, and he observed, "Isn't it fascinating that Elizabeth's specialty is literature of fantasy? Especially in light of the world of the past Kingsley has recreated for Will. I sometimes wonder how much she contributes to that illusion as she's home alone with the child all day."

"An interesting point—but as I understand it, Kingsley assumes primary responsibility for the home-schooling regime. They do their lessons in the evenings, and Will has homework assignments he performs while Elizabeth works. The child writes all sorts of scenarios into a notebook, which he and his father enact on their puppet stage."

"Violet, when I stopped by there last week, Elizabeth appeared more depressed than ever. She was still in her night clothes and quite unkempt. Elizabeth and Will seemed like mirror images, both sitting alone, both scribbling in jotters. The boy was all in black and neither was very responsive or engaging to me. The boy does not resemble his mother in looks at all, but they seemed the depression twins. Will answered my comments in single words."

"Not unusual for the boy. It's either that or iambic pentameter," I observed.

"But Elizabeth's condition! What a falling-off there's been. I asked if she was moving from editing to writing, and she said, 'Just jotting down the thoughts that flood my mind. I've done so since I began carrying Will.' She made an automatic motion of rubbing her belly. And then, Violet, she gestured to a portion of the bookshelf that was crowded with rows and rows of these journals, like annals of these past years."

"Well, writing can be good for the soul. Did she give you a look at any of them? I wonder what she's recording."

"Just thoughts, she said, going nowhere in particular. Nothing to leave one's job for," Gordon reported.

"This eclipse of her sanity does not bode well."

We heard a light rap at the door, and Gordon stood up, saying, "Oh, forgot to mention I asked Kingsley to stop by on his way home from lab. I have a book about emotional intelligence I want to lend him. It must be him now."

I set down my drink and rose to greet my son. "Kingsley! My darling, you look worn. We hardly catch a glimpse of you these days!"

He gave me a perfunctory hug and kiss on the cheek. "The duties of fatherhood, Mum. As a single parent, I'm sure you understand."

"Yes, but *you're not* a single parent!"

"Will is *my* baby, Mum . . . in a manner of speaking. A son needs a father figure. Elizabeth occupies herself with her own concerns."

"What's happened to her, Kingsley?"

"A spot of vodka and tonic?" Gordon interjected.

"Yes, thanks, old man." Kingsley perched on the sofa.

I continued. "She used to be vibrant and lovely. Lately she seems drab and despondent. She's let herself go. And she doesn't get out. Now we hear she's leaving her job."

"It's her decision, Mum. After all these years it may just be wearing her down." He accepted the drink Gordon brought him, and I took up my own again.

"The tedium of work wears everyone down, dear, but still we trudge on without going off our heads."

"You're not implying Elizabeth is mad?" Kingsley exclaimed.

"Haven't you noticed her condition? Doesn't she confide in you? Husband and wife should be best friends."

Gordon shot me a loving glance.

"Will and I are busy with home-school, and she's much withdrawn into herself."

"And you, aren't you much withdrawn as well, into Will?" I blurted out. Kingsley gave me a cold look. "The two of you have created a world to exclude Elizabeth."

"You and your husband, always interfering. Unlike you, Mum, to tread so heavily into private matters."

"Now, now," said Gordon.

"That's just the point, Kingsley. A child is not a private matter, nor by extension are the parents. We all have circles of context. You are my flesh and blood and we'll always be connected. Elizabeth is my adopted daughter. Will, as your flesh and blood, is mine, too. Showing our love is not intruding."

"We're all fine, Mum. We appreciate your concern." Kingsley seemed to dismiss my reasoning.

The drink had lowered my usual threshold for decorum and circumscription. "Kingsley, you are blind. You're not listening. Don't try to brush this off. We've stood by while you fashioned Will into a Tudor doll, and we're not going to let you push Elizabeth away from her life. This has gone too far! Open your eyes before it's too late to make changes."

Again the cold look. Steel doors closed over Kingsley's entire face. He shut out all access to the concerned parental touch. I'd seen him in his teenage years assert a cold independence but never to this extent. The three of us endured an uncomfortable silence.

At last Kingsley downed the rest of his drink in one gulp and stood. "Must be getting home now." Then his gaze softened a touch. "Mum, Gordon, you know Will is a prodigy, and I'm devoting my life to his welfare. Elizabeth has always been her own person—but I do hear you, and I will look to her. Maybe some anti-depressant medication would bring her back. I'll speak to her doctor."

Relieved, I stood and hugged my son. "That's all we ask, Kingsley. 'The voice of parents is the voice of gods, for to their children they are heaven's lieutenants.'"

* * *

Chapter 50

After our confrontations with Kingsley about Will and Elizabeth, he warmed up to us again and for a while resumed the weekly calls. This is not to say that their home situation changed or improved. All of them continued as before or, in Elizabeth's case, in a downward spiral. Kingsley performed his work at the lab with meticulousness and responsibility; Will received his father's attentions during off hours with a sense of entitlement and chill. But poor Elizabeth, relieved of work duties, stayed at home in her robe sitting in her easy chair scribbling in those journals—which she would show to no one. After we expressed interest in her writing she removed the rows, the years, of books. Kingsley said she had locked them away in a hidden place.

His buoyancy in all things pertaining to Will and his apparent indifference to Elizabeth's state both concerned me. Gordon had, I could sense, wearied of the small circle as a topic of conversation, so I fretted quietly, constantly, to myself. My mind was on the three of them as I sipped my tea, when the phone rang. It was Kingsley checking in.

"Hullo, Mum, how goes it at the old folks' home?"

"Hello, darling. Gordon and I are fine—and as you well know, fit as fiddles and bustling with activities. No ribbing allowed for a condition we cannot change. Time and the hour run through the roughest day."

"I wanted to tell you about the marvelous outing Will and I had last week. In honour of his thirteenth birthday, I took him down to the New Globe. Have you and Gordon been there? It's an authentic reconstruction of Shakespeare's own theatre built with the input of scholars and archaeologists to essentially recreate the original."

"Ach, Shakespeare again and again. That boy needs some other experience. Take him up in the Eye of London, for Pete's sake, or even on the Jack the Ripper tour. That ties in to your work and would be historical and educational."

"Well, I took him on the Globe tour instead. He absolutely loved it. Mum, he was right at home there. I've hardly even seen him so animated, so happy."

"That would indeed be a welcome change in the boy. But it's not surprising given his complete immersion since birth in the Bard."

"We stayed on for a performance of *Othello*. He was rapt and I could see him mouth the words to every speech as it was spoken on stage. My efforts have really paid off."

"Yes, we know the boy is apt. But really, Shakespeare to what avail? Right now all you've trained him for is a career as an actor with the RSC to the exclusion of all else. And I'm not sure he has the empathy to play a role convincingly. He may know the words, but can he feel the emotions?"

"Mum, you've hit it on the head. He says the actors on the stage are his puppets all grown up and moving about of their own accord. For him it was like discovering a new technology: humans! A life in the theatre, that was all he babbled about on the way home."

"Anything that can make that child babble must be good. Working in theatre would be a simple extension of his present home life, it seems. But I do hope you'll expose him to other kinds of plays. The Shakespeare focus is quite limiting. What about something light-hearted—say, musical comedy?"

"He has a serious bent, Mum. He's so gung-ho about Shakespeare I think we'll take a motoring trip to Stratford next. Maybe we'll even see that pipe I worked on, on display there. I'd love to share some of my work with him."

"Well, I'm sure it would do Elizabeth good to get away. Maybe you could even motor on to the shore. A little sea air for all of you."

"Oh, Elizabeth really doesn't get out, Mum, and she leaves Will's education in my hands."

"You don't mean to say she'd refuse a brief family vacation? Is she feeling poorly?"

"She's quite a scribbler these days. She's given up endless reading for endless writing."

"I must drop over. Is she working on something in particular?"

"Just thoughts, she says, thoughts about being a mum."

"Well, plenty to express in that topic. Once a mother, always a mother. The job is never done."

"I think you're right. She's developed a strange gesture of rubbing her belly sort of automatically. She says it's not because of pain, but I do wonder."

"What does Dr. Knowles say?" I asked.

"He's given her a mood-elevator and says otherwise she's spiffy. No physical problems to address."

"Do consider taking her north with you. And I'll try to get over this week. Even if she's not working, the city is full of stimulating possibilities she might enjoy."

"All right then. 'Til next time, Mum."

Kingsley's tone had been bright, but he seemed oblivious to the seriousness of Elizabeth's decline. More needs she the divine than the physician. God, God forgive us all! I thought.

 *   *   *

C hapter 51

Gordon still dropped in at the lab one or two days a week, and late Friday afternoon he rang me up from work.

"Violet, I've got Kingsley in tow, and I've persuaded him to come out to the pub before taking off for Stratford tomorrow. I wonder if you'd care to join us—a quick drink and perhaps some starters if whatever dinner you're cooking up can hold. Can you meet us right away at the Scarsdale Tavern in Kensington? A happy threesome, colleague, mother, and son?"

"What a nice invitation, Gordon! Are you sure I wouldn't spoil the fun?"

"Nonsense. It'll be a festive event. Time for us all to stop fretting so much and let our hair down."

"All right, then. I'll motor over and we can come back home together in my car."

I set the oven on "warm," hoping the shepherd's pie wouldn't dry out, and I freshened up quickly before getting my coat and taking the lift down to the carpark. Traffic was heating up, but the Scarsdale wasn't far, and I snagged a space on the same block.

Gordon and Kingsley were already seated and had ordered pints of bitters and some chips.

"Here we are, Violet!" Gordon waved to me from the banquette and I made my way towards them through the crowd. Kingsley was all smiles for a change and he rose and embraced me. Gordon lumbered over to the bar and returned quickly with a wine spritzer in hand. "Something sparkly for the light of my life," he said, setting the glass before me and winking at Kingsley.

"So, you're leaving tomorrow for your holiday up north?" I broached, sipping at my drink.

"Right-o, Mum," Kingsley said brightly. "Will is all prepared and enthusiastic. This will be the capstone to his Shakespearean studies. I'm looking forward to experiencing it all through his eyes."

"Any luck on getting Elizabeth to join you? I see that she's perkier."

"No, no. This is a trip for the boys, don't you know. Father and son only. She's pretty much avoided our Shakespeare activities. She's left that all up to me. I know she's told the boy some other tales, but the Bard is our main man. How about another round, Gordon?" Kingsley downed the last of his pint and approached the bar, returning with a pitcher in hand. "This will save us some steps," he said, refilling both their glasses with the foamy brew. "Cheers!" They each chugged the dark liquid.

"Don't forget we have dinner waiting for us at home," I said to Gordon. "I don't want to have to roll you into the flat."

"Just a little oil for the art of conversin'," he replied. "You don't mind a bit of shop-talk, do you, my dear?"

Gordon turned back to Kingsley and mentioned a relic that had recently been sent to the lab.

"That stone mortar and pestle they brought us from the dig near Hadrian's Wall could be rich with DNA samples, and they might help fill in the profile of pre-Norman, pre-Roman indigenous clans. Wouldn't it be exciting to isolate a female genome from the first millennium?"

"The scientist's imagination loves to take these possibilities to the limit," Kingsley mused in response. "But as you well know, my friend, that encroaches on dodgy ethical ground."

My mind wandered as they considered the addition to knowledge this sample might offer. Then I saw a friend from the gallery wave at me from a table across the room.

"Excuse me for a minute," I interrupted. "I see Imogene and want to say hello."

Imogene and I caught up on the recent exhibits, and I made my way on to the loo. I could see the fellows were still in earnest conversation. The ladies' room was situated down a partitioned hall behind the banquette, and as I returned I could hear the animated voices of Gordon and Kingsley. My son seemed on the edge of inebriation. I paused at the end of the wall to observe and listen.

"But what if you could bring a Pict back to life?" Gordon posed. "We have the technology. It's a common error to think of different versions of *homo* existing on a chronology in an orderly sequence, one at a time. But in reality, several strands of humankind lived simultaneously, side by side. I ask you, what would be the harm in bringing one of them back into our world?"

"Ah, but the responsibility, there's the stickin' point," I heard Kingsley reply, slurring his words. "How would you nurture the cave man? What would be the ethical imper'tive? You'd have to be heroic in tendin' to him as a person from his own time. And you could never, ever reveal to anyone the secret of his identity and birth." He paused and gulped at his bitters. "It would be a burden I'm not sure anyone could bear. If society found out, you'd be judged and censured. And in a way, that life would take over your own, for you would be the sole parent of this bein' from the past. In a sense you'd be the God, certainly the creator. And a God is accountable for his creation." He drew from his mug again and ran his fingers through his hair, making it stand on end.

"And a God is alone. The scientist would have to devote his life to the result of this one experiment, neglectin' all other entanglements. It would set him apart, yes, but at what cost to him?" Kingsley's face had become red and blotchy. "He'd be sacrificin' his own future for the benefit of science—in an act he could never share or reveal in the light of day. And heaven forbid if he would involve others in the project. They'd be . . . ruined . . . by his choice to follow through on the experiment." His voice faltered and cracked.

"You speak with such passion about this, Kingsley, almost as if you've considered the possibility," Gordon observed. "Did you ever try it on the sly? See if you could get an old-time embryo going?"

Kingsley's eyes pierced Gordon's face. "Well, haven't you been tempted on occasion, my colleague? It's the crux of our discipline—pushin' into unknown territory."

Gordon leaned back on the banquette. "I must say, when we found the pipe that old Shakespeare might have smoked, the thought did cross my mind. In a way we were saved by the ambiguity of our results. But if we could have said with certainty, this is the Bard's DNA, I would have loved to bring him back to life. What insights he might have shared with us!" Gordon chuckled at the thought.

Kingsley gulped hard, and I heard him respond, "Per'aps horror rather than delight, Gordon. But who could've known? Who could've known?" he repeated softly.

I rounded the corner and sat back down by Gordon. "Have you two resolved the future of genetic research?" I asked. Kingsley's face had dropped and his mood had darkened. He was staring stoically at his mug. He looked a fright. Before he'd always taken delight in the possibilities of science. But now somehow he seemed tormented. Or haunted.

I couldn't help comparing him to Elizabeth. What had happened to this promising couple? I had witnessed their alienation from each other and a physical and mental decline—brought on apparently by the birth of Will. Both seemed to dismiss or avoid facing their new reality. I felt increasingly more helpless, an astounded on-looker with no remedy.

"Oh, just idle talk, my dear," Gordon replied. "'Imagination bodies forth the forms of things unknown,' for scientists as well as poets."

"Per'aps the unknown should be left where it lies," Kingsley said. "Conscience *should* make cowards of us all. . . ."

* * *

Chapter 52

While Kingsley arranged for the boys' trip north, I had spoken to Elizabeth on the phone and made her promise to spend time with me when they were away. As Kingsley predicted, she had elected not to go along. She was lacklustre and much dwindled away both physically and mentally. Because she seldom left her chair in the flat, her stamina had ebbed. She was becoming an invalid, afflicted, it seemed, in both mind and body.

At breakfast in our flat, Gordon and I spread the arts and culture section of *The Daily Mail* across the table and scanned upcoming events for an outing she might find stimulating, something that would not be taxing or strenuous. That stipulation excluded long walks, gallery and museum tours that necessitated hours on one's feet, or even lengthy concerts she might find enervating.

"Here's something, Violet," Gordon said as the morning streamed in through our window. "It's a public lecture at university on genetics."

"That might interest *you*, my dear, but Elizabeth?" I responded.

"Don't be hasty to dismiss the topic. She and Kingsley met and courted during the pipe episode, and he shared some of the DNA profiling process with her. With her expertise in science fiction, she found the possibilities fascinating. Of course, she's given all that up now, but who knows? It might rekindle her mind, pique some interest."

"Well, a lecture would be sitting down, and they usually go about an hour, right?" I inquired.

"Yes, about three-quarters hour of lecture and then Q and A."

Kingsley and Will had headed north that Saturday morning, and Elizabeth half-heartedly agreed to accompany me to the talk. I decided to drive us there as, if we could park easily, it would mean a shorter walk for her than using public transportation. She held my arm as we walked towards the hall, and it was a fine late summer evening with fragrance of the last roses still perfuming the air from trellises in the gated gardens we passed en route to the theatre.

"It's so good to get out," Elizabeth said, taking a deep breath. "Thank you, Violet, for bringing me. This should be fun."

"Topic a bit out of our sphere, but of concern to us all."

"It's always been part of Kingsley's conversations about work—how difficult it can be to trace a genetic line even in a small country like ours."

"Yes, as I recall, that was the stumbling block with that Shakespeare pipe all those years ago. There was a gap in the genetic line, and they just couldn't make the connection . . . Shakespeare again. Sorry, darling, you must be weary of the man."

"Well, truth be told, between constant quoting of lines and puppet dramas at night, it's almost as if I live with him. It's a good thing I love a turn of phrase, or I would truly be mad by now," Elizabeth confessed.

"Had you the foggiest notion that Will would grow up to be such a . . . prodigy?"

"There's a bit of the swot in Kingsley, Violet, and he's devoted himself to the boy's education. What with my occupation with literature, it doesn't seem entirely unnatural."

"Ah, here we are," I said. We approached the hall and found seats in a sparse audience within the theatre. Right on time a young man strode onto the stage, the lights dimmed, and the talk began. The lecturer was in his early thirties, full of vigour and enthusiasm. He focused on the ability of genes in the human species to alter over time. Of course we know this as evolution and think of it as a lengthy process, but he emphasised that changes constantly occur, even over a few hundred years. Often the changes do not manifest themselves in particularly observable phenomena, so we don't notice. But there are constant mutations.

And even with an identical set of DNA as in twins from the same egg, the genes may reveal different qualities through something called "gene expression." A single gene may have potential that might show itself differently if its acid-forming process takes a path of choice. At this Elizabeth sat at attention in her seat. I had been worried that the talk might bore her, but she now seemed fully focused on the lecturer. Further, if these twins had been raised in different environments after birth, the differences would be even more profound. Nutrition, climate, health care, education—all can alter who we become.

The lecturer darkened the room even more and the faces of identical twins appeared on the large screen. "These two people are monozygotic twins, from the same egg. Thus they have identical genomes or genetic blueprints. They are essentially clones," he said. "But even in the womb each had a different experience, and even small changes in our environment can alter how our genes become expressed. You'll note that one of these twins is taller than the other and one considerably heavier. How can this be if their genes are identical?

"The process is called 'missing heritability.' For a single trait as many as 500 different genes in combination may be involved." There was a slight gasp of disbelief from the audience. "A biological process called methylation can activate a certain gene—in essence turn it on—or accelerate its activity. Apply this process to 500 genes in combination, and the variables of potential grow exponentially to a dizzying figure."

Everyone in the audience seemed wide awake. Most of us had thought your genes determined your destiny, that it was cut and dried. Identical genes would produce identical results. But he was proposing a much more fluid and even malleable process.

"We've also seen changes occur through gene adoption, something we call 'horizontal gene transfer.' An organism can appropriate an advantageous gene, even across species. We're not clear on which processes worked on the genomes of these twins, but one died at thirty-five of a stroke, and one still walks this earth happily today at age seventy-five. Different gene activation means a different destiny."

He switched off the overhead and brought up the house lights. "So," he concluded, "all of us carry marks of our ancestors within us, and each of us has a unique DNA profile. But genes adapt, genes evolve, genes contain variables. The final product we call the self remains shrouded in mystery. And now I will entertain your questions."

To my great surprise Elizabeth's hand shot into the air.

"Yes, you, ma'am," he gestured towards her.

She rose and said, "Has anyone done experiments with actual clones of humans?"

He laughed. "Not that we know of . . . or speak of. That's a universally prohibited application. Identical twins are the closest we come to comparing the expression of a single DNA profile."

"Oh, and more, if I may . . ." she went on. "Could the human species have changed in character in, oh, say four or five hundred years?"

"We generally conduct genetic research on species with brief lifespans and a quick reproductive cycle, like the fruit fly. That way we can note genetic changes over generations in, for us, a short observable time. But yes, we've noticed small alterations within twenty generations and sometimes even a single generation. The point is that mutation and evolution are constant on-going processes, and if you factor in gene expressions and missing heritability, we find that even with a single profile there can be—if not alterations—at least alternatives. With more than 3 billion base pairs in the human genome, the possibilities are dizzying."

"So would, again as an example, someone from the Elizabethan age have been a different sort of human from how we are now?"

"We are all *homo sapiens*, the knowing man, but there certainly could be small instances of evolution in our species profile across the board. And until we can examine several complete profiles from that era in detail, we'd be unable to say what precisely has changed. They would certainly look much like us and speak much like us. We know this from portraiture and from literature. But at the cellular level . . . ? We simply can't be sure. And now . . . anyone else?"

The questions went on, but Elizabeth sat back down and turned to me with shining eyes. "Oh, Violet, that was so illuminating!" she whispered. After a smattering of applause, we rose and began to make our way back to the car. Darkness was descending, and the streetlamps cast pools of isolated light upon the sidewalk. We moved from halo to halo.

"I didn't realise you shared Kingsley's enthusiasm for genetic study," I commented. She seemed as if she'd received a shot in the arm. She was animated, almost frenetic, and there was a revived energy in her step.

"Over time you just pick up bits and pieces from the on-going conversation," she said. "They are making all sorts of new discoveries, and I am fascinated by what shapes the nature of man. I think that's always been the question of literature as well. What is given, and what do we choose? And then, what are the consequences?"

"Yes, for a while there we seemed to think it was all written in our genes, as if in the stars," I said, looking up at a sky in which Venus was ascending brightly.

"Oh, but how wrong that is, didn't we learn tonight? If the genome is a blueprint, it is vague. The genes may build the human with gingerbread embellishment or crown mouldings or wainscoting or turrets and porches. No wonder sometimes a child seems like not a member of the family. He may be a head taller than everyone and carry a musical talent no one else shares. But it was there in potential, in some mysterious genetic combination.

"Maybe it's a quality that has lain dormant, even from ancient ancestors. Then the right conditions occur for its activation and combination with other genes and environmental factors, and you have what seems like some kind of mistake. I suppose this accounts for strange personality differences too—or even criminal behaviour. It's in the genes, but we can't really lay the cause at the parents' feet."

It was clear that Elizabeth was thinking deeply about the concepts we'd learned in the lecture, and I couldn't help wondering if she was making a personal application to Will. We reached the car, and I said, rather boldly, "I mean no offense, but I've always marveled at your own son's strange qualities and preferences, I must say. Although he follows Kingsley's lead, he seems so unlike either of you really. He's always been his own person and rather like a stranger in our family. I suppose this lecture helps clarify the child's character and personality." I silently wondered how much Kingsley's schooling had shaped Will into a Tudor anachronism.

We seated ourselves in the car, and Elizabeth bowed her head. She seemed exhausted now, or perhaps transported into another world. Like me, perhaps she was considering the possibilities.

* * *

C hapter 53

Early next week I received a brief text from Kingsley, with Will in Stratford. "Arrived safely. Will absolutely in his element. Having a brilliant time. We'll stop at Stonehenge en route home. Talk then, Kingsley."

I shared the message with Gordon, who said, "Well, good on them. I can't see any harm in father and son spending quality time together. I know Kingsley missed that in his own childhood—no fault of yours, my dear—and he's compensating for that with Will. Never let it be said the child lacked a strong parental role model."

"I just wish his maternal parent were equally involved," I sighed. "If only Elizabeth had gone along with them, as a complete family holiday. Kingsley's bound to make it schooling rather than fun. And she did liven up so much at that lecture. I think she lacks stimulation. Getting away would have done her a world of good."

"You've helped as you can, sweetheart, and they must be free to make their own decisions. She'll have a lark listening to the both of them tell their tales when they return."

"If the child will converse. He's generally so laconic, almost secretive."

"Well, he's a teenager now. The troubled years, rebellion, all that. Never easy to keep in tow."

Towards the end of the week Kingsley himself stopped by at tea-time. Gordon fancied a bit of the sweet, so I'd begun weekly baking episodes. Today I'd just managed some orange scones and a lemon cake; the aromas of baking filled the flat. From the kitchen I heard the voices of my men in the lounge, the lilt of Gordon's accent, the reasonable steady baritone of my son. I quickly dried my hands and rushed out to greet him.

"Kingsley, so glad you're home safe! And Will, did he survive the rigours of holiday?" I hugged him and kissed his cheek.

"Hullo, Mum. Oh yes, we're both in one piece despite crazy motorists on the M40." A brief memory of Kingsley's father flitted through my mind.

"Sit, sit. Tell us all about it. I have scones and cake! Gordon, could you bring out the tea tray?" We situated ourselves with the abundance from my kitchen.

"Mmm, scones are still warm, Mum."

"Takes me back to my childhood days," added Gordon.

"Well, this vacation was simply extraordinary," Kingsley began. "I was able to discuss English history with Will as we drove north. Events and places came alive for him as never before. We stopped at Banbury Cross and Warwick Castle and took the tours—lots of good historical lessons johnny-on-the-spot. And when we arrived at Stratford, it was as if he were at home. We wandered the older section of town, walked along the river, and of course did our Shakespeare visits, to both Holy Trinity Church with his bust and monument, and to the Birthplace."

"Have they made a prominent display of our old pipe?" Gordon asked.

"Ah, yes, there it was, in a glass box," Kingsley replied. "Will meandered through that house almost as if he knew it, lingering particularly by the hearth and in the garden. I felt he was absorbing the vibes of what it would have been like to live in Tudor times. When we contemplated the monument with that cheery round-faced effigy of the Bard, Will recited a line, 'Age cannot wither him, nor custom stale his infinite variety.' I tell you, as a father I was thrilled beyond words. He was making an emotional connection and an homage. I think our Shakespeare lessons have paid off."

"How exciting to bring an historical awareness into the present," I said. "I feel that way when I meet and speak to an artist I have known only through the paintings, or when I visit the site that inspired a great painting—the gardens at Giverny, for example."

"Ah, yes. And then we took in a matinee at the RSC, a fine production of *Hamlet*. As at the New Globe, Will was rapt, and I noticed him mouthing the words to the great soliloquies right along with the actor—almost as if he were stage-managing the whole thing. And when the Ghost of Old Hamlet appeared—well, I thought Will would jump from his seat with wonder."

"I'm so glad you've found the key to animating the boy. He's generally so self-contained," I commented.

"'The play's the thing' for Will, eh?" chuckled Gordon, taking another serving of lemon cake.

"Two strange things occurred, though, when we were at the Birthplace," Kingsley went on. "First, Will was in his usual black, and in the spirit of the place he had added a white collar to his outfit. The Birthplace guard stopped him as we entered, putting a hand on Will's shoulder. Calling to the other room, he said, 'Georgie, take a look at this. We've got the spit 'n' image of old Will returning home after lo these many years.' His fellow guard came over, and they scrutinised the boy. 'What's your name, lad?' he asked. "William Shakespeare Armstrong,' replied Will confidently. 'Ah, so,' he laughed. 'And how was your day at grammar school?' And they waved us on without charging an entry fee, the guard giving me a wink as we passed."

"Well, Kingsley, you set the boy up for this years ago with your custom-made doublets and hose," I observed. "He does resemble a little Shakespeare. It's uncanny, I've always said."

"Will was honoured and thrilled. He took it as a sort of right. 'Father, they recognised the Bard I am within,' he said to me. Always that iambic rhythm—don't know how he manages it." Kingsley took another scone.

"If you hear enough of that cadence, you'd have it settle into your bones," said Gordon, munching away. "Sort of like the bagpipe hum. It begins the drone, and your feet want to march."

"What was the other event?" I asked.

"Well, Mum, very strange. We were in that lovely rose and herb garden in the back of the house. The bees were buzzing all 'round, and the heady fragrances transported us into a timeless realm. We were alone; all other tourists were occupied with the house itself."

"Sounds heavenly on a rare summer's day."

"Will was pensive as usual, but animated. He paced around on the gravel path. His eyes darted here and there and then he stepped into the garden proper. Kneeling down, he scraped the dirt away from one spot of earth until he could see something glinting. He dug until it came loose into his hand."

"What on earth was it?" Gordon asked.

"My question precisely. He stood and came over to me back on the path holding out a muddy palm with an equally muddy blob deposited on it. He began to clean the dirt away until the item shone. It was a Tudor gold coin, what they call an angel, dated 1576."

"My stars," said Gordon. "Quite the find. Should be rather valuable now. As I recall, it has a gorgeous depiction of the archangel Michael on the obverse. I'd think the Birthplace would want to put it on display. Then we'd be connected to two items there in the museum. What did they say when you turned it over?" he asked, rising from his chair. As we continued to talk, he left the room.

"Well, there's the rub, as they say," Kingsley responded loudly enough for Gordon to hear. "Will simply would not relinquish the coin. Although he had absolutely no logical or rational way to locate something buried in a garden over 400 years ago, he claimed it was his and he was merely reclaiming it. I have to say, it was odd, the way he went directly to it. And the coin was not on the surface; he had to dig into the ground two inches or so. But he appeared to know right where it was. Perhaps there was a slight mounding up of the earth there that he detected."

"But Kingsley, you can't think for a moment the boy has a right to the coin," I admonished.

"Well, no . . . but yes, in a way, Mum. Finders keepers."

"Ach. Child's play, child's logic," I replied.

"I tried to use reason with Will, but he became agitated, and I didn't want to have a scene. He clutched onto it and would not let it go. He kept saying it was his. Just to get us out quietly I let him pocket it."

Gordon came back to his easy chair. "I just checked the internet, and that coin is valued at over £7000. I'd say that's more than petty larceny, Kingsley. You don't want to be committing a felony now, do you?"

"It couldn't be helped. Will's already had it pierced, and he's wearing it on a cord around his neck."

"Well, that will have diminished the value," said Gordon. "But surely you need to make some kind of amends."

"I was thinking of making a yearly donation to the Birthplace Trust as a recompense. I'll make up the complete sum to them over the years."

"What's happened to your ethical sense, Kingsley? You seem complacent to compromise these days. I'm disappointed," I remarked.

"Mum, it couldn't be helped," he responded. "Sometimes you're 'stepped in so far returning were as tedious as go o'er.'"

"Ah, the Scottish play!" said Gordon. "Isn't that followed by 'things bad begun make strong themselves by ill'?"

Part IV: The End and the Beginning

 * * *

William Shakespeare Armstrong-Montague

Chapter 54

Brilliant 'tis, wearing this shiny angel near my heart. It carries the year 1576 engraved upon it. Somehow my head had known it was there under the mud, and I must have it. It called out to me. I think the old Will buried it in the garden behind his house, perhaps when he was just my age. I could sense his presence upon it, as if the archangel represented the old Will himself, my guardian angel.

It isn't just that Father has primed me up in Bard lore. True, I can quote just about any line from any Shakespeare play or poem. Father's been drilling those words, those rhythms, those characters into my head ever since I can remember. That old-time face smiles down at me in my room, watching me grow all these years. He'd created those characters who were my only real friends. For my whole life, these fourteen years, Father and I have brought them to life in our puppet theatre. I know the thoughts that lead to their words. I see the way the villains read people to get what they want. They have taught me the way to succeed.

I've always used those tactics on my Mum, and Father has let me do it by turning a blind eye. He's been my ally against the world. Mum has a fear in her I can play on. When I come near to her, she shudders. Women can be so weak sometimes. Anything to keep me quiet and keep me away from her. She scribbles away in those books of hers, a furtive act. I love to amaze her by speaking in iambic pentameter. It isn't such a challenge to perform: da dum da dum da dum da dum da dum.

But I don't write down my thoughts. Someone might find them and then I'd be discovered, uncovered. I just think and talk to myself, a dramatic monologue. When I do speak iambic Grandmum gets unsettled too, but I sometimes find her watching me, studying me. I know that look, that evaluating look, because I'm a watcher too.

If you hold your peace and observe, you can see straight to what people desire and what they fear. And that gives you all the power. Never show your mind to anyone. Keep them guessing. All this smiling and pandering they do, just to keep it all rolling smoothly. I don't laugh. I don't try to get along—unless there's something for my pleasure or my advantage. The fools! Most of them are.

Except Granny. I wonder what she knows about me. Once at the gallery when I was playing a random prank I caught her figure out of the corner of my eye, spying, watching. She tries to draw me out, but I stay mum. I think she's judging me. That old buffoon Gordon, he's an easy one to mess with. So honest, so sincere. One time he was "helping" me play with my soldiers. When he looked away,

I murdered one of them and left the evidence fully visible. He hemmed and hawed and turned all ruddy in the face when he discovered the corpse. He couldn't handle thinking it was me, innocent child that I am. And of course I just gave him the fish eye in return. If they can't know me, they cannot control me. I've always been my own man. I'm not one of them. I don't belong. "Lord, what fools these mortals be."

Not that I'm immortal myself—but you can be like a god sometimes. This world is like a stage, and people are the players. They cry out for a script, for action, for a stage manager. It's them behind the scenes that pull all the strings. That's me. That's where I want to be. That's the role I was born for. That's what I live for.

Father gives me everything I need. For him I'm the living and breathing centre of the world. He's blocked out everyone else from our partnership, our projects. The only question now is where does it all lead? I can't go on with my puppet theatre for long. I see those actors moving around on a real stage, expounding those lines I know so well. Now I need actors with moving parts and stentorious voices. I need a larger platform for my own plots—a kingdom for a stage.

* * *

Chapter 55

Father always leaves a lesson plan for me to complete during the day while he's at work. Today it focuses on the history of world geography and map-making. I am to look through atlases containing views of the world as it spread out from England, its centre, from 1500 forward and note the changes, then write an outline of how this altered mankind's self-conception. My favourites are the older maps, as they are the smallest and most self-contained. Not far from England's coastline are squiggly lines representing waves of the ocean, deep waters I surmise, and then a drawing of a dragon or sea serpent with the legend "Here be monsters."

Humankind as a whole seems ignorant of their environment. For my domain I have almost exclusively this flat on Yeoman's Row, London SW3, England, and I try to be master of my space. Occasionally Mum might take me on a walk to the park, but there is little for me to do there. She and I have evolved a style of minimal conversation. She often appears lost in thoughts of her own, and I do not like to reveal my own mind—to anyone. Self-sufficient is sage. And if no one knows the real me, then no one can predict what I might do. I can pull their strings as I like, always appearing innocent.

If we are not on a silent walk, Mum and I are alone together in the flat. She has her chair and I my room. My puppet theatre spills out onto the floor of the lounge, and I sit for hours there putting my cast through their parts. But sometimes I just get the itch for mischief.

Once, when Mum took a trip to the loo, I rushed to her lamp and unscrewed the bulb so it just made minimal electrical contact. This meant it would randomly and unexpectedly flicker on and off. If this worked to unsettle her, I planned to sabotage the lighting of every room she frequented. Pranks were best when they were perplexing to the victim.

Mum returned to the lounge and I continued manipulating my puppets. She resumed writing in one of her books, and soon enough the lights began to flicker.

"Hmmm," I heard Mum say.

I saw her from the corner of my eye look up at the lamp with a quizzical glance. I pretended not to notice. The light flickered again, then steadied. She resumed writing. Minutes later, the light began to flicker again.

"Will? Did you see that?"

"See what?" I asked from the floor.

"The light," she said.

"I don't know what you mean," I said, continuing to walk my puppets on their stage. She reached up and clicked the lamp off, then, after a brief pause, on again. It glowed steady. We both continued our activities, and then the light blinked again.

"Are you saying you didn't notice that?" she asked me.

"To what do you refer?" I looked up and gave her a steady and confused gaze.

"My stars," she said. "I think my eyes have had it for today." She rose from her chair and took the laundry from the hamper into the kitchen to begin a load. I stealthily crept into her study, protected by the drone of the washing machine, and doctored the two lamps there, also unloosening the bulb in the overhead fixture. Tomorrow I'd work on her bedside lamp. I returned to my spot on the floor—and my puppets.

She moved from the kitchen to her study. I heard her click on the overhead and then say "What the—?" I smiled. "Ah, the desk lamp works," she said softly. We were both quiet for a bit, the washer making the whooshing and humming sounds of its cycle. Then, "Ach! How can this be?" came from her study. "Will!" she cried out.

I rose and walked into her room, where she sat in the gloom.

"What is happening to the lights?" she said.

"What ever do you mean, my Mum?" I asked.

"Isn't it dark in here?"

"Not dark. No, just as usual," I said, looking up and around, although I wasn't sure how well she could see me in the half-light coming in from the curtained window.

"Well, I can't see," she said. "Will you help me back to my chair?"

I took her arm and together we returned to the lounge. I got her situated under the now-steady light and returned to my spot on the floor. She picked up one of her books and paged through it. The light flickered. I made no remark but rose and sat in the chair across from her, walking my puppet on my leg, giving her my direct gaze.

"Oh fool, I shall go mad!" I heard her mutter. With my head turned away, I smiled, utterly satisfied. No monsters in our territory, but mischief for sure.

* * *

Chapter 56

Mum's going to stay in hospital for a while. While Father and I were at the Birthplace she got giddy. I showed her my angel 'round my neck when we returned. Her eyes grew glistery and round, and she swooned. Those books she writes in are piling up again. When she woke up in ER she was babbling gibberish. It's all about monsters and magic. Father and the doctors say it's those manuscripts she scanned for so many years. The plots sank into her brain and took it over.

So now I'm in the flat by myself while Father's at work. He's told me to stay inside and do my studies. But I like to wander the halls. The people come and go, and I watch them. Mostly they're like clockwork and like mice in a maze. They don't know they could end up in my little mousetrap. I'm just the kid in black. They pay me little mind. I could be a ghost.

I'd like to comb hair over my face and be a fright. Or disappear into the woodwork. But I've never had much hair unless I grow it long in back. My forehead takes over my face.

Down in the cellar there's an echo, and that's the place I can use my voice. I shout the lines I know so well, with just the right inflection. No one can hear. My daily stoicism is not discovered as a pose. It's the role I play. And I am invincible.

Yesterday I was shouting those lines, "Alas, poor Yorick, I knew him, Horatio, A fellow of infinite jest, of most excellent fancy: he hath borne me on his back a thousand times. . . ." I turned and there it was—she or he, I wasn't sure. Rosalind and Viola both pretended to be boys. This creature seemed to be their scion. It stood silently in the corner regarding me, listening to my speech. Its face was pale, with thick black lines outlining its eyes. On its slender body it wore a basic urban teen outfit, black on black, black jeans, black jersey jumper. Its hair was layered to the shoulders and mussed. Studded ornaments sparkled—in the ears, along the nose, at one eyebrow—with strange eye- and skull-shaped jewelry on the fingers and wrists. When I espied it, I ceased my oration.

"What are you doing?" it asked.

"I might have queried you in the same way." In times of stress I slipped into pentameter.

"Huh?"

"Do you reside within this edifice?" I needed to find out the nature of this potential character.

"Yeah, third floor. You?"

"We occupy the flat along the front." Pentameter again. "Ground floor," I added in a single foot spondee.

"I haven't seen you before. Do you go to school?" it asked.

"Home education keeps me occupied."

"Me too, home school. I have a condition. Can't go out much. I'm Cecelia, by the way. Papa calls me Cece."

"I'm Will." Where to go from here? She—now revealed—intrigued me, and I needed—if not a friend—a live body for any convenient purpose that might arise—

ally, puppet, operative. "Why do you haunt the building's nether world?" I asked.

"Huh?"

"What occupies you in these cellar walls?"

"It's my place just to get away and be myself. Nobody is ever here. 'Til today, 'til you."

"What do you do when you are most yourself?"

"Don't laugh. . . . I hum. No words. Just music, tunes I make up. I hear it in my head, and then I hum it. . . . But you, you fancy speeches? I heard you talking. Was that from a play or something?"

I was completely taken aback. Was there actually someone on the planet, here in London no less, who did not recognise some of Hamlet's most famous lines? All this language had constructed my world, and it was second nature. I perceived she was not joking.

"Um, well, my studies have been mostly in the Bard," I responded gently.

"That mouldy twit? Does anybody even care? Silly costumes, swanning around, sword fights, people complaining all the time. . . . Why don't they just say what they mean?"

I shuddered involuntarily. She shifted in my mind from possible ally to operative, no doubt about it.

"Want to perform some mischief and some fun?" I asked.

"Will we get caught?"

"Not if we're careful. We'll be safe and sound."

"What is it?" she queried.

"We can slip into the car park from here and unscrew the valve on the back tyre of someone's Rover. Then when they're in a hurry for work, they'll see a flat working and have to ring up for a tow. A bother for them, a lark for us. Come on! No one will ever know—we're the Stealthy Scourges."

"Really? Do you think we can get away with it?" Cece wondered.

"It's cloak and dagger, really just a prank. It's what teenagers are supposed to do. Put us all in pairs and then beware!"

She tittered. I knew I'd found her weakness, a desire for companionship and belonging. If we got away with it— and we would—she would trust me. And then whatever came next would be easier.

"Now, crouch your body down and walk like this." I mimed a cat-like skulk, and she followed my lead. Even better than puppets. As two small dark-clad figures minced towards the door to the car-park, I smiled with satisfaction. The game was afoot.

 *   *   *

C hapter 57

Father had forbidden watching telly while I was home alone, but sometimes I sneaked it on. I enjoyed flipping from serial to serial, just catching random episodes. Some of these stories seemed to me direct descendants of the plays I know so well, filled with intrigue and manipulation, with desire and revenge. The words, true, do not scan, but the emotional drama is clear.

I was clicking the channel button and paused on the news station. They were showing a picture of what looked like that silver Rover from our car park, and it caught my eye. A blonde woman with perfect stage make-up was speaking in the Queen's English about how it got bashed. The car had been traveling along Lower Thames Street when the rear tyre went flat and it zoomed down the embankment into the river. The driver and passenger had both been trapped inside and drowned before emergency help arrived. The two had been residents of our building.

Well, I thought. The world could be a dangerous place. People were in charge of themselves and their own safety. If they fell prey to misfortune, bad judgment, or error, whose fault was it? If this episode implicated me, it involved Cece even more. I had simply planted a seed, made a proposition. She's the one who'd decided and followed through on the action. Somehow I suspected she had the mischief within her. Or maybe she was just weak. I smiled as I munched on the last of the blueberry scones.

There came a rap at the door, and I switched off the telly. I wondered, was it Cece? Had she too heard the news? I peered through the peephole and saw Grandpa Gordon.

"Will, my lad!" he said as I opened the door. "How are you faring at home all alone?"

"Well enough, Gramps. Well enough. Are you checking on me?" He bustled into the lounge as if he were at home.

"Thought you might like some company. Or perhaps an outing. Is that scones?" he asked, spotting my plate.

"Just finished them off, sorry. What did you have in mind?"

"Well, we can start with the tea shop, just get our energy up. With all the recent rain there's been minor flooding of the Thames. I don't know if you're familiar with this phenomenon. When the waters recede, there's a line of rubbish left by the lapping waves. They call the deposits Bones of the Thames."

"Bones!? In the river?" I asked. For a moment I flashed on the bobbing Rover and its bodies.

"Not actual bones, but what looks like 'em," he replied. It's fragments of little clay pipes from days of yore. That's what's brilliant about London, son. We have history layered around us and under us. Sometimes nature unearths that for us, makes us see clearly how we're connected to our past."

"Pipes. What for?" I wondered aloud.

"Come along, lad, get your coat. I'll fill you in on the way."

We bundled ourselves up against the mist and walked the few blocks to a tea shop. Gordon ordered scones and tea for us both, and he tucked in eagerly when the plates and steaming mugs arrived. I sipped at the tea.

"Until the age of discovery, England sat drab on the palate, lad. No refrigeration, no way except salt to preserve food for winter eating. Dry bread, stale cheese, desiccated apple, maybe some cured venison—it all lacked spice."

Another lecture. I sipped at my tea.

"Seeking a quick passage to the east, rich with pepper and spices, they sailed west and found unknown lands. Home they came with savages, red in skin, along with maize and dried leaves you could grind up and inhale. Old

Ralegh showed folks how to fill up pipes and suck down the smoke," Gramps finished up.

"Was it tobacco? Shakespeare says 'love is a smoke.'" I gave him a wry smile, thinking of the hashish I'd heard about on telly, popular with gangs on the London streets.

"It was indeed, lad, tobacco, not love. They thought it might stave off a load o' pain—make you euphoric, curb your hunger pangs. When they'd used up the smoke, they tossed the pipes into the river. And now they wash up by the hundreds. If you're lucky, you can find one intact. The rain might keep people away today, and maybe we'll have the luck."

"Hmm," I responded. "I have to visit the loo."

I wandered towards the back of the shop thinking about how I might vex Gordon today. He was such a big buffoon. Down the hall a door was ajar, and I pushed it open to the jitty. Three geezers with skinheads started at the sound, and they scattered, scampering away by scaling the short fence behind the shop. Within seconds they were gone and away. There was a small pile of something where they'd been standing, and I probed at it with a stick I found in the rubbish heap. Something black and burnt—just aromatic ashes. Other refuse also lay around, and in curiosity I poked it too. Under a sweets wrapper was a small intact pouch, and I collected it and pocketed it. I'd investigate it later. My heart quickened with the novelty of discovery and anticipation, but I knew I'd better get back to Gramps in the shop.

"Ah, there you are, lad. Finished up and ready for Bones of the Thames?" Gordon asked as he paid the tab. 'Heaven take my soul, and England keep my bones,' eh, laddie?"

* * *

C hapter 58

It was misting heavily as Gordon and I walked along the wall near the Pelican Stairs in Wapping. Despite the damp, small crowds had gathered in various places where waves had lapped the shore and then receded, leaving a line of residue. Flotsam or jetsam—I wasn't sure of the word, but it sounded Shakespearean. Down on the shore Gordon spotted a section thick with the residue, and we bent over it together. It did look like fragments of bones, but it was broken bits of light beige clay pipes. You could see a portion of a stem or bowl among the other undistinguishable parts.

"Here," said Gordon. "Look, Will. It's a section from the bowl of a small pipe." He held it out in his palm. "Did you find anything good?" He put the fragment into his pocket. I remained silent and continued to cull through the piles. With the old man so intent on his search, it seemed a good time for a prank.

"I'm going to take a look down here a way," I announced and began to meander slowly along the residue line, my head bowed towards the ground—my eyes glancing sidelong towards Gordon. I moved further on, and when he bent down to pick something out of the pile, I turned on my heel and quickly climbed the bank. One second and a half, and I was out of his view but still within earshot. I heard him pronounce my name, but I moved down the path and found a niche in a doorway. Standing within the recess, I could glimpse the activity on the bank and as a private audience watch the drama unfold.

Gordon was satisfyingly predictable, and he cut a comic figure with his stocky build and bulky overcoat. I smirked as he straightened up, looked around 360°, and called my name louder and louder. Clearly I was nowhere to be seen.

He began waylaying passers-by. Had they seen a teen-age boy dressed in black? No. No, sir. He stumbled a way along the river, first one direction, then the other. No Will. He paused, doffed his cap, wiped his brow and his eyes, scanned an entire circle of vision yet again. No Will. He looked intently with some fear into the river itself for a long moment then cast his eyes up the embankment towards the path. I could see the wheels of his mind turning. Soon he'd muster the energy to climb back up, but I wanted to prolong the agony a bit longer.

The doorway I hid in happened to be a knick-knack shop, the window actually displaying some of those famous pipes, completely intact. Lest Gordon might achieve the path and spot me immediately, I ducked inside—cases and cases filled with the miniature clay pipes, all arrayed on deep red cloth, looking like the dismantled skeleton of a gnome. I was carrying some of my allowance money—I hardly ever had a chance to shop, except on the internet. I pointed to a small pipe that was in such good condition it looked almost new. The clerk removed it from the case and let me hold it.

"Hard to conceive some bloke from Shakespeare's day tugged away at the smoke from this little beauty then chucked it in the Thames," he said. In a moment of whimsy I moved it close to my mouth and mugged a deep inhale, making a nasty face and then coughing. We both laughed heartily.

"Wrap it up for you?" he asked.

"Um, no—I'll take the pipe but I won't need a bag," I replied. Iambic pentameter again. I hoped he hadn't noticed. I handed over £20 and held the pipe carefully as I laid it into my coat pocket.

"Now don't try to puff on that relic," he said, returning with my receipt. "It's a delicate piece, and, well, we're not sure just what places it's been over all these years. 'Full fathom five' and all that." He was satisfied at his own wit, and against my habit I gave him a smile. "Ta, now," he said.

When I re-entered the street I saw Gordon about a block away talking to a bobby. A group of people had gathered around them, and Gordon was gesturing towards the Thames. As they all looked downriver away from the shop, I slipped back down the embankment. Putting on a casual air, I meandered downriver until I was even with where the throng had gathered. I retrieved the pipe from my pocket, dampened it, and rolled it through the sand. Then I climbed the bank, pipe in hand. At that moment the crowd was all gazing towards the river and someone was pointing a finger towards the swift current. All eyes were on me as Gordon shouted.

"Will! Oh, Will, thank God you're safe!" You could almost hear the collective sigh of relief from the crowd. I put on my most innocent look.

"Safe? Of course I'm safe, and here I am. Look what I found along the edge, old man," and I held out the intact pipe in my palm.

"You've had a good bit of luck wi' that," said the bobby. "Most are smashed to smithereens by the ebb and flow of the tides. Is this the lost boy, then, found again? So, all's well that ends well, eh?" He addressed Gordon, who was losing some of his fluster by my reappearance.

"Yes, thank you," Gordon replied and turned to the crowd. "And thank all of you for your concern and help. It takes some vigilance to rear a child, you know, especially a teen-ager. As you can see, the boy is alive and fine. Alive and fine." Some folks chucked him on the shoulder in congratulations. A couple of them came over to me to examine my pipe. And then they slowly dispersed and Gordon and I were alone.

"Quite an unexpected adventure, eh?" he began as we walked quickly back towards the bus. I remained silent.

"Now you've seen the bones of our river—and found a memento of your own. *Memento mori*, as they say, a reminder of death. That pipe should be a warning to you of the dangers of smoking and a spur to cherish the gift of your own life, lad. The years are gall'ping steeds who pass us by."

Despite my own prankish state of mind I smiled with satisfaction. Now I'd infected Gordon with the iambic. What might I accomplish next?

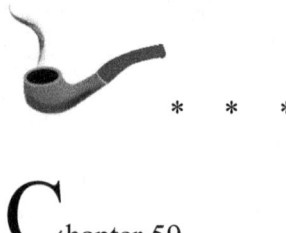

*   *   *

Chapter 59

"Will, I'm home, son!" The door slammed as Father came in.

Upon returning home from my adventure with Grandpa Gordon, I had extracted that pouch I'd found in the alleyway from my pocket. I was pretty sure it was some kind of contraband—perhaps hashish. I'd opened the bag and sniffed at it. It had a potent herbal aroma. I was sure I could find a good use for it so Sello taped it to the frame of my dresser behind the bottom drawer. I could get at it pretty easily, and I didn't think Father would run across it there. And the realisation flitted through my mind that the tiny pipe from the past had come into my life just in time.

"How was your day with Gordon? Did you have a good time despite the rain?" He strode into my room, where I was sitting innocently perusing books spread over my desk. I turned, reached into my pocket, pulled out the pipe, and without a word extended my palm towards Father.

"What is this?" he asked.

"Bones from the Thames washed up along the shore."

"You found this?" Inexplicably Father turned pale. "A pipe?" He turned away, and I thought I heard him mutter "Why did it have to be a pipe?"

"Quite a treasure, son," he said as he regained his composure. "Tobacco was brought back from the new world, and everyone considered it a miracle. Shakespeare himself might have smoked that wee pipe. You'll want to preserve it carefully. Stow that pipe away now. Let's have a quiet supper, and then we're off to see your Mum. Strange not having her here with us, isn't it?"

Father went into the kitchen and I followed, perching myself on a stool near the counter. He took some bangers out of the fridge and started the flame on the cooker. Steamy aromas began to fill the flat.

"I picked up this baguette on the way home," he said, as he sliced it and placed it in the toaster oven. "We'd better have some fruit." He rummaged around in the fruit bowl and came out with some oranges. "Ah, these will round things out," he said. And he asked me to peel the oranges.

He set out two plates and some kitchen paper. I deposited the peels onto the towel and placed orange segments in a fan on each plate. "She doesn't talk to me very much anyway," I ventured. He brought over the skillet with the sausages and lined up two on each plate. Then he retrieved the bread from the toaster and buttered it, laying it alongside the sausages.

"People can sometimes get distracted," Father answered after a long pause, still fussing over our supper.

"Is there any cheese?" I asked.

He located sliced cheddar, which he sat atop the warm crusty bread, where it melted slightly.

"You remember what Falstaff says about 'a piece of toasted cheese,' eh, lad?" he asked. I recalled something about choking to death and smiled briefly.

Quietly companionable, we ate with enthusiasm, cleaned up, and without further discussion left for our visit to Mum in hospital.

She was in a darkened private room, sitting in a recliner and staring blankly at nothing. I wasn't sure why she'd been taken away from us. At home, too, she'd done little more than sit unobtrusively in her chair. Now, seeing us, she began stroking her belly in a repetitive automatic motion.

"Kingsley, my love. . . . Will. How nice of you to come." Father gave her a kiss on the cheek. "Could you please turn on the light? I loathe the darkness. The nursing staff keeps closing the shades and lowering the lights. They don't know it's the darkness that will take me away. Tell them to leave the lights on, won't you, Kingsley? For me?"

"Of course I will, darling. And let's stop this silly talk of going away. Will and I want you at home where you belong." She rubbed her belly. "Are you getting enough rest? You look a bit drawn."

"Nothing to do but rest—and wait. But all is amiss, I fear."

Letting her comment pass, Dad looked at me and gestured with his head towards her. "Tell Mum about your studies," he said. I looked at her and reached into my pocket, where my hand fell upon the little pipe. On an impulse, I extracted it and held it out in my palm.

"Look, Mum. Bones of the Thames washed up along the shore," I said.

Mum visibly shuddered. "Away! Get it away! Out of my sight!" She rubbed her belly even more vigourously. "Why are you taunting me with a pipe?" The nurse came bustling in as Mum talked louder and louder.

"You must go now. The patient is agitated and needs to rest," said the nurse. She nudged us towards the door and automatically reached out to dim the lights.

"No!" Elizabeth cried. "No more darkness! The lights, Kingsley, the lights! You promised!"

I pocketed the pipe. Father glanced at me and said to the nurse, "Please calm her by leaving a lamp burning. It's her specific request."

"Often the patient does not know what's best," she replied.

"Look here," Father said. "I can speak to her doctor if need be, but for now humour me, will you? Leave the light on. Can't you see she's desperate?"

We left Mum crying out and rubbing, rubbing at her belly. And I did not realise at the time that would be my last glimpse of her alive.

 * * *

Chapter 60

Next day when Father left for work I hoped to find Cece. I had three possessions to show her, and I wanted to gloat with her about the Rover. I made sure my coin was on its cord around my neck, and I pocketed the little pipe and the pouch. She'd mentioned the third floor. I took the stairs up and walked the entire corridor, running my hand slowly along each wall. I encountered no one, and I didn't feel bold enough to begin knocking randomly on doors. If I tried that, word would probably get back to Father, and my wanderings would be revealed.

At loose ends, I repaired to the cellar to try out my voice with some of my speeches. Father had left me science homework, but I much preferred revisiting my Shakespeare. I placed myself just at the spot producing a fine echo. Running passages through my mind, I selected "Blow, winds" from *King Lear* and began my stylised oration. As my eyes accustomed to the cellar gloom, I discerned Cece's form. She seemed spectral as her shape emerged from the darkness, first the pale face and darkened eyes, then the outline of her body, black clothing against the murkiness.

"'And thou, all-shaking thunder, / Strike flat the thick rotundity o' the world! / Crack nature's moulds, all germens spill at once / That make ingrateful man!' . . . Ah, there you are!"

"Yes, Will. Here I am and here we are again."

"Cece. Did you see the telly news at five last night?"

"About the Rover, you mean? I don't know what to think. We didn't mean to damage people's lives."

"It's not our fault, a prank is all it is. They should have checked the tyres before they left. . . . But what a brilliant show to daze the eyes! I wish we'd been bankside to witness it. Did you see the Rover dripping from the Thames?"

She seemed not to share my glee at the vision. I approached her and extracted the coin from beneath my shirt.

"Here, look. I want to show you this, my angel guard."

"How pretty! What is it, really, Will? Where'd you get it?"

I pulled the angel on its cord away from my chest and extended it towards her. She fingered the coin, running her thumb over its shiny, smooth, embossed surface, and she examined both sides carefully, staring at the archangel.

"I found it in the garden of the Bard. He left it there specific'ly for me."

"Oh! Huh!" she said, dropping the coin back to my chest. And then she extended her arm and hand, bunching up the sleeve so I could clearly see her rings and bracelets, costume jewelry. Instead of angels, they were leering skulls and skeletons, symbols of death. "These are my protectors," she said. They were of a base metal, already tarnishing around the edges. I didn't really see how bones of the dead would protect her, except maybe as haunts—or *memento mori* as Grandpa Gordon had said—but I let it go. She had shared something of herself with me, and all indications were that she was a rebel and would be ready for more mischief.

"I found another thing upon my trip," I told her, extracting my herbal pouch from my pocket. I handed it over, and she unsealed it and gave it a sniff.

"Brilliant!" she said, her eyes shining.

"Have you tried it in a pipe before, my friend?"

"No, but you inhale the smoke and feel fine. And it's forbidden," she said. "Do you have papers?"

"Something even better. Looky here." I pulled the little pipe out.

"Oh, it's so wee!" she said and set about filling the bowl with the mixture and tamping it down tightly. "Matches?"

"Oh, rot!" I hadn't thought of how to light the mixture. My family did not smoke, and our fireplace was electric. We lit the occasional candle but other than that had little use for flames.

"Not to worry," Cece said, as she walked towards a dark corner of the cellar. Ducking behind boxes piled towards the ceiling, she re-emerged with a victorious "ta-da!"

"Just what goes on back in the cloistered space?" I asked.

"It's my little lair," she answered. "My getaway haunt. Sometimes I light a candle or an oil lamp, so I have matches. Lucky for us."

We squatted down together with the pipe between our lowered heads. She struck the match and held it out towards me.

"You go ahead," I told her, so she wiped the mouthpiece with her jumper hem, placed it between her lips, applied the flame to the bowl, and sucked. The contents glowed briefly and then smouldered as wisps of smoke began to rise. At first she sucked lightly then inhaled more deeply. A paroxysm of coughing overcame her, and, her body convulsing, she handed me the pipe.

I wanted to try it, but first I wanted to make sure by watching Cece that inhaling the mixture was not harmful or perhaps fatal. She stopped coughing and began giggling. She rolled her eyes and said, "Gosh, I feel sort of woozy and lightheaded. It's like my head is growing out right by my eyes. Let me have another puff."

This was good. Let her take the lion's share, then try it just at the end to know what it was like. And then I'd see what opportunity might present itself. She puffed away without coughing this time, and the pungent aroma circled us in eddies of smoke. Again she passed me the pipe. I placed it in my mouth and could taste the potent mixture.

"You know, if inhaling gets to you, they say you can eat it in brownies," she said and giggled.

I inhaled lightly and the smoke seeped into my lungs. It felt harsh, and I choked back a cough. I held the smoke in as long as I could, then blew it out, and quickly I felt a lightheaded giddiness. My world view altered slightly. I surmised that more puffs would bring a stronger skewed vision, and I could see the attraction of the drug, the high, especially for someone living a drab life. This smoke evened out the edges and made all ills seem inconsequential.

Cece took back the pipe for another puff. She had not even inquired as to why I had the pipe or where it came from. She was a strange creature, and now that she stood near me, I could examine her more precisely. I already knew she was at loose ends, isolated in the building like me, her only door to the world at large music, the telly, the internet. I thought her not terribly bright, or at least inarticulate if she did have acute perception. For my purposes she seemed naïve and easily malleable.

Up close she appeared less ethereal. The reality of her physical embellishment struck me—the uneven black eye-liner, ragged inky hair against pale skin, macabre jewelry and facial piercing. But strangely, her apparent vulnerability excited me, and for the first time in my life I perceived a possible sexual conquest. Her figure was slim and not at all voluptuous. But I found her androgyny in some way less daunting, and I wondered how she would respond to an advance. Now, with her in a giddy state, could be the opportune moment.

I lifted my hand and rubbed it along her jawbone as one might stroke a cat. She said "Mmmm" and tilted her head into my hand in what I took as an invitation or at least an encouragement. The pipe had burned its last, and she handed it back to me. I set it down on a nearby crate and sought her eyes in a direct gaze. They rolled upwards languidly, dreamily. I took both her shoulders in my hands and her body softened, so I pulled her close in an embrace. She was warm and smelled of the herbal mixture. I began caressing her back, and, sensing no resistance, I sought out her mouth for a long kiss. She tasted strongly of the pipe.

"I really like you, Cece," I said, in an age-old lie or at least half-truth.

"Me too," she slurred back as she closed her eyes for another kiss.

My roving hands found their way under the waist of her jumper. She felt smooth but bony. She was a wisp of a girl in all ways. She wore no underwear but a camisole. I grasped the edges of her jumper hem, and she lifted her arms for its removal. Eager to see where this might lead next, I said, "Now may I join you in your hide-away?"

She led me through the shadowy maze between the crates to a dark corner furnished with some cushions and candles. In the dimness she seemed almost to disappear, and I joined her by instinct in making the beast with two backs.

* * *

Chapter 61

The next several days Father spent in vigil at hospital with Mum. I was in the way, he said. Besides, my presence seemed to upset her. Physically she was sound but her mind was profoundly distracted. The rubbing had become automatic and continuous. She raved with meaningless phrases and insisted the light be always beside her.

I did not miss her as her, but I was alone and a bit lonely. Mum at least had been company, and it was amusing to try to make her jump to my desires. After the pipe episode in the cellar and our sexual encounter I felt connected to Cece in some way. I had combed the halls and lingered near her lair, but she had not reappeared. Aside from the third floor or the cellar, I didn't know where else to seek her.

I sat in Mum's chair and stared at the falling rain— always the rain here in London town. My eye scanned the lounge and lit upon the shelf where her journals had been lined in a row. She and Father had locked up the prior years' volumes somewhere I'd not found. But in their haste to take her away and Father's urgency to be by her side, these few had been overlooked. They were forbidden territory for me—but who would discover that I'd taken a peek? I didn't know Mum well. She'd always kept an arm's length, and I even felt I was a bane to her at times. That involuntary shudder.

Curiosity drove me, and I removed the volume to the far left. Her handwriting was neat, a small but clear script. I sat back down in her chair. What followed shattered my world.

The creature—always lurking around me—how can I bear my lot? He only gazes, assesses, judges. I don't think he feels human. He is cold, and he withholds his words and affection. It hits me like malice, and my skin crawls. I am a prisoner with him as my torturing cell mate. Day after endless day.

Who can I talk to? K. seems blind to the creature's character. He even encourages his behaviour. When my belly aches with memory of the torment of bearing him, I try to ring up Tessa. As fortune goes, no answer. But I couldn't tell her anyway. I'm doomed to die carrying my secret. I can only try to calm the memory.

For K., this is the Bard of England *redivivus*. For me, it is a horrible nightmare, *quelle cauchemar*—worse than any science fiction plot brought into our world. Yet we continue as if all is normal, presenting our façade to the rest of society. They know, though. They suspect something amiss with the boy—always have. But in their wildest dreams they could not imagine the truth of the matter. I am glad K. home schools him. We keep him away from other children and other opportunities for malicious mischief. To keep the creature contained is our only salvation.

I knew all of this instinctively from the beginning, but I allowed love of K. to blind me. The creature is not the culmination of science or of evolution. I convinced myself to believe that logic. I thought we were building a family. But Will is a true creation. He is an aberration, an error, an anachronism, patched together by a kind of laboratory magic. He was an alien inside me. He tortured me then; he tortures me now. I cannot face my part in bringing him to life. K. has abandoned me for the creature. I am alone, and I am guilty. I cannot tolerate this daily life, the creature a constant reminder of our sin. He never should have been. What have we done? And now, what is to be done? For me my life can only be a walking shadow, my own story "a tale, told by an idiot." There is only the darkness of our deed and no promise of a brighter future.

Shaken and even moved, I carefully replaced the volume. For the first time I'd heard Mum's true voice. And how was I to take this in?

I was the creature!

* * *

Chapter 62

The room seemed to spin, and for the first time in my life I felt out of control, no longer in charge. I couldn't quite put all the pieces of this story together. Could I even credit it as truth? Perhaps it was merely the rant of a mad woman— and I'd played my own prankish part in pushing her over the edge.

But somehow it contained the candour of reality. I wasn't sure what she meant by *creature* and *creation*. I knew I had been born in the usual way and that these were my parents. They had created me. I had not been found on the doorstep, nor was I a fairie changeling. True, I resembled them very little in both appearance and character. And I had small fellow-feeling or affection for any of the lot. They were so good-hearted and predictable, so easy to manipulate. I scorned their gullibility.

I wished I had someone to talk to about my discovery. Father was my only friend, and he was out of the running as confidant. Cece was nowhere to be found. I ran Mum's story over in my mind again. "Bard of England *redivivus*," she'd written. That must be a clue. I scrambled to the shelf in my room and found the dictionary. My finger raced down the page. *Redingote, redirect, redistribute*, ah, there it was, *redivivus*: "brought back to life; reborn."

Reborn. The Bard Reborn. I hadn't questioned Father's Shakespeare theme in my life. I'd thought he was just building on my own talent and interest. But maybe there was a stronger tie-in. He'd fashioned me into a sort of modern walking and talking Shakespeare. And at the Birthplace, hadn't they taken me for a Shakespeare lad?

My eye caught the glint of the angel around my neck. The location of this coin in the mud had called out to me in a mystical way. And it may well have been buried there by Will Shakespeare. Inexplicable, unless. . . . What? What were the possibilities? Father was a scientist. Was there a secret magic he had worked at my inception? For a moment I mused on the possibility of adoption—but then why the Shakespeare focus?

I stood and contemplated my image in the full-length glass in my room, assessing my appearance as objectively as I could. I bore little physical resemblance to my family. Father was tall and had sandy hair, an elongated face. I was more squat with dark hair visibly receding beyond a substantial expanse of brow on a rounded face. Although I no longer wore Tudor costumery, I still had an antique look. My eye moved upward to the poster that had been on the wall as long as I could remember.

My eyes—identical to those in that Puritan portrait. My brow—there it loomed the same in that portrait from the First Folio. The roundness of my face and the slope of my nose—not Father's, but Shakespeare's! It was there to be read clearly—somehow this Shakespeare had begotten me. "O heavens, this is my true-begotten father!" The Bard *redivivus*, Mum had written. What did that actually mean? How could it be a reality?

Confusion overcame me. Oh, how I wished for a confidant. What was the secret of my birth? I strode quickly back to Mum's forbidden books and selected a random volume further along in the sequence. Maybe she would reveal more. I scanned the pages full of anguish and woe, not so much a linear tale but a circular story, repeating the same themes.

> The creature is tormenting me. Or maybe it's just his malicious presence that alters the space he inhabits. Right now I'm not certain if it's a metaphor or a reality, but when he is near the lights seem to dim. He puts me in the dark.

> What was the moment of my error and sin? I loved K. Surely it was no sin to marry. But then to agree to carry his unholy creation—that was my undoing.

> When I saw that pulsating egg I should have run in terror. But instead I became its host, and it tortured me as it struggled to re-enter our world—out of its proper time in history. To allow an egg from the past to be placed in my womb was an unnatural act. And the creature protested then as he has ever since.

Some sort of secret surrounding my birth lurked beneath these words. For a moment I felt a small pang of regret for having treated Mum so mischievously with the light bulb pranks. I hadn't actually meant to harm her. It seemed antic and funny to trick her—and to be secretly in control.

But she'd mentioned something about an egg being implanted into her. I wondered now if maybe they were not my true parents. Father had talked to me in clinical terms about sex and the risk of making a baby, so I knew the rudimentary facts of the basic process. I supposed Father had access to the technology for getting a fertilised egg and finding a surrogate mother. That meant I had real parents— my genetic parents—somewhere else in the world. Perhaps my father was a descendant of Shakespeare. That would explain my looks and Father's emphasis on my mastering the Bard.

Among the books of my library was, of course, a biography of Shakespeare, and I turned to my own shelves to locate it. An entire chapter devoted to his family tree made clear that his line had died out with the death of his son Hamnet and no issue from the grandchildren Elizabeth Hall Nash or the Quiney boys. But how else then might I have something to do with the Shakespeare family? I was at a dead end and pondering this, going nowhere. I needed a friend, a human validation of my existence as me, whoever that was.

   *   *   *

Chapter 63

Stepping out of the lift, I accustomed my eyes to the gloom. I could hear a soft, lilting hum, and I knew that was Cece. I followed the sound behind the crates to her den. She blended so well into the darkness—with her brunette hair and black clothing—that she seemed invisible. I saw only her pale face floating in the air. The humming stopped when I approached, but Cece said nothing.

"Hi. I hoped to God I'd find you in the gloom. I need your friendship now: I need your ear."

"My ear?" Cece smirked. "But Will, I gave you my whole body."

Our intimacy had been more monumental an event than I had intended. For me it had been an experiment, a necessary step. But now she assumed a connection between us. I could take advantage of this and use her today as my sounding board. I joined her on the cushions and put my arm around her shoulders. Her small candle flame fluttered slightly with the air of my movement.

"Do you ever wonder if you landed in the right family?" I asked after a short pause.

She stared at me, her eyes dark.

"I wonder, Will, if I landed in the right universe."

I hadn't meant my question quite so philosophically, but it was clear we shared a like feeling.

"Do you resemble your mum and dad?" I didn't even know if she had siblings.

"My Mum is gone, and Dad is . . . a very tall man," she said with a strange tone.

"I look nothing like anyone in our clan," I said. "In fact, I know this sounds weird, but I look like William Shakespeare." The fact that I bore his name suddenly struck me hard.

"You always sound like him," she said and managed a feeble smile.

"Can you talk much to your dad?" I asked. She was quiet for a while.

"Not about anything that matters," she finally answered.

"Same here. But I looked in these journals Mum is always writing in. She calls me 'the creature,'" I blurted out. "I wonder if I'm adopted—but I know they brought me home from hospital, and I've seen photos of Mum very pregnant."

"I only feel who I am in this spot—and now with you," she said, leaning into me. Cece obviously was fighting her own demons and would not be of much help to me in this matter.

She reached towards the hem of her jumper as if to remove it, an almost automatic gesture, it seemed.

"Cece. I would like a repeat performance but I can't just now," I said, pulling my arm out from around her and edging away. It occurred to me that the answer must be somewhere in Mum's scribblings, and I could find no peace until I knew something for certain.

"Your coin is shining," Cece said, her eyes dropping to my chest as I stood.

In the darkness my angel seemed to attract the rays of the dim light from Cece's faltering candle. The coin had a preternatural glow to it, as if it were giving off heat, and the figure of Michael gleamed forth as if in victory.

The lift took me back up to our flat, and I returned to the shelf to continue in my discovery. In the meantime Father had evidently returned home from hospital briefly, realised his oversight, and taken the journals somewhere, as the shelf was empty. He hadn't had much time to hide them well. I went into their bedroom and began to search. Nothing under the bed. Nothing in the bedside tables. I pulled out each drawer in the dresser and rifled through the contents. Nothing. On an impulse I pulled out the drawers completely, beginning with the bottom one, and there they were, fastened apparently hastily with gaffer tape to the flat of the drawer's base.

I eyed Mum's array of journals and carefully removed one volume at random. I'd noticed how her ramblings seemed to always return to the same topics of torment and anguish—with me cast as the villainous *creature*. For me it was not an easy story to read. The narrative moved ahead only in jumps and starts. I played a large part but seemed dehumanised. I did not care for my characterisation through Mum's eyes, but I thought that somewhere amongst the woes my secret would be revealed. I picked up the saga:

K. hoped he was bringing the Bard back to life. But the creature is not Shakespeare. No matter his training, no matter his talent, his genes found their separate way. He is a type of *homo* but unevolved, I fear. Old DNA, different conditions, different gene expression. Who knows?—according to the lecturer the difference might have been simply his nutrition. Or perhaps spending his first weeks in a mechanical incubator. And how significantly have we evolved in 400 years? Who is to blame? I just wanted to make a baby and have a family with K. Should I be angry at him for invading me with his experiment? He did it and then abandoned me. He shut me out of the project and his own emotions. And then to be shunned by the child as well! I can admire K. for his dedication to the result,   but yet. . . . Loyalties matter. Love matters. A mother matters.

I cannot blame the child. Even as a baby he shrank from my touch; he refused to smile. He is a cold, manipulative demon. I am sorry to have been the vessel for that mass of cells, their DNA gleaned from an old pipe. For Will to have a chance at a future, he must never know. Damn, damn pipe! The experiment has been an epic failure, and now I must bear the consequences or give in to the darkness.

My stomach plunged as if I had leapt from a high cliff. Dread crept 'round my heart. Was I a true part of my own family—or some kind of outsider? Why had Mum shrunk from me all these years? Why had Father kept me inside and drowned me in Shakespeare?

"Old DNA," she wrote. "Mechanical incubator." "Vessel of his birth." A horrendous picture was taking shape in my imagination. "400 years." "Cells on an old pipe." When Father and I visited the Birthplace, there had been a pipe encased in glass.

"Son, that's our pipe," Father had proclaimed proudly. I'd heard Grandpa Gordon speak of it as well—a pipe maybe belonging to Shakespeare they'd examined in the lab before I was born. Father had commemorated this event—so important to the lab—by a second poster he'd hung in my room. It was a painting of a pipe, and underneath was written in lovely script, "Ceci n'est pas une pipe," this is not a pipe. Father said it called attention to painting as the art of representing rather than reproducing reality, since it obviously was the *image* of a pipe. Yet not the pipe itself.

But now I was beginning to think my parentage had stemmed from that pipe, and that the poster in my room was an homage to my beginnings. Could a person be created from old cells on a pipe? You'd need an egg, I thought, and my mind was awhirl. Had Father played some kind of scientific trick to cause my birth? Anger rose like a dark cloud inside me. The journals had dropped clues like bread crumbs—I had to follow the trail to the secret of my self.

I carefully replaced the journal under the drawer and left all as I had found it. I returned to my room and turned on the computer. In the search box I typed "human baby from skin cells." Eight million entries appeared in a queue down the screen.

"This is actually happening," the first article read. ". . . In principle we could take a biopsy from skin of a man and turn it into either eggs or sperm, so he could have a genetic child from his own skin cells." The next article: "Scientists have created cloned embryos from human adult skin cells to harvest for organ implants." And another on what constitutes a human being: "an entity is 'human' if it is an organism that has possessed, at some point in its past history, a structure made up of one or more cells that have the same basic genotype as your cells and my cells have right now." I scanned through several of the following entries, all on the same theme. A human skin cell *from any era* could be turned into a human being with the identical genetic profile as its parent.

I clicked off the screen and tried to process what I'd read. And my mind rehearsed events from my own life that seemed to implicate Shakespeare. I bore His name. I looked like Him. Father had trained me in His words and thoughts. I found His angel. And more tenuous evidence: I felt out of place in this family, in this age. I was drawn to the stage and to manipulation of characters. I'd seemed very much at home when we visited Stratford, and I adored going to His plays. It must be so: Will I am.

The gorge rose within my throat, and I rushed to the loo. Cold beads of sweat twinkled on my brow and trickled down my back inside my jumper. Father had created me to carry on the heritage of our Bard. I was not exactly His son, nor was I exactly Him. Who was I? Who in fact was I? People everywhere used His words—now mine too—on a daily basis. I felt like a sort of crypto-currency, the bard but phony in genuine value, a copy only. I breathed deeply to find resolve and, calming my mind I repeated: It must be so: Will I am.

 *   *   *

Chapter 64

Old Polonius had given his son that sage advice, "To thine own self be true." The sticking point was in discovering the nature of your own self. It was a shock to read about Mum's fear and loathing of me, yet Father loved me, and I had made a friend in Cece. Even if somehow I was a man reborn from the past, I was still a human being, now alive and healthy and thriving in the second millennium. Few doors would be closed on my own corridor to the future. And with the power of the Bard's genes as my sustenance, I would need no one else.

I had thrown myself onto my bed, and I was rehearsing all the clues to my identity from Mum's book and my own life experience. The Shakespeare connection made everything fall into place, all mysteries solved. I could imagine a creation scenario with Father as the passionate scientist. Somehow he'd garnered the Bard's DNA—ah, from that pipe we'd seen at the Birthplace. Father and

Gordon were so proud it had been brought to their lab, and that story was part of our family lore. It had happened, not coincidentally I realized, just prior to my birth.

Mum must have played surrogate mother to my egg, and she'd said as much in the journals—"the vessel of his birth." A slight pang of regret passed through me as I thought of how she had shrunk from me from infancy and then how I'd tortured her through my pranks and manipulations. They had made me and in a sense I'd made them too. And that's what the plays had taught me. We humans fashion a tenuous co-existence through our words and actions.

From my room I heard the front door close. I rose and walked to the lounge. Father was sitting slumped over in Mum's chair with his head in his hands. He lifted his head at the sound of my footsteps and his face was wet with tears.

"Father?" I said.

"Will. Come close to me, son," he replied. I sat down on the stool near the chair.

"Your mother is gone." He caressed my shoulder.

"She found a way to leave the hospital?"

"No, son. She's gone from us forever, gone from this earth." His caress became a grip.

"But she has always been at home with me." In the plays people died all over the place, during battles and struggles, famously at the end of tragedies. I hadn't thought much of it. They would spring back to life, at least briefly, when the play began again. As characters they came and went. If they were dispensable, they would succumb to someone's machinations and to the dynamic of the drama. But this sounded much more final.

"She didn't seem that sick when we were there," I protested.

"Her mind became diseased," he explained. "She became fixated on surrounding herself with light, steady, bright light. When they dimmed the lights, her spirit weakened. She reached over and turned up the dial on the sedative metre. It was her own choice, Will, her own action. The drip increased, delivering a fatal dosage, and she fell softly into the sleep of death."

"But why would Mum decide to leave us two? And who will tend to me while you're at work?" My lightbulb prank flashed across my mind.

"We must face our sadness first, Will, and then the changes her death will bring to our life together, what's left of it. Your Mum we must leave to heaven." He reached down and gave me an awkward embrace.

As Father sobbed on my shoulder, I stared out the window towards the sky. "We must bear our going hence even as our coming hither" echoed in my head. My own eyes were dry.

 *   *   *

Chapter 65

I was quickly becoming accustomed to the idea that I was a new version of the Bard of Avon. All my doubts about what I enjoyed doing to people disappeared, and I felt comfortable if not slightly smug with my identity. Manipulation was the playwright's trademark. It was only natural for me to size up a character and motivate it to action.

Mum's journals had hinted that perhaps, being actually more than 400 years "old," I was in some way unevolved. I wasn't sure how she meant that. I looked like a modern person—nothing of the Neanderthal about me despite my broad brow. My mind worked quickly, and I could stay at least a step ahead of even the smartest people I'd met. But aside from Cece, I loved people only as something to manipulate, not as connections to or extensions of myself. I truly felt like a puppet master, and that made me superior. It set me apart, and now I knew the reason. I was a legend! An historical monument!

Regarding Cece, I wasn't certain that I actually cared for her, but her oddness attracted me. I liked using her as a sounding board. And my body had enjoyed our sexual experiment. I was hoping for further scenes in that act.

A pall had settled over the flat with Mum's death. Father was going through his usual motions, but his spirit seemed empty and dull. While he was still attentive to me and even affectionate, I perceived that he regarded me with a cooler eye—at times even icy. I knew he was fully aware of my identity, as he had created me. But my true character remained a secret to him. Did he have any suspicions about my interactions with Mum—or my lack of regret?

Today we were preparing for Mum's memorial service. Father had laid out a modern dark suit for me, and I combed my hair neatly back away from my face. Regarding myself in the glass, with Shakespeare smiling behind me as always, I looked fully a man, a modern man. I was not as tall as Father—probably never would be, from the news of my genes—but it was clear I was no longer a child. I intended to embrace my destiny, now reborn, and manifest my identity fully in my actions.

Father looked me over when we convened in the lounge, ran a finger through my hair, and nodded approvingly.

"You're a fine testament to your mother's life," he said.

We made our way to the chapel in a big black limousine sent from the mortuary. I had wanted to bring Cece along but knew that could not happen. I couldn't reveal her in the light just yet. We rode along in mutual silence. I enjoyed watching London pass by the car window. My day-to-day world had been small and limited up until now.

Father and I walked solemnly down the centre aisle of the chapel and sat in a front row. A large casket covered in sprays of flowers lay at the altar of the church. As we passed through the rows I noticed Grandmum and Grandpa Gordon and others who had visited the flat when I was younger—Tessa and her mum and some colleagues from the lab. The audience contained many people I did not know, writers and editors from Mum's work. I was surprised at their number.

During the comforting music Father sat stoically by my side. A young priest spoke in emotional tones about Mum's contributions to the world.

"We have lost today a woman taken from us in the prime of her life. Elizabeth Armstrong-Montague was beautiful inside and out, as all of us who knew her can testify. Only God sees clearly the inner workings of the individual soul. A darkness had recently fallen on our Elizabeth. She struggled for the light, but the darkness won, tragically."

This harping on darkness and light kept reminding me of my prank. I didn't often think of consequences, but every action set into motion a chain of causality. Each of us could feel isolated, but ripples of our being extended out in ever-widening circles.

I refused to think her death was my fault. I noticed that Father's shoulders had begun to tremble. A hand reached from behind us to give his arm a squeeze, and then another hand for the other shoulder. I turned to see the concerned faces of Grandmum and Gordon, the silly old couple.

The priest continued as Father began to sob audibly.

"Her contributions to the world of publishing were substantial. Over the years she sorted through thousands of manuscripts to recommend the titles you've come to know so well as entries in our catalogue of fine letters. She worked steadily and quietly with a discerning eye—all the while keeping the home fires burning for her distinguished scientist husband and their son. She read manuscripts and she mothered her son, with us today grown into a fine young man."

Father reached his hand over and placed it on my knee. All this joining of hands to bodies had fashioned us into a circle of family members right there in the pews. I felt the eyes of the audience on me as the priest described me, and my face burned. I much preferred to remain out of the spotlight, working behind the scenes.

The priest persisted on the same theme.

"The most glorious memorial to this extraordinary woman will be the flowering of her son's future. It is he who now carries on the tradition of her talents and her contributions to society. With his father's continued guidance and counsel, the child will no doubt devote his life to glorifying and sanctifying the memory of his mother."

I could not understand the priest's reasoning. My life was my life, and, as I now knew, it had little to do with this woman I'd called Mum, this woman who for years had shrunk from the sight of me. At best we'd lived as prisoners in the same cell, by little more than accident.

"Elizabeth's husband has requested that you honour her memory and her life's work by writing about her effect on you, or something, some act of hers, that will remain with us in the world, as a tribute to her own belief that text lives on even as we succumb to our mortality. Words remain, carrying traces of our selves, long after we individually are gone. We also extend our loving support to Kingsley and their son William in what we know will be, for a while, difficult times."

After the memorial we gathered in the hall with a table laden with food. While I sampled each dish Father spoke with everyone individually. One by one they left, and he sat with me quietly while the staff cleaned up.

"These little sandwiches are full of taste," I said to make conversation.

"All is lost, all is gone," he replied.

I did not know what to say to this.

He continued with a kind of moan, "I have no wife. Oh, insupportable! Oh, heavy hour! Methinks it should be now a huge eclipse of sun and moon, and that th' affrighted globe should yawn at alteration."

I heard the emotion of this outcry from *Othello*, but it seemed to me pure histrionics. I felt little compassion and wondered if Mum had been right about my lack of emotional evolution. She was gone now, and that might change what was in store for my own life.

 * * *

Chapter 66

"Son? I'm going to work now." Father's voice woke me from a sound and dream-filled sleep. "Make sure to finish up the lessons I've laid out on your desk. I'll ring up at lunch."

I heard the front door close and latch. I rose and made myself some tea and toast—Father's distraction had caused neglect to the fridge—not much fuel for foraging. Munching, I idly moved my puppets around on the stage. I knew what needed to happen today. I must locate Cece and catch her up on the news.

The lift took me down to the cellar, where the darkness welcomed me. I found a spot and began orating a speech, the one on the seven ages of man. The subtext was an admonishment to seize the day. Time and tide wait for no one, and after we'd lost Mum prematurely, it seemed appropriate. I'd just reached "sans everything" when I detected movement in the corner, and there was my dark darling.

"That was a good one," she said, without moving.

"I wonder if you've missed me these few days," I broached.

"This is the empire of darkness, touched by neither night nor day," she said dramatically. "Did I sound Shakespearean?" She giggled.

I walked towards her, and she led me into her den. We plunked down in our usual spots on the cushions. I leaned in close to her.

"Cece, my Mum is dead."

"Hmmm. So is mine," she replied.

"No, I mean my Mum just now has died. We laid her yesterday into the grave."

"Was she old?" Cece asked.

"Not older than a parent just would be," I said.

"Did her car fall into the Thames?" she ventured.

"No, not at all. She just went off her head. They took her to her bed; return she never could."

"Does that mean you are also a madman?"

"At the present moment maybe that I am. I've been reading scribbles in the books of Mum's," I told her.

"And the words have burrowed into your brain, infecting you with her rare genetic disorder. Soon you will turn a shade of grey and develop a taste for human flesh."

"Can we be real for a minute?" I chastised. "I found something written therein that has unhinged my life. . . . I . . . I am not of this time."

"Sometimes I forget what day it is too. Or lose track of the hour. But you are sitting right here. In the cellar. On Yeoman's Row. In London. The year is 2016 A.D. Your angel is gleaming. Do you want me to pinch you?" she concluded.

"How can I explain? I think Dad cooked me up inside his lab," I confessed.

"Huh?"

"I think I came to life from long ago."

"Like . . . back to the future? I never thought those stories were real."

"No, not time travel. Something more . . . biological."

"You look pretty normal to me," Cece said.

"Do I resemble Will-i-am Shakespeare?" I asked her. I turned my head in profile so she could take in my broad brow.

"You look like Will to me," she said, and she reached over to pull me close. I sighed and gave in.

This time Cece removed all her black clothing, and her skin gleamed pale in the half light. I examined all her parts as I could, her body much like that of a slender boy. I gave her a quarter turn, and something dark marred the clear expanse of white, just near the small rise of her buttock.

"Cece, what's this?" I asked, touching her skin at the dark place. "Does it hurt?" It seemed like a substantial bruise.

"Huh?" she said dreamily. Hastily she recovered and replied, "Oh, nobody knows. It's Dad . . . oh, it's nothing." She turned and looked me in the eye. "It's nothing." And then she continued in her caresses. Again, eagerly, we joined in a quick union. I felt manly and grown up. The image of my parents flashed through my mind, and it hit me that no such action had created me. My inception had been cold and clinical. Somehow my essence was a reanimation rather than a new creation. I felt a kinship with Caliban, sprung mysteriously from the magical witch Sycorax.

Lying there with the strange Cece in my arms, I wondered whose destiny would determine the course of my life. Would I be doomed to relive the past, or would I be allowed by the Fates to make my own path? The philosophy of it was too hard to piece together. Was I really a man like no other? With Mum gone and Dad so distracted, now I would come into my own. I longed to discover for myself my place in this brave new world.

 * * *

Chapter 67

More and more, things were chaotic at home. I woke to find Dad not yet even awake, and it was time for work. Tripping over shoes and clothes strewn near the door of his room, I made my way to his bed and shook his arm.

"Dad. Dad!"

"Mrmph," he muttered.

"Dad! You're late for work."

"Huh? Oh, I was dreaming about your Mum. She was here with me in bed on a chilly afternoon. We were planning your birth. Let me go back to sleep. And maybe she'll return." He trailed off and tried to roll away from me in the bed.

"Dad!" I shook him harder and put a parental tone in my voice. "Get up right now and shave and get dressed!" I shoved back the covers and pulled at him until he was balanced uncomfortably at the edge. "I'll make some tea and toast. Now get moving!" I gave him one last nudge that forced him to put a foot on the floor.

He rubbed his eyes then focused on me and glanced at the clock on his bedside table. "Oh! Half eight! Will you ring up Gordon at the lab and tell him I'm on my way? The number's in my mobile."

I went to the kitchen and made the call. Dad's coat and things were simply dropped where he'd left them, and his mobile was on the worktop. No one had cleaned up the kitchen, and I saw a nearly empty bottle of whisky near the sink, along with a glass with a few dregs in the bottom. I took a whiff of the glass. Any other time of day I might have downed the remains myself, but this morning I emptied it into the sink, put on the tea kettle, and began filling the mechanical dishwasher.

When the kettle whistled I put a tea bag in a large mug and popped some bread in the toaster oven. I carefully wiped down the countertops, now cleared of the clutter, and scoured the sink. At the last minute before the toast popped, I returned the bottle to the liquor cabinet. Dad walked quickly into the kitchen still knotting his tie.

"Here's your tea," I said, swiping the butter knife across the slice of bread, "and here's your toast." Still standing, he took a few hasty bites, washing them down with gulps of tea.

"You saved me, son," he said between bites. "I still feel groggy, but off to the salt mines it is. You can look over your lessons from yesterday."

He brushed the crumbs from his face and put on his overcoat. "Now, don't get into any trouble!" He smiled at me feebly.

"We're out of groceries!" I called out as he began closing the door.

"Call Grandmum." His voice trailed off, and he was gone.

I stared at the calendar. Mum had been gone just six weeks, and my birthday was coming 'round in April. Dad was fraying at the edges, it seemed. I had begun to feel imprisoned by our circumstances and my increasing responsibility. Cece was my only distraction, and I found our encounters both comforting and unsettling at the same time.

I made myself a small plate of the last few muffins and a mug of tea. Dad had tossed the *Daily Mail* onto the table, and I arranged my cup and plate at my spot, opening up the paper to page through as I ate. I wasn't much on the world news, but it was fun to look at pictures and catch a few headlines about the royals. All this gave me information on people's antics.

In the advert section something caught my eye. An amateur theatrical group was seeking volunteers for a production of *The Comedy of Errors.* No experience required, and the address was an old church in our neighbourhood. Also in my favour was the 5 p.m. meeting time. I could make the event and still rush back to the flat about the time Dad would return home from work. I noted the address on a pad nearby and then phoned Granny.

"Hullo. This is your grandson Will upon the line."

"Will! How good to hear your voice!" she said, warmly as usual. "How are you this lovely morning? How go your studies?"

"Oh, fine, Grandmum, just fine. Always the same. Dad asked me to ring up to get your help. We are completely out of kitchen stock."

"What? Kingsley's not keeping up on his shopping?"

"Well, he's, um, kind of feeling low, I think. Of late he's been in bed most of the time."

"Only to be expected. It's so soon after your mother's passing. And you, how do you feel, son?"

"I'm making my small way in this wide world. What shall I do about the lack of food?"

She arranged to add our list to her own, and she or Gordon would bring the bags by later. I set out to tidy up the lounge and Dad's room. I knelt down and felt where the journals had been carefully retaped under the bureau but felt only a blank space. I lay completely down on the floor and peered under. Nothing. For a moment my heart pounded, but I realised that Dad must have remembered them and secreted them away to join the rest of the collection, wherever they were. I had read them just in time—and no one the wiser except myself.

Now that I knew who I was, the world was opening up to me in a new way. I would accept my birth and my destiny, and, alone, I would, like Caliban, be king of my own island.

*   *   *

Chapter 68

A young man stood near the side door entry to the chapel hall, smoking. He eyed me quizzically, so I said, to set him at ease, "I'm looking for the group that puts on plays."

"You've found 'em, mate," he replied, blowing out a large volume of smoke and crushing the burning stick under his boot sole with a twisting motion of the foot. "Follow me."

The small red door in the masonry wall led to an anteroom and then a pedestrian meeting hall.

"Look who I found lurking near the door," my guide said to those assembled in three small groups. "It's Will Shakespeare himself."

I wondered how he knew who I was. Everyone looked up. Some smiled and waved at me, and there was soft snickering at my name.

"We're just dividing up duties and responsibilities, and then we'll proceed to casting," a tall young woman said to me. "Actor, or behind the scenes?"

Her question caught me by surprise. "Um, dramaturge, perhaps, or stage manager," I replied. I tried to think of something resembling what I did with people at large and with my puppets at home.

"Ah, expert in Bard lore, then? So you can clarify the language for us? Dramaturge it is, and you can be in charge of diagramming the blocking, scene by scene. Frankly, I'm relieved. We have enough thespian types. We're in need of some anchors behind the curtain. I'm Amy, the director."

"I'm Will," I replied. Her eyebrows raised. "Um, Will . . . Armstrong," I added quickly. She seemed like a decisive person, so unlike Cece. I resolved to make an ally of her rather than an operative. She handed me a very large book full of blank pages.

"This will be our atlas," she said. "You'll make an x or y or zed for each character and then line out their movements on-stage for each scene. It's the movement that grounds the action and makes the lines possible."

I hadn't thought of it that way before. Even though I'd seen plays, somehow I believed that the actors had memorised the words of the speeches first and then walked about on stage as the spirit moved them. But now she was saying that spot and movement came first, then the words. It made sense. If actors knew WHERE they were, that would place the speech in a context. And that might help with memorisation and motive. I could see how important the book of blocking would be. I would pull the strings. I would tell everyone where to be and where to go next.

"What is your experience in dramatics?" she asked.

"I specialise in plays by our own bard. I've staged all of the plays in puppet-size," I lit upon as a fair response. "And, I know all his words complete by heart."

She gave me a hard, unbelieving look. "No way," she said.

"Oh, yes. My father has a thing for Shakespeare lore. He's read to me from e'en my very birth. I couldn't say how many times we've passed through all the thirty-seven plays and poems. After a while it simply takes and stays."

Her eye dropped to my pendant. I thought this might validate my credentials, so I said, "This is my guardian Michael on a coin." I held it up for her to examine. The piece was in pristine condition and simply glittered with the presence of any light. "I found it in the bard's own garden plot. It's called an angel, Tudor, '67."

"Brilliant," she said. "Amazing. You're an odd duck, Will, but I think you'll fit in well here. I'm glad you found us. And now, are you ready to help with casting?" I nodded, and she turned to the others and clapped her hands briskly. "All right, listen up!" she called out. "We'll begin with the Dromios and Antipholuses. Find someone of a similar height and colouring and make two lines. . . ."

* * *

Chapter 69

I kept my master blocking book under the mattress of my bed. Not that Father would have noticed it anyway. He dragged himself to work each morning, returned after 6, prepared us a simple dinner, and then began drinking. He sat in Mum's chair with head in hands 'til bedtime.

As usual I did my lessons, and he inquired about them perfunctorily. I cleaned up the kitchen and picked up the flat. Other than that I was free, and I was happier than I'd ever been. In the early afternoon I met up with Cece in the cellar, and after tea time I ran to the church and my theatre family. More than a year passed in this manner. We moved from *The Comedy of Errors* to *Titus Andronicus* and then on to *The Winter's Tale*.

Always I was master of the book and a bit of stage manager too during production. Amy thought it amusing that I mouthed the words of all the speeches right along with the actors, and I was always ready with a cue. Many of the patrons noticed my resemblance to the Bard, and it lent a bit of notoriety to our troupe to have me backstage. In our matinees I always took a bow at the end with the rest to enormous applause.

It was as if I had three separate selves, three separate lives, all a part of me but each quite different. I was still Father's boy but more and more our roles had been reversed, and I was taking care of him. Thankfully, he was so distracted that he couldn't notice small changes in the operation of the flat or even indications of my prolonged absences. The troupe had become a replacement family for me. Among them my quirks and predilections were welcome, and they gratefully acknowledged my dramatic expertise. Cece remained my dark darling. She too accepted me as I was. She was the only human creature with whom I shared an open and intimate closeness.

And she needed me. I came to understand this fully during one of our afternoon trysts. As usual she emerged from the gloomy light when I began an oration, and then she led me to her den. My angel pendant seemed to take on life in the cellar, glowing purely in the darkness. We communicated more through touch than in words, but this day Cece seemed pensive.

"Cat got your tongue?" I ventured, stroking her arm. I saw a single tear roll down her cheek. She reached for me, and as we hugged tightly, she began to sob. Her eye make-up mixed with her tears, and she appeared to me either ghoulish or forlorn, her face streaked with the dark lines. She released her hold and looked at me directly for a while. Then she began.

"You don't know the story of me," she said. "And it's like a sad song that plays over and over in my head."

"Cece, you light up my very life, every day and every hour we meet."

"Why do you think I'm here in the dark?" she asked. "I am unworthy of the light. And I cannot bear the look of myself, of what I've become."

"But you are barely nearing an adult," I reminded her. "How could you have turned into something bad?"

She choked back a sob. "I miss my mum so much," she said. I hardly missed mine at all so did not respond. "And for Dad, well, I've become . . . everything."

"Lucky for me that he's away at work and even more that I have found you here." Her eyes opened wider and had a far-away look.

"Will. He takes me. Has done for years."

"He takes you where? . . . He takes you where, Cece?"

"No. He never lets me leave the building. And he takes me in my bed at night."

I was silent. So others also harboured dark secrets. This made sense of the bruises I'd seen on her body and of her sometimes nearly automatic motions of love-making. For an instant I thought of her pain and the suffering of betrayal. And then I felt anger, that I shared her with another. A vision of a large man smothering this waif in an unholy act appeared to me.

"But are you hurt? Does this man inflict pain?" I asked.

"Not any more," she said. "Not any more. But I thought you needed to know."

"Is there somewhere that you can go, or someone you can tell?"

"It's far too late for that," she said. "And there is only you."

My mind struggled.

"Which is his car?" I asked suddenly. "Which is the one he drives?"

"Oh, Will, we couldn't . . . could we?"

"We did it once before. We can again."

"But then where would I be? How would I live? Who would take care of me? I would be alone in the world."

"Unspeakable, unthinkable," I told her, running through the evil acts perpetrated in the plays. This rivaled them all. Having only recently discovered my own freedom, I was not ready to take on another's life. I needed to be responsible only to myself and find my own personal destiny. But "I will take care of you" escaped from my mouth.

"We're too young," she said with an uncharacteristic practicality.

"What can I do to help make sure you're safe?" I asked.

"If I lie still and close my eyes tight, I get through it," she said. "And I can think of you."

I vowed to find a way to avenge my dark darling, and I would bide time for the perfect opportunity. The plays showed a kind of cosmic justice at work in the world, and for myself, I was beginning to believe in karma.

 * * *

Chapter 70

Gordon knocked on the door of the flat. I peered through the peephole to see him standing there in a deerstalker cap, holding two large shopping bags. I opened the door since I was keeper of the castle.

"Weekly grocery delivery, son," he announced and bustled in with the provisions. He headed directly to the kitchen and, after shedding his coat and hat, began stowing things in their proper places.

"I picked up some nice quince jam for your toast." He held up a small jar as evidence before placing it into the cupboard. As goofy an old gent as he was, he took his own care to tend to me. He put the kettle on to boil, then he walked forward and put both his hands on my shoulders.

"Let's have a good look at you," he said, scrutinising me up and down and then turning me around. "My, you're as tall as any fine man now." He smoothed the hair away from my brow. "But you are as pale as fresh-driven snow," he proclaimed. "You have been too deep in grief. We must get you out into the sun and air."

"I'm quite all right at home here in the flat," I replied.

"Rot and poppycock! What you need is exercise and diversion, and I know just the thing for it. You lads raised in the city have no sense of the power of the forest, the thrill of the hunt. You've not learnt to pull the string of a fine ash bow taut with your finger, sight down the line, and let her fly straight into a handsome three-pronged buck. Maybe deer to poach are scarce near London proper, but you can still master the art of it. Fetch your coat, lad. We're going out to shooting practice." He turned off the fire under the kettle, grabbed his own coat, and headed to the door.

The folio in my mind paged through the Bard's works for a precedent. Ah, yes, there was the Forest of Arden and those who hunted within the woods where Rosalind disguised as Ganymede. With firearms in their infancy, of course they plied the bow and arrow. And my Tudor parent himself had been accused of poaching deer on the Lord's territory as a youthful lark. It behooved me to learn this weapon.

Gordon had his car, and before starting the engine he made a call on his mobile. "Henry?" I heard him say. "Have you an open bay? It's Gordon McLeod, and I've my grandson in tow. The boy's green about shooting. Can you prepare him a light-weight starter and give us an hour? And my usual bow as well, just to join in. Yes, quarter of an hour to you. We're on the road."

He smiled towards me and said, "All set then, lad. Today you become even more of a man."

Gordon steered us to Queen Elizabeth Walk over Putney Bridge. It was not raining today, but we stood under a wooden canopy with bull's eye targets visible some distance out in the open air. Henry brought out an array of shooting accoutrements and outfitted me like William Tell. He placed a quiver full of feathered arrows over my head and situated it behind my shoulder. He gave me a leather glove for my trigger-hand and produced a stunning ash bow with a taut string like that on a guitar running end to end. I held it in my left hand. They plopped a green felt hat on my head to complete the picture.

"Helps shade the eyes," said Gordon. "It's a medieval version of the Roman pilaeus." Both men regarded me and grinned.

"You've stepped off the pages of an antiquary," said Henry. Gordon studied his mobile, then held it up and snapped a shot of me in full archer's garb.

This felt like play-acting, and I thought it might actually be fun—perhaps at some point even useful.

Henry left us and Gordon picked up his own bow, taking off his mackintosh for better freedom of movement. He began a series of detailed instructions for placing the bow, arming the arrow, sighting the target, pulling the string, steadying down, and letting the arrow fly, Bob's your uncle. I tried to copy his motions, but it was a complex matter. We both shot. Gordon's arrow, to my surprise, pierced the hay just to the right of the bull's eye. His arrow head was touching the red of the centre. My arrow flew straight like a bird on a mission and landed with a plop on the ground a metre wide of the target.

"Not bad for a virgin shot," said Gordon. "Now arm up again. Make sure your eye sees the spot you want to hit. Hold steady, and the arrow will follow your aim."

This time my arrow hit the hay, although outside the target area. We loaded and shot for the best part of an hour. I had mixed results, I was sweating, and both my finger and right arm had begun to ache.

"Enough for today," Gordon eventually proclaimed. "A valiant first effort, son. Did you feel the joy of the challenge?"

"You shoot so well! It's harder than it looks," I replied. I had developed a new admiration for this old geezer, my step-grandfather.

"If you like it, I'll pick you up Wednesdays at one, and we'll practice together. Before long you'll be outshoooting this shaky old arm of mine. Eyes too watery to draw a clear bead these days," he confessed. "Now let's go home and you can put some Deep Freeze on that shoulder. And I'll be sure to clear our standing date with your father. I doubt he'll object."

My father. No, I too doubted he would object. These days I was troublesome small fry to him. His mind was with Mum in her grave.

* * *

Chapter 71

Rushing home from my theatre family, I closed the door of the flat just minutes before Father followed me in. I had plunked down at the desk in my room, pretending to be studying. My mind was spinning, instead, with a new possibility suggested by Amy. Our little troupe had achieved some small notoriety with our productions, and she had invited representatives from the RSC at the New Globe to one of our matinees of *The Winter's Tale*. They had remarked to her particularly about the effect of Hermione's statue coming back to life. Amy told them that I had been responsible for both the blocking and coaching of the actors for delivery of lines. Here was the crux: "I'll make the statue move indeed, descend and take you by the hand; but then you'll think—which I protest against—I am assisted by wicked powers.... It is required you do awake your faith." They wanted to give me a "local production commendation" along with an invitation to apply for a position at their theatre.

I was itching to look at their on-line site when Father came in. No greeting. I heard ice clink into a glass. I knew I'd find him in Mum's chair. We hardly spoke anymore, and when I tried to talk to him, he seemed in a world of his own—of his own making. Tonight I had much to share with him. I wandered towards Mum's chair in the lounge.

He sat with glass in hand and his head reclined back, eyes towards the ceiling but closed. Without changing his position or opening his eyes, he heard my approach and spoke.

"Will," he said softly. "You are the very thing."

"How was your day at work and how's the lab?" I broached.

"Always the iambic pentameter," he remarked. "But have I made you into a poet? Can you feel things 'like a man'? I do wonder." He lowered his head and sipped at his whisky. I sat across from him.

"Can you forage in the fridge for dinner?" he finally asked. "I have no more hunger." He sipped at his drink.

"Dad, I wondered if we two might share some words," I said.

"I'll put together some new lesson plans tonight," he replied. "Meanwhile, try staging *The Tempest* with the puppets. There's a challenge for you, implying the storm and the movements of Ariel the spirit."

"This is about our staging, actually. I've been at work with locals doing plays."

He sat up straight and looked directly at me. I could not tell if he was pleased.

"You've been going out on your own? And without permission?"

"I cannot be a prisoner of the flat! It's very near; I'm using all my lore."

"Are you an *actor*?" he asked with a strange tone to his voice, almost fateful, almost scornful.

"No, I work for them behind the scenes is all. I tell them where to stand and what to say."

"Ah." He laughed and sipped at his drink.

"They seem to like me there—and what I know. A bloke from RSC wants me to come, see how I'd fit in at the New Globe site. May I attend and find out what they say?"

"Ye gods. The wheel has come full circle." He clutched his head in his hands.

"Father?"

"Let me think on it, Will."

"Oh, and something else if you still have the time."

"What more?" He raised his head.

"Grandpa Gordon takes me shooting arrows."

"He mentioned that to me, Will, and I approve. It can be a hands-on re-enactment of Tudor weaponry, good for your immersion studies."

"It makes me think of good old Robin Hood."

"A historical figure become legend, all quite Shakespearean."

"I thought so, too. I've broached a play about him. I did some research on the internet."

Father threw back his head and laughed heartily.

"First *The Two Noble Kinsmen* and now you—another new play by Shakespeare!"

"By William Shakespeare *Armstrong*, Father. I am *me* alone."

"Or a rose by any other name. . . ." He downed his drink and walked over to the bar to pour another, laughing softly. "A rose by any other name," he repeated again and again.

*   *   *

Chapter 72

If I were to claim my own identity, my sixteenth birthday offered the moment to fuse all parts of my life. A party had been Grandmum's idea. She'd come by with the weekly supplies and probably to check up on me. I sat on a stool at the counter as she sorted through the items she'd brought. There was a colourful bouquet from the corner florist, and Grandmum was snipping off the tips of the stems and making a pleasing arrangement in a vase. This was not something either Father or I would have bothered with.

"We will make our beds of roses, and a thousand fragrant posies," she said, humming softly. Her eye caught the calendar hanging on the wall. "I see we have a gold-letter day fast approaching." She beamed at me. "In some cultures a boy becomes a man at twelve or thirteen," she added. "Here you are—what will it be?—sixteen, isn't it?" As if she didn't know. "We all miss your Mum, it's true, but I think we should brush away the black crepe and celebrate your future. What do you say to a nice party here at the flat? I'll bake a cake."

"I think my Dad's too sad to celebrate."

"Your Dad will need to tend to his grief in his own way. But life goes on—your life, especially."

"Would it be for just the four of us?" I asked, thinking of Cece.

"Well, that's a beginning. There's always Gladys and Tessa, who've been around since your birth, and what about Henry from archery? Who would you like to invite?"

"I've been a volunteer down at St. Crispin's," I said.

"You have? On your own?"

"Yes, going on a couple of years now. I'd like to ask director Amy too. Perhaps another of the actors, Gareth."

"Well, of course. Young people in the mix, couldn't be better."

"And, well, I've made a friend here in our lot. Her name is Cece and she's just my age."

"Splendid! That's ten including you. We'll have a cake and play charades. You invite the youngsters and I'll take care of the rest. Say a week Saturday at 2? Now we're set."

*   *   *

"What have you there, my dear sweet one?" I asked, as Cece pulled on her jumper and rummaged around in her den, producing a small cello-bag. Just tetrameter this time as I was comfortable with her.

"I think it's just regular tobacco," she said. "I nicked it from my dad's bottom drawer. He's trying to stop, so the stash is piling up. I don't think he'll even notice a bag gone now and again. He rolls this in little papers," she added, "but I'm sure we could stuff it in the pipe."

We'd used up the hashish blend I'd found in the alley, but I still had my "bones" pipe, and Cece had her candle matches.

My lungs had become conditioned by the harshness of the herbal blend one of the actors was supplying me and this mixture felt mild and calming.

"He's quitting smoking after all these years?" I ventured, blowing out an enormous puff.

"Yes, and cutting back on the bottle too. Mid-life matters and pressure at work, he says."

"My dad attacks the bottle every night."

"He misses your mum. . . . You're lucky you're a lad." I passed her the pipe.

"There's something more that lies beneath the skin. His mind dwells on a darkness from his past. It seems to be a demon haunting him. He's always been look-on-the-bright-side, but suddenly he's only doom and gloom."

"Hmmm. Just opposite from yours, perhaps changes for the better in my little family," she said.

"Cece?"

"I don't want to jinx it, but Dad's not been coming to my room anymore." She took a small puff from the pipe.

"So now you are completely just my girl," I said, relieved—relieved that I wasn't sharing her, relieved that I would not need to shoot her father in his own bed with my arrow—an action I'd been contemplating and rehearsing in my mind. But I knew the damages would remain with her for a long, long time.

"He's actually begun to look at me, and tries to talk to me. He wants me to ditch the studs. Not lady-like, he says." She returned the pipe to me. I was certain we reeked of smoke. I always threw my clothes into the washing machine as soon as I returned to the flat, showered and shampooed my hair, and brushed my teeth thoroughly.

"I am about to have a birthday come," I announced.

"Which one?"

"Sixteen. Will you attend a party in our flat?"

"Who would be there?" she asked.

"Mostly adults, since I don't go to school. If they'll come, Amy from plays, and Gareth, who first introduced me there. You've been my little secret long enough. Just cake and some malarkey. No present is required."

"I don't think they will like me. And how will you explain who I am?"

"You're my friend and that is just enough."

"What would we talk about?" More questions.

"Me and myself, no doubt. Just smile and be yourself."

"Whoever that is," she replied.

*   *   *

Amy and Gareth walked to our flat from the church and joined the other adults in my life. Everybody was exactly who they seemed to be. Henry told stories about the making of bows and the fletching of arrows. Grandpa Gordon sipped some whisky and recalled tales—seemingly apocryphal—about stalking twelve-pronged buck in the highlands. Tessa'd gotten married and brought her toddler Emma, who threw all my puppets wherever she wanted. Father sat in Mum's chair and did not speak. Grandmum brought out a cake all lit up, and everyone sang "For he's a jolly-good fellow…." On the third "hip-hip-hooray" I blew out the candles, which immediately re-ignited, to everyone's great pleasure.

We acted out the titles of classic novels in honour of Mum, but Father refused to play. Grandmum produced a special package, which was a framed photo of me that first day of archery, looking much like one of Robin's Merrie Men. Somewhat in his cups, Grandpa Gordon offered a toast in honour of me.

"Here's to Will, whom I love as if he were my own flesh and blood."

"Hear, hear," everyone said, but Father began a spasm of choking and retired to his room.

Amy cornered my grandparents to tell them about the RSC commendation and invitation, a good building block towards permission for my application. In spite of my usual reserve, I had fun with all these well-meaning people who'd stood by me and supported me.

"Happy birthday!" "Many happy returns!" they called out as they bundled, two-by-two, out the door. I was reminded of the Dromios, who exit at the end of their play with "We came into the world like brother and brother, And now let's go hand in hand, not one before another." As I turned back to the flat, I saw the puppets were everywhere, and Gordon was dozing on the sofa. Father was in his room, and Grandmum and I began to clean up.

"Wasn't that fun, birthday boy?" she commented. "But where was your little friend from the building?"

"She's somewhat shy. I fear she's hid away," I ventured. "I wanted her to meet my family."

"I can tell she's important to you, and I'd like to meet her, too. Shall we ring her up now the crowd's thinned out?" Gordon offered soft snoring sounds. I thought for a moment.

"I cannot ring her up, but I know where she might be."

"Will you take me to her, then?"

I wasn't clear on whether or not to trust Grandmum that far—to reveal to her our secret realm. If we just went into the cellar but not into our den, we'd probably be safe.

"Well, all right." I led Grandmum by the arm to the lift, and we pressed "C."

"She lives in the cellar?" she asked.

"No, but for a lark that's where we spend our time. Kids' antics, don't you know. She must stay in the lot, and there's little place to go. This is where we play," I added quickly.

The door separated upon the cellar's dank gloom. Grandmum gave an involuntary shudder. It was an unfriendly space, I could see with her eyes. We stepped forward into the semi-darkness.

"Where is she?" Grandmum whispered.

"I have to speak the speech," I whispered back. When she looked at me askance, I added, "trippingly on the tongue" and grinned. I assumed an oratorical stance and launched into Cleopatra's speech, "It is my birth-day: I had thought to have held it poor: but. . . ." My words rang out and echoed resoundingly in the space. No Cece. My eyes scanned her usual positions for the paleness of her face and then scoured into remote corners. Nothing. My heart dropped a bit. Until now, she'd never let me down.

"Will? Son? There's nothing here, nobody in the shadows. And it smells stale down here, like old smoke. Can we look for her somewhere else? Perhaps you were mistaken." Grandmum put her hand on my arm and drew me back towards the lift. There was disbelief and a small amount of pity in her gaze. We rode up in silence, both looking straight ahead, and, at our floor, re-entered the flat. Gordon was still snoring quietly. We walked back towards the kitchen. I was nonplussed and plunked down despondently on my stool.

Grandmum began drying glasses, running the towel carefully along the rims and into each glass, again quietly humming.

"Will. My darling." She finally spoke. "It is time to put away childish things."

 *   *   *

Chapter 73

"Trevor Redmond," the clerk announced clearly in the anteroom of the RSC offices at the New Globe. A slender chap with spiked hair said "Oi" and rose. I noisily shuffled my blocking book, which I held under my arm. The other person remaining in the room was a striking girl with reddish hair, and she looked at me, smiling warmly.

"Nervous?" she asked.

"Um, no, not actually," I replied.

"Did you bring a stack of head shots?" She gestured towards my book. "Forgive my being so bold, but you actually look a bit like a young Shakespeare. They're sure to capitalise on the resemblance. I'm Pamela. Rhys-Jones. Your next Lady Macbeth."

"Ah, you're here to try out for an actor's role," I said.

"Aren't you? I was rather hoping you'd play my thane and my king. You've got the iambic down pat already, it appears."

It crossed through my mind that she was flirting. She was clearly more aggressive than Cece, and she recognised metre.

"No, I'm not an actor. Only behind the scenes for me, my dear. My name is Will Sh---, William Armstrong."

"Hullo, Will Sh---, William Armstrong." She came over and sat in the loveseat with me. The corners of my book poked into us both. She pulled a slender portfolio from her bag then tugged my book away from me and laid it flat like a tray and opened up her own folder on top. "What do you think of these?" she asked.

The file contained 8" x 10" glossy pictures of her in various actor-like poses and some actually in Tudor costumery. She sorted through them, holding each one up for my consideration.

"Do you think I look old enough to be Lady Macbeth? Probably still too young for Cleopatra. But you know, there's innovative casting now, and I might have a chance for a meaty male role. Probably not Lear but maybe Prince Hal, or even Hamlet! Diane Venora did it first." Her eyes lit up at the thought. "See, when I pull my hair back"—she did so—"don't I look rather manly?"

"So you'd like to hold a mirror up to nature, but with a twist, perhaps a flaw in the glass," I responded.

"You do know your lines," she commented.

The clerk returned. "William Shakespeare . . . um, Armstrong!"

"Just here!" I called out. Pamela Rhys-Jones eyed me with wonder.

I struggled to rise, pulling my blocking book out from under her folder. Her head shots scattered onto the floor. She quickly scuttled after them, and as I entered the sacred chambers she, on her knees on the floor, cried out to me, "Break a leg, William Shakespeare, um, Armstrong, and I'll be waiting for you!"

The executive who'd seen my Hermione come back to life sat at a short table with another man and woman. A single chair faced their table, and I perched on the edge of its seat clutching my large book.

"What have you there?" the executive asked.

"This is my blocking book for all the plays," I answered.

"*All* the plays?"

"Our troupe's done four with me throughout the past. And all agog, I've gone and blocked the rest."

"You've blocked out all thirty-seven plays of the Shakespeare canon?" the woman asked.

"Yes, and *The Two Noble Kinsmen*, and one little effort of my own called *The Merrie Tale of Robin Hood*. In five acts." They raised their eyebrows in unison, which had a comical effect. It took all my energy to remain serious.

"And you so young," the other man said. He consulted a paper on his desk. "Sixteen, is it? And where have you received your training?"

I heaved my heart into my mouth and replied, "Only at home. My father's led the way."

They brought their heads together and whispered, then the executive said, "Would you mind letting us take a good look at your book? You could wait in the lounge, and we'll call you back in soon."

"Really? All right! I'll leave you with my book." I stood and placed it on their table.

The waiting room was empty, and I wondered about Pamela. At that moment Cece's image faded into the shadows of my mind. Surely this Pamela had not been a figment of my imagination. I remained standing, surveying the costume sketches that adorned the walls, designs that had been used in productions right here at the Globe over the years. Some were historically accurate, but more and more there was a tendency towards anachronistic period dress or modern dress. These walls offered a history of one aspect of twentieth-century Shakespearean production.

I heard a door click and turned. Pamela emerged, all smiles.

"I'm hired on!" she bubbled and rushed over to hug me. She smelled like hyacinths and felt soft and robust at the same time. It turned into a long embrace.

"Did you hear anything?" she asked.

"They have my book. I'm waiting 'til I'm called," I replied.

"Well, I won't be Lady Macbeth at first. They think I'd be right for Celia in *As You Like It* or Miranda in *The Tempest*—roles in keeping with my age and appearance, you know." She struck a dramatic pose. "Oh, wonder! How many goodly creatures are there here! How beauteous mankind is!" She giggled with delight. "With those parts behind me, I'm sure to graduate to a lead." She radiated a halo of excitement I found compelling.

The clerk re-entered the ante-room and pronounced "William Shakespeare Armstrong. Please follow me."

Quickly Pamela reached into her bag and produced a small card, which she thrust into my jumper pocket. "Here's my address and number. Stop by after to let me know how it went!" I could still smell hyacinths as I returned to the audition room. The panel members were positioned as before.

"How clever of you to choose the Bard as your stage name," the second man said. "We can see you're following in his tradition."

"Oh, no, that is my given name . . . by birth," I corrected him.

"Another fine tradition, a wise parent giving the child a name to live up to," he went on. "It's been decades since a William Shakespeare worked at the Globe, and we're glad to have you on board."

I could not speak. This seemed a holy moment of destiny.

"Now about this Robin Hood drama. We'd like to do a reading to see how it plays. If you can leave us your manuscript, we'll make copies and return it to you at the read-through—say Thursday at 3? We'll use members of the repertory company who are available."

"Where shall I come to hear you read my play?" I asked, my heart pounding.

"Enter by the stage door and tell the clerk you're headed for Rehearsal B. He'll show you the way. And, son, welcome to our enterprise." They stood and each shook my hand. I extracted *The Merrie Tale of Robin Hood* from my book and left it on the table. The waiting room was empty and I walked on, out of the theatre into the sun.

I examined Pamela's card in the brightness. I was beginning to explore more of London, and I recognised her street, actually in a neighbourhood near our own. With Cece's whereabouts uncertain I needed a confidante, and I wanted to share my good news. And then there was the imprint of Pamela's body still lingering on my own. . . .

* * *

Chapter 74

I found the building and pressed the buzzer. Pamela's voice crackled through the speaker.

"It's Will . . . um, Armstrong."

"Ooh, you came!" she crowed and buzzed me in. I was hoping not to have to meet parents on this day. She was standing near a doorway on the ground floor bouncing from foot to foot. She gestured me into the flat and gave me a gleeful hug.

"This is the first day of the rest of my life," she said, dancing around dramatically. And then she began striking poses. "This is my shocked look. Now I'm distraught. How's this for amourous?" She shifted her body and face with each new emotion. And then she hugged me again. It was hard to tell when she was play-acting and when she was for real. "So, what'd they say to you? Will you direct me in my greatest role?" she asked.

"They signed me on. They're looking at my play!"

Pamela Rhys-Jones squealed with elation and threw herself at me in apparent happiness at the news. But this hug became prolonged, and since the third time's the charm I found myself snogging her wetly, and she responded with enthusiasm, maybe even experience.

"Are your parents here? Or are we all alone?" I asked, catching my breath. She snatched a feathery scarf that was hanging from the coat rack and wrapped it sexily around her neck. Then she began a seductive dance, using the scarf to highlight the erotic areas of her body rather like a striptease. She hummed a raunchy tune and slithered in front of me.

"They've gone to Scotland on their holiday . . ." she chanted. "They've left me on my own . . ." She swiveled her hips. "With auntie checking in from time to time . . ." All the while she'd been backing up, and she disappeared into an open bedroom door. I took a couple of steps forward, and then a piece of lingerie flew out of the doorway and landed directly on my head. I heard giggling. I extracted the bra from my hair and held it by a strap at arm's length as I entered the room.

Pamela was lying completely naked on the bed, propped up against plush pillows in a seductive pose resembling one of those odalisque paintings I'd seen as a nipper at the BM. She was much rounder than Cece, and I found her curves exciting.

"Dah-ling," she drawled, pretending to inhale from a long fag holder she held between two fingers. "Wel-come to my bou-doir," and she exhaled as if puffing out smoke.

Although I wasn't much for public acting myself, I did know how to play a role, especially when the script was so evidently laid out. "Shall I join milady in that bed of pleasure?" I asked, beginning to remove my jumper.

"I shall languish here alone," she placed the back of her hand over her brow, "without you by my side."

Her skin was silky and she seemed more engaged and responsive than Cece had ever been. Our encounter was over quickly, and it was thrilling. Cece and I always shared my Tudor pipe after. I rose and rummaged through my coat pocket. From the bed Pamela sang out, "I see the full moon rising, and it's somebody's white bum!" I found my pipe and the cello bag and jumped back into the covers.

"Will pater mind if we inhale in bed?" I asked.

"Oh, no for-real smoking in the flat . . . but maybe just this once if we air out afterwards. WHAT do you have there? It looks like a prop."

"This is my Tudor pipe, bones from the Thames."

"BONES from the Thames! Oh, it's so tiny and twee!" She took it and ran her fingers over its smooth edges.

I gave her the bag and said, "You fill it up and tamp the leaves down tight."

We passed the pipe back and forth, puffing contentedly until the meagre contents burned out. Pamela coughed a bit at first. I suspected she was experienced only in pretend smoking, but love-making she seemed to do for real.

 *   *   *

Chapter 75

Cece still lingered in the back of my mind, and I felt her disappearance as a mystery—perhaps a timely one—yet I wondered where she was. Upon my return to the flat, I took my pipe and the cello bag with its dwindling contents and rode down to the cellar. It was gloomy as usual, and I assumed an oratorical position near a stack of old crates. Feeling sated with Pamela, wondering if I should tell Cece about her, I launched into Richard III's speech, "Was ever woman in this humour woo'd? / Was ever woman in this humour won?" and I got completely through it without Cece's face emerging from the dark shadows. When the speech ended, the last word echoed briefly and silence resumed.

"Cece?" I ventured. Nothing. "Are you there?"

I moved slowly through the narrow corridor of stored boxes that led to our den, hoping perhaps to find her asleep on the cushions. No Cece. Instead, the area seemed hastily vacated. Only a single cushion remained, and all the small creature comforts had disappeared, except for one upended candle and a nearly empty matchbook. Something had happened, and I was in the dark, feeling forlorn.

I sat on the remaining cushion, and, in hopes of rekindling our feeling of homeyness, lit up the small bones pipe. I mused on possibilities. She'd not actually lived in our building except as a solitary transient. . . . She had lived in our building but her father had precipitously moved, taking her along. . . . She never existed at all except in my imagination. . . . She was my desire projected as a practice woman preparing me for Pamela. . . . With smoke wreathing my head, I wondered if the baggie had contained traces of that potent hashish, as I felt light-headed. With no answer to my speculations, I shook myself and put out my arm to push to a standing position. My hand fell upon something crinkly. It was a cello bag full of aromatic leaves.

I had just finished showering and tossing my clothes into the washing machine when Father came into the flat.

"Will, I'm home!" he called out. I heard him move to the bar. I heard the clink of ice into a glass and then a slight swooshing sound of something being poured. Ten seconds, then again the pouring sound. Then footsteps to Mum's chair.

"Father, hello! Just closing out some work!" I finally replied. I hastily dressed and strode into the lounge, where he sat, head in hands as usual. I lowered myself onto the stool nearby facing him.

"Father, I've had such a brilliant day!"

"Oh, son," he said, raising his head. "There must be balance in the universe, for mine was miserable." I weighed his response and decided that misery trumped glee. He took a sip of his drink.

"What happened?" I asked.

"It's difficult to explain. I *have* been late for work a couple of times, but they say my performance has fallen off and they've lost trust in my work. I've been put on administrative leave, and they're calling Grandpa Gordon back full time to run the lab."

"Oh, Father, I'm sure it's because of your grief. Like Hamlet, you feel your loss too deeply. It's not alone your inky cloak—you bear that within which passeth show. With time things will improve."

"I've given all my being to science. The lab has been my life. What will I do at home except sit in your Mum's chair and mourn? This is a blow to me, Will, a blow to us."

I wanted to tell him my news about the RSC, but I tried to focus on his topic. "We can open and air out your lab here at home, get it back to shipshape spiffy quick. Then you can work on projects once again."

He moaned with a sort of horror I did not fully understand. After all, I had been his last home experiment, and I was quite the success. Impulsively, I seized the opportunity.

"Father. The secret's out and I know who I am," I confessed.

"And who are you, Will?" he responded absently.

"I know the origin. I'm William Shakespeare, and now I'm at the Globe."

"You are William Shakespeare Armstrong and a home-schooled teen-age boy," he said matter-of-factly without changing position.

"I read Mum's journals," I continued. His body jolted, and he stared at me with bleary eyes then emptied his glass.

"Get me another drink, will you, son?" His voice wavered.

Reluctantly, I did as he asked, in silence. I handed him the icy glass and our eyes met.

"Ah, you found them then. How much did you read?" he asked numbly, and he downed the refilled glass in a single motion.

"Enough to know the story, the full truth of my birth."

A long silence filled the room as we regarded each other. On stage it would have been ten beats—an unbearable lapse in the dialogue. His face seemed an expressionless mask. I could not read the thoughts clearly fulminating in his mind. Father stared into the melting ice of his whisky, and finally he spoke—creator to creation, as it were.

"I am still your father."

"Of course. Of course," I reassured him. "You are all I've known.

"But a voice speaks to me from another time as well, and it I also must heed. Dad—I've written a play, and they've signed me on to work backstage at the New Globe.

"They delight in my name, and I will make it famous once again, to the glory of you and my own identity."

He had paid close attention to my speech, but now he muttered "It's out of my hands" and again hung his head.

"The die is cast, Will. I knew not what my actions would beget. And now your mother, gone, because of me." He shook his head slowly and moaned softly.

"But I will make my way within this world. And I will tend to you; we'll be just fine," I assured him.

"Ah, your predecessor had the human heart. 'We know what we are but not what we may be.'"

   *   *   *

Chapter 76

The flat was quiet when I walked towards the kitchen to get some breakfast. Father wasn't in Mum's chair, and his bed was rumpled but vacant. For an instant my heart sank in worry. Since Mum's death, Father's and my roles had reversed, and I cared for him like a child. I noticed the door of the lab—for years closed and locked—slightly ajar, and I put my eye to its slitted opening. Father was sitting at the microscope, staring, still as a glacier.

The phone rang while my bread was in the toaster. On the fourth ring I knew Father would not pick up. The caller ID specified the lab. It was Grandpa Gordon.

"'Morning, lad. Just wanted to reassure your father that all's well at the lab. Is he up yet?"

"He's looking through the scope in his home lab," I replied.

"Can you fetch him?" Gordon asked. I walked with the receiver to the lab door and nudged it open.

"Father?" He did not move.

"What is it?"

I walked towards him and placed my hand gently on his shoulder. "Blower for you." He did not move.

"Can't you see I'm busy working?" He continued to stare through his scope.

I squeezed his shoulder then returned to the kitchen.

"He can't talk right now," I said into the receiver.

"Oh, right-o, then. Tell him everything's swimming along here . . . And, Will? We'll need to postpone our archery sessions for a while, I'm afraid."

"Okay. Bye." No problem about the archery. I enjoyed the challenge, but I had already used the situation as a stimulus for my play. It had served its purpose.

I wondered if Father's being at home was going to hinder my freedom. I planned to visit Pamela today. Cece passed through my mind. Her disappearance was still a mystery, and that nagged at me. It wasn't that I would miss her as an individual exactly, but she had been just what I needed when I needed it, and she had brought me into my manhood. Her otherworldly oddness still intrigued me, and it had been comforting to know my dark darling would be waiting for me down cellar. I hoped she was all right wherever she was. My only clue to her disappearance was a "To Let" sign that had materialised in the window of our building. Here and then gone. First Mum, then Cece. And now, what about Father? "Our little life is rounded with a sleep."

I'd learned from the strongest of the villains that you only ever really had yourself to rely on. That was fine with me, actually. I enjoyed occasional interaction, especially if I could manipulate scenarios to my advantage. I carried the ability in my genes to create separate worlds. Now if only I could keep those worlds in their own compartments where they belonged.

I polished off the last of my toast and walked quietly to peek into the lab. Father seemed frozen in the same spot as before, hunched over the scope and staring into it. In a way I was relieved rather than concerned. He was out of harm's way, and with him so occupied, I could move about at my own will. This afternoon I'd have a tryst with Pamela and then prepare myself for tomorrow, which was to be the staged reading of *The Merrie Tale of Robin Hood*. It occurred to me that since Mum's death my life had taken wing. I found it hard not to make some kind of connection, especially with my knowledge of the larger story. At what point had she become the sacrifice for my successful existence? Perhaps from the very beginning.

Now only father and I knew the secret of my birth— and Father was coming unglued from this world. Mum's death had nudged him towards a precipice into which he was slipping. He seemed fixated on cause and effect, on unforeseen consequences, and his coping strategy was to replay that monumental past event, staring through his scope as if a new insight might appear before his eyes. So far he'd not directly come clean with me about my origin, even though I had confronted him with my information from Mum's journals. He could not think clearly about the present and its possibilities. He seemed stuck in the moment of choice about those cells on that pipe, all those years ago.

But I was living, and I was young. I planned to make the most of this second chance. I would try to act humane, but the path to my own future might of necessity be strewn with occasional casualties. "Collateral damages" they called them on the telly. You had to make way for yourself, and you had to try to write your own script. In my case, I wanted no one else directing my actions and movements. I carried my plot in my genes—my genius laid out the way before me. Shakespeare's angel was like a headlamp, sending beams forward towards my destiny.

After breakfast I showered and shaved, combing my hair forward as I could over my large round brow. By habit I still wore black, and I found a clean jumper and dark jeans. The laundry wicker was full, and I toted it towards the machine in the kitchen. The lab door was standing open, and I could hear Dad in the loo. Snatching the opportunity, I set down the hamper and strode quickly into the lab. Assuming Father's position on the lab stool, I adjusted the scope to my height and peered with curiosity to see what so mesmerised him. The scope held nothing at all, not even a blank slide. Father was staring through his microscope at empty space! And I knew at that moment I was living with a madman, who claimed to be my Father. The wheel had turned, and I was ascendant.

 *   *   *

Chapter 77

When I arrived at Pamela's parents' flat, the front door was ajar, and a note was taped on it saying "Who chooses me shall gain what many men desire." I smiled and pushed the door open. This was nothing if not a romantic invitation. Inside was a narrow table graced with three small homemade cardboard boxes painted metallic gold, metallic silver, and a dull, dark grey. Each box had a removable lid with a hinge made of tape. They resembled stage props—substantial looking from a distance, flimsy upon close inspection. New age music was plunking softly in the background—and no sign of Pamela, who I knew was playing an erotic game with me.

I recognised the quotation as borrowed from the casket game devised for Portia by her father prior to his death. He was trying to ensure that she would select a husband with correct priorities, one who valued character over wealth. Pamela apparently had appropriated the form of the game without much attention to its thematic intent. In *The Merchant of Venice* each casket contains a picture, one of a fool, one of a skull, and one of the lady herself.

I flipped back the lid of the metallic gold casket. Instead of a skull, there was a snapshot of Pamela in Cleopatra garb, reclining on a chaise longue and dangling a clustre of grapes before her waiting mouth. Nothing like mixing up the plays in service of your point. She seemed like sexual desire personified. The middle casket, metallic silver, instead of a fool also contained a picture of Pamela, cross-dressed as a boy, perhaps Cesario or Ganymede. She was as entirely erotic androgynous as she was in womanly dress. Her self-absorbed presentation amused me and attracted me. It seemed naïve—if *not* innocent.

I also found submerged humour in these photos linked with the epigrams. Cleopatra was paired with "what many men desire." The androgyne went with "as much as he deserves." And now for the leaden casket, Portia's triumph: the epigram read to "give and hazard all," and the photo was a nude shot of Pamela in a pin-up pose. Suddenly I felt ready to give what I had.

"Woo-hoo!" I called out, and I heard tittering from the bedroom. Pamela's lithe yet curvaceous figure appeared in the doorway. She had put on a diaphanous robe that hid nothing, yet was alluring in its pretense of coverage. She also wore a come-hither smile.

"Romeo, Romeo, wherefore art thou Romeo?" she uttered, posing in the doorway and mistaking the sense of the line as "where are you?" rather than "why are you Romeo?" She opened her arms. I fought the urge to correct her literary interpretation and strode to her, impetuously picking her up—and carrying her to the waiting bed. I realised then that both the language and the actions of courtship and love-making were based on literary models. We repeated lines of love poems as our own. We mimicked the actions we'd seen lovers perform on stage and on screen and in our imaginations through the words of novels. The force and power of this literary tradition coursed through my own veins, and I felt its cadence.

Shakespeare—my father—or actually my very self—had brought this girl and me together, and we would as fully vibrant beings bring to life once again the emotions that drove his drama and his poems. This was somewhere beyond poetic justice. It was more like poetic vindication, poetic reanimation. I was the living bard, and Pamela was every desirable character he had created. At this moment my mind and body were completely one, and I was transcended—thrilled to be alive once more, strutting and fretting upon our little globe.

And it was the readers and viewers, those story-lovers and language-lovers, who had kept me alive and fueled my reanimation. Pamela kissed me long and deep then opened her shining eyes and said with conviction, "I'll set a bourn how far to be beloved . . . find out new heaven, new Earth." Whether she was sincere or merely playing her role as paramour I could not tell. As an actress she seemed, in life, always "on." But it did not matter to me. Pamela was quoting the language of lovers, appropriating it as her own.

The way we talked about love followed its own age-old codes. We may even have conceived of the emotions from the words and phrases themselves. It was much like modern-day texting—OMG, IMHO, TMI. These were shortcuts to emotions. After a while the emotions themselves disappear and the symbols stand alone, live as independent entities, and we mouth them as actors reciting our lines.

What did matter to me was that, while I felt enormous desire for Pamela, I was not moved by emotion. Nonetheless, I too knew the lines of love so I replied as the avatar I was, "Love's not Time's fool. . . . If this be error and upon me prov'd, / I never writ, nor no man ever lov'd." Thus fooling ourselves into some sort of intimate connection, thus comforting ourselves that we were the heirs of all the lovers who had preceded us through the generations and in our stories and poems, we gazed into each other's eyes and made love over and over again, with haste and urgency.

 *   *   *

Chapter 78

It's a truism that during our teenage years we "find ourselves." At fifteen I had lost my foster mother, my birth mother, but discovered the truth of my parentage in her books. My play—that best manifestation of the father, myself, within—had made a hit with the RSC producers and would go into rehearsals for next season. Wherever I went I carried the signs of my origins, the shining angel around my neck, the Tudor Thames bones-pipe in my pocket. After rehearsals I would regularly retreat to Cece's old den in the cellar and pull out my little pipe for a contemplative, reflective moment. I was, in my own estimation, living up to my genetic heritage. I could take what I experienced and observed about the human race and render it into effective art. I felt vibrant, strong, and vigourous.

On the debit side of the ledger, I sort of missed Cece. Her disappearance was still a mystery that haunted me. I realised that I had known her hardly at all. She was a body with a voice at first, then a pathetic tale. And then a warm and comforting refuge from the adult world. I wasn't sure we had connected, except physically. If I loved her, it was only in the most general sense, concern for the welfare of a fellow creature, and in my case I'd almost always name my feeling curiosity rather than love. People's antics delighted me, and if I could read their character and manipulate them according to my whim, I felt fulfilled.

I wasn't completely a cold fish. I did value others' concern for me, especially demonstrated over time. I recognised love when I saw it. But I knew it only as words and forms of behaviour—*I shall languish for love, I shall die for love*. These were the extremes His plays had taught me. I was grateful to Cece, my dark darling, for bringing me into the world of physical connection—which I was now practicing with the divine Pamela at least twice a week. We were grateful for permissive—or neglectful—or trusting—parents. It was difficult to pin down their motives, but Pamela's mum and dad left her to her own devices, and devices she had, in spades.

We'd made love on just about every surface in that flat, and each time Pamela assumed a different dramatic persona, costuming herself in the appropriate garb briefly— before doing her provocative strip-tease. I'd never known such a chameleon, and that suited my own temperament. It did not vex me that the genuine Pamela eluded me. I was comfortable in the company of characters I'd known since I could hear and recognise words. Pamela always seemed like a very old friend—whoever she was that day.

It comprised an odd genealogy. In a sense I had created her—well, my parent, who was myself, had invented the fictional selves she donned like jumpers and jackets. So her familiarity resonated deep within my genetic memory, if such a thing existed. And now we mouthed the words the historical I had created, and I coupled with her, the creator with some personification of his own creation.

If I pondered this arrangement too deeply it seemed un-right, almost incestuous. But then what actions in my life *could* be genuine and untainted? All the traces of my former life surrounded us, on the news, on everybody's lips, on posters and in theatrical coming attractions. Careers had been made by virtue of my caché, as vigourous and powerful now—perhaps even more universal—than 400 years ago. In a single summer season more people saw my plays now than had during my entire first lifetime.

And I was adding to the canon with *The Merrie Tale of Robin Hood*, which, in a satisfying arc of completion, would be performed at the Globe, His theatre. My theatre. The author was listed as William Shakespeare Armstrong. This play was the vessel of His language but in my voice. It truly revealed my parentage. I was my father's son in a strange rendering of "the child is father of the man."

My head felt dizzy with a combination of smoke and inscrutable relations reasoned out. I turned my mind to my sad modern father with his eye glued to the viewing scope over nothingness in his lab upstairs, and I sighed. I pretended Cece was present, and I unburdened my heavy heart.

I could see now that I had been his undoing—not the actual I—though I'm sure my presence was a constant reminder—but his choice to reanimate the Bard's DNA. Once I was "hatched," his control was gone, except for his educational plan, which was meant to immerse me in the product of His genius. And it had. My first friends were all the cast lists of all the plays, and that iambic pentameter coursed through my veins with the pulse of my heartbeat.

Mother had not been able to accept my being—and her part in bringing me into this world. Father was suffering now, no doubt from his role in convincing her to become his partner in this experiment. That initial decision to clone the DNA, whatever the professed reasons, was like the lead domino in a long file. Once he nudged it into motion, the rest was inevitable, unstoppable, and uncontrollable. My DNA was my roadmap, and it expressed itself through my new body with only the slight modifications of my modern environment. They had taught me the canon of Bard literature, but I would have had the playwright's turn of mind anyway—keen observation, character manipulation, poetic expression.

What they hadn't realised was that I would be a separate organism; I would exist beside them, despite them. In a sense they were irrelevant. And while Mum had influenced the world by her choice of stories to publish, and Dad had brought truth to light at the molecular level, I was the one who would be remembered. Mum had even said it in her journals: the Bard *redivivus*. Everything about me was *re-*: re-born, re-animated, re-invigourated, re-stored. And ready.

Perhaps because I was my own parent, I lacked that feeling of fellowship with others. Like any actor, I could find the words and actions to be convincing at human connection. As Stanislavsky had proposed, the actor needs to react on the stage, to garner energy from the words and movements of the others to find his own feigned emotion and make it seem convincingly genuine. That described my entire life. I had taken my father's—my own—metaphor "all the world's a stage, and all the men and women merely players" and realised it as my own reality.

Was manipulation evil? I thought of it as morally neutral. I listened and watched and then created the conditions for characters to realise themselves. They were responsible, not I. If any blame were to be laid at my doorstep, it would be that I did not distinguish the boards of the theatre from the ordinary walks of life. ALL the world's a stage. My genes told me so. And then there was my lack of affection—but that was my own business, and so long as I could behave convincingly "normal," I got on in the world just fine. I too would guard the secret. No one ever need know the truth of my origins.

I shivered slightly and realised I'd whiled away an hour or more, still missing Cece's warmth here in the dank cellar. It was a good place to think: sub-terranean, sub-conscious. I rose from the floor feeling stiffness in my limbs and hobbled to the lift. Back in the flat, all was as before. I peered through the lab door. Dad was still staring through the scope, but now he was muttering under his breath.

"What are you looking at, Father?" I asked, hoping perhaps to bring him back to reality.

"Yes, I saw it move! My ovum—it's alive!" he exclaimed.

I knew he stared at nothingness, yet I walked and breathed, son of a Bard and a madman.

 *   *   *

Chapter 79

Despite Father's steady decline, I'd never felt more myself. My play was in rehearsals at the Globe. When I walked along the banks towards the theatre, modern London spread out before me, my Tudor relics around my neck and in my pocket, I felt the old Bard pace along with me, in me. I truly walked in his footsteps, but even more so, with his own stride, with his very cells.

I was used to people I passed doing double-takes when they saw me, for even though I did not wear a ruffled collar, I resembled Him remarkably. I'm sure some thought I was an actor or impersonator, here near the Globe, and some called me Will and asked for my autograph. I was identical to him yet not—in another time, with different opportunities. I was the heir to his literary production, and now I would build on it. The name William Shakespeare was about to gain new currency.

It had been two fellow actors from the troupe's joint stock company we had to thank for preserving the Shakespeare plays. John Heminge and Henry Condell had recognised their friend's genius and laboured to collect the draft papers and the quarto editions into our grand First Folio. I felt equally grateful to Amy and Gareth for offering an outlet for my talent and fostering it. The local theatre was like an island of the past where I had discovered my destiny. Grandpa Gordon had inadvertently given me the subject for my first play in our archery sessions, and I'm sure that all of the rituals surrounding my days and nights with Cece and Pamela would make an appearance in my writing. I had Mum to thank for showing me the value of the written word and Dad for the spoken word. He had immersed me in the Bard's own language for nearly two decades.

As I walked towards Pamela's flat, I felt the power of the future compelling me forward. All was well, and the thinly-veiled London sun still warmed my shoulders. My angel glinted and I grasped it in my palm, re-warming it with my own living heat. Although somehow I would have to deal with Dad's decline in the years to come, I was launched and coming into my own.

Pamela answered my buzz with a serious face. I wondered which dire matron she was playing—Margaret or Calpurnia, perhaps.

"Will, we need to talk, and I'm not sure how you'll take my news," she began.

My stomach lurched momentarily. I didn't recognise the lines, then it hit me she was in earnest. "My darling girl, what troubles can you bear?" Nerves, and again the iambic pentameter reappeared as a tic.

"Sit with me." She took my hand and led me to the sofa. "I don't know how it happened. We've always been so careful, but there must have been a leak or tear or something. I haven't had a visit from Auntie Flo for two months in a row. I feel sort of bloated, too—and look!" She stood and turned in profile, pulling her clothes tight around her belly. She looked like her normal self, fit but provocatively rounded as usual.

"Pamela, my dear, are you with child? Isn't there a test to verify? We need to know the truth, and then we'll think."

My initial reaction was purely physical, a combination of pride and dread.

"Yes, I took the test. It came out plus, and I did it twice, same result. Will, we're so young. But I do think I love you, and I don't have the nerve for an abortion. Do you think this would keep me from getting roles?"

"Certainly for a few months," I replied. "But then what? It's too soon to marry—but I will not abandon you." The idea of my genes continuing into the future at my instigation delighted me.

"I want to keep the baby."

"I will help you as I can, my dove."

"Just think of the artistic genes our child will inherit," she continued, walking over to the full-length glass and regarding her own image. "Beauty and talent—there's a life in the theatre ahead for sure."

I smiled at this, although Pamela did not know why. I had not and I would not—I could not—tell her the secret of my birth. Through all that might materialise in the decades that beckoned ahead for me, I must find a way simply to capitalise on the Shakespeare resemblance without revealing my origins. If the truth were revealed the media would take my news and make it a circus. The entire world would be changed by knowledge of my reappearance. It would seem even more miraculous for me to make my way as a newly-sprung individual—rivaling Shakespeare but as a new man of the twenty-first century, millennial, not Tudor.

I was sure Pamela would work out the details for rearing the child. Her parents would continue to support her, no doubt, probably even take up the child. While I found it hard to cast myself as a father, I would remain in the scene, although I would try to keep my distance. I enjoyed the historical significance of this thought, a child carrying the Bard's genes, the potential of begetting a new branch of His family tree. The clan of Shakespeare would be reborn, revitalised, like me, through me.

Pamela turned back to face me. "So, you're okay with this?" she asked, stroking her hand across her belly in a gesture reminiscent of my mother's. She looked plaintive and completely endearing. She seemed ready to play the role of expectant mother with full investment.

I opened my arms and Pamela flew towards me. As we embraced, I could feel the slight swell of her belly against me, and I smiled again. Othello's speech ran through my mind: "I cannot speak enough of this content. / It stops me here, it is too much of joy."

   * * *

Chapter 80

When I returned home, Father was as I had left him, hunched over the lab table and staring into the scope, which I knew held nothing at all. He was muttering softly to himself. I saw traces that he had moved from his spot, however briefly. The lab door itself stood open, and the remnants of lunch were on the kitchen counter. Later I would try to get him to eat some supper, but for now I lay down on my bed to process the day's events. I was grateful for this quiet time alone.

A stray thought niggled at me about Pamela's baby, my baby. I realised my own oddness. In some ways I always felt not of this era. Even though my context was completely modern, a slight divide separated me from everyone I knew. I simply did not have the evolved emotional investment in others that they demonstrated on a daily basis. I looked like them. I spoke more or less the same language. But at best I was indifferent about their connection with me. I enjoyed observing human character, and I liked making things happen. I knew what to say to get what I wanted. Everything else was simply by the book, according to the script.

Was this a product of my genetic make-up? I wondered if my precursor carried the same stamp of calculation and coolness. He could personify villainy like no other. He created cynical self-congratulatory manipulators like Richard and Iago and social opportunists like Falstaff and Edmund. Yet he knew how to model the language of love, loyalty, mortality. Upon which side did His own character fall? If I were truly His child—or more accurately His modern twin—then He and I were cut from the same cloth.

And if He and I were the watchers, devoid of deep attachment, perhaps this baby, with our genes, would be of our colour. Had Father considered this when he first created me? The Bard excelled at dramatising ill-conceived choices and their consequences. In fact, that seemed to be the crux of tragedy. A temptation loomed and a generally well-intentioned person succumbed. That initial decision set the future in motion, horribly outside the individual's control. By bringing me from the past into the present, Father had altered the future, not just for himself or for me, but for humanity.

From the instant I drew breath—actually before that, from the instant my first cell divided—the experiment left Father's control. I thought I could understand something of why he followed through on his temptation. And I felt some pity for him now, my creator, the man who had reared me so meticulously to know the words and the world of my true father, myself. That single choice had set in motion a chain reaction: my manifestation in the modern world, my reading Mum's journals, Mum's decline and death, Father's own unhinged fixation on his moment of fateful decision, and now, now a new avatar to enter the world, my child, one who would be a hybrid of old and new. I doubt Father had followed the time line through to that possibility. Here was an inevitable chain of consequences and more unseen consequences.

For a moment I wondered if a baby from my semen would be viable. Certainly I was a *homo sapiens*, but my DNA was more than 400 years old. I wondered what small evolutions might have occurred in our species over the centuries. Was I really like these modern folk? And what about my own child? Would a merger of old and new result in a devolution, a kind of tainted return to the affect-less condition of my own emotions? That sort of individual could survive and pass without notice in the twenty-first century, as I had. Or would the DNA merger spawn a minor sub-species, the character yet to be determined? This could result in a super-strain of man as yet unthought of. Super-Bard, I thought, and smiled. And my father—myself—and I would be its progenitor.

In that moment I felt proud. I glanced up at the portraits poster that had been with me ever since I could open my eyes and focus. All these varying images seemed to me to represent possibilities. In the same way that generations had envisioned their Shakespeare in alternative images, now I—Shakespeare, myself—would be the progenitor of these images brought to life as actual living beings. These could be all my children, smiling down at me, and the Shakespeare family tree alive and well again.

My reverie was interrupted by the buzz of the intercom. A voice announced "special delivery" for a

"Will" at our address. I opened the door to our flat and padded down the hall to the building entry. The envelope bore an immature hand—perplexing. Who knew where I lived? Who would write to me?

I glanced into the lab on my way back to my room. No change, Father as if frozen in that position. Sitting at my desk, I opened the letter and my eyes zoomed directly to the signature. Ah, Cece! In spite of myself, my heart began to pound. Sort of automatically my fingers sought the pipe in my pocket, and it came to me that I should read this missive in our place in the cellar as an homage to my lost dark darling.

As the lift descended Pamela passed briefly through my mind, Pamela now pregnant with my child. I felt no betrayal of Cece in this new development. Each girl occupied her own place, her own function within this flow of my life. I made my way to our corner den and took a minute to tamp some herbs into my Tudor pipe. My angel caught a bit of light amidst the cellar's gloom and glinted sharply. I lit the candle and unfolded Cece's letter.

    Dear Will,

    You prolly wondered what happened to me. Sory to keep you in the dark. Dad hit me hard and I landed in hospital. They said I'm preggers. Dad took me far away where no one will know. He thinks it mite be his but it isn't. He never got in that far, and I washed with a little bag and plunger. It's your baby Will. Our baby. And I'm so happy about this. They took a little picture from inside and it's a boy. Of course I'm going to name him Will. He'll come into the world any day now. When you read this I mite be holding him.

Please don't look for us. It's safer that way and we'll be just fine. My family is my lot alone to bear. Think of us from time to time and know there's another Will like you walking about. Maybe giving speeches. ☺

Cece

I inhaled deeply from the pipe and my heart steadied. Wisps of smoke encircled me like an embrace. Who could have predicted my situation? Only sixteen, and two of my children were germinating to enter the modern world. Not long and they too would have children, and our family tree would sprout new and vigourous branches. As the smoke clouded around me, I smiled in satisfaction recalling my own words from more than 400 years ago, the real secret of life readers searched for in my works, "the world must be peopled."

—"Genetic engineering, a family mystery, a mad scientist, and a precocious incarnation of the Old Bard himself—just the stuff of a thriller. 'Shakespeare's Pipe' takes us through the riveting story of bringing Shakespeare back to life from some stray DNA on a Tudor pipe and of the consequences that befall his creator and his family. Packed with suspense and Shakespeare quotations to liven the parallels, Alexandra Mason's story offers us a plot worthy of the Bard himself—with devious wit, intrigue, and pathos. As the plot and its characters slowly unravel under the strain of this experiment, we enjoy a fascinating look into the human nature of our reincarnated playwright. 'Shakespeare's Pipe' is a page-turner, brimming with the mysteries of genetic codes and surprising plot twists. The final section offers a stunning insight into the nature of identity and the connection between language and reality, between art and life." —Ellen M. Caldwell, Professor of English at University of California, Fullerton

—"Move over, Mary Shelley; you've got competition! 'Shakespeare's Pipe' is the story of unhinged, megalomaniacal scientist Kingsley Armstrong, who, like his literary forebear, wants to create life, but more specifically than that, to re-create the genius of Shakespeare by cloning DNA from an old pipe found during repairs at the Bard's birthplace. The results of his obsessiveness unfold in this brilliantly crafted contemporary morality tale. American scholar Alexandra Mason proves herself to be a talented and highly engaging storyteller, weaving together age-old patterns of character and language into models of actual behavior. This novel takes its place within the well-established literary tradition of Shelley and her descendants." —Marilyn Ewing, Professor English at Eastern Oregon University

—"Alexandra Mason's newest novel will delight Shakespeare fans while giving a nod to the brilliance of Mary Shelley. What Shakespeare lover hasn't dreamed of sitting in a London coffee house eavesdropping as Will and his friends gossip about the people and events in their everyday life or perhaps read aloud bits of their latest poetry? Just imagine being able to ask Will why his female characters are always silent at the end of the comedies or how much Latin and Greek he really had. Mason's novel, however, goes beyond these blithe thoughts to explore the intersection between pleasant dreams and the obsessions of scientific genius when a DNA lab is used to clone Shakespeare. What could go wrong? Mason asks. Why wouldn't we want to bring to life a person with unparalleled ability to delve into the darkest reaches of the human soul? Today more than ever the warnings Mary Shelley gave us about the dangers of attempting to create human life in the laboratory are resonant in 'Shakespeare's Pipe.'" —Marilyn Sandidge, Professor of English at Westfield State University, Massachusetts

—"Mason's writing is truly spot-on and her characters well-developed and engaging. The movement of the narrative is smooth, believable, and intriguing. Definitely a best seller here. What gives it backbone is attention to the emotional landscapes of the characters and how they evolve and intermingle."— Brenda Croghan, Literary Editor